L[illegible]

"Lori Wilde has created a rich and wonderful story about the charm of small town life combined with the power and passion of first love. Delicious!"
New York Times bestselling author Robyn Carr

"Delicious details, a small town full of memorable characters, great dialogue, and humor all combine to make this a highly enjoyable tale about two people who find healing—and each other."
Booklist (*Starred Review*)

"Wilde's clever combination of humor, sorrow and love brings a deeply appealing sense of realism."
Publishers Weekly

"Sexy and a hoot . . . a delicacy that really hits the spot."
Romantic Times BOOKClub

By Lori Wilde

THE CHRISTMAS COOKIE COLLECTION
ALL OUT OF LOVE
LOVE AT FIRST SIGHT
A COWBOY FOR CHRISTMAS
THE COWBOY AND THE PRINCESS
THE COWBOY TAKES A BRIDE
THE WELCOME HOME GARDEN CLUB
THE FIRST LOVE COOKIE CLUB
THE TRUE LOVE QUILTING CLUB
THE SWEETHEARTS' KNITTING CLUB

Available from Avon Impulse

ONE TRUE LOVE
THE CHRISTMAS COOKIE CHRONICLES:
CARRIE
R'AYLENE
CHRISTINE

Forthcoming

THE CHRISTMAS COOKIE CHRONICLES:
GRACE

LORI WILDE

AVON
An Imprint of HarperCollins*Publishers*

This is a work of fiction. Names, characters, places, and incidents are products of the author's imagination or are used fictitiously and are not to be construed as real. Any resemblance to actual events, locales, organizations, or persons, living or dead, is entirely coincidental.

AVON BOOKS
An Imprint of HarperCollins*Publishers*
10 East 53rd Street
New York, New York 10022-5299

ISBN 978-0-06-213630-5
www.avonromance.com

First Avon Books mass market printing: November 2013

Printed in the U.S.A.

10 9 8 7 6 5 4 3 2 1

To Linda Brooks Bagwell,
PR director at Weatherford College.
Your love of books and authors
has enriched our community,
and your personal support has led
to a friendship I treasure.
You are appreciated!

Acknowledgments

I want to acknowledge the quaint lakeside community of Granbury, Texas, that inspired my fictional town of Twilight. The local legends, historical landmarks, friendly welcoming faces, beautiful lake, and Old West charm are simply irresistible. Granbury is truly unique.

Author's Note

Twilight, Texas (pop. 6,000), is a quaint tourist town on the banks of the Brazos River that feeds into Lake Twilight. The hamlet was founded in 1875. How the town got its name is a subject of heated debate, but the prevailing legend among romantics involves two teenage sweethearts separated during the War Between the States. Circumstances tore them asunder, but they never stopped loving each other. Fifteen years later, they met again at twilight on the banks of the river in the spot where Twilight now stands. A statue in their honor has been erected in the park next to the town square.

There's a rumor that if you throw pennies into the park's fountain you will be reunited with your high school sweetheart. Many reunited high school lovers come to Twilight to get married, and, in fact, there is a thriving matchmaking business in town, focusing exclusively on helping people reconnect with long-lost loves.

With its stately courthouse, surrounded by lovingly refurbished buildings of Old West–style architecture, *Texas Monthly* voted Twilight the Prettiest Town Square in Texas. The combination of the pristine blue lake and the intriguing history—lore has it that Jesse James used hidden river caves near Twilight as a hideout, and the real John Wilkes Booth escaped the law after shooting Lincoln and took up acting at the Twilight Playhouse—lend a magical air to this quirky but close-knit community filled with warmth and small-town camaraderie. In the summer months, tourists flock there, drawn by the water, the odd little curio shops, acclaimed community theater, and lively town events.

But Christmas is the season when Twilight truly shines. There's the Dickens on the Square weekend that includes a Dickensian parade to kick off the event. Visitors can meet a one-shoed Miss Havisham, express their respect for Sydney Carton, shake hands with David Copperfield, and hoist Tiny Tim upon their shoulders. There are free trolley rides, horse-drawn carriages, and pajama parties for the kids at Ye Olde Book Nook.

The theatrically inclined can learn about the town's romantic history from the annual holiday play at the Twilight Playhouse, often starring local-girl-turned-movie-star, Emma Parks. Afterward, grab a hot chocolate at Rinky-Tink's ice cream parlor, where a seat at the front window will allow full view of the locals decorating the tree on the town square. Romantics can stroll hand in hand through an over-the-top light display at Sweetheart Park and throw that penny into the Sweetheart Fountain. And when it's time for bed, spend a night in the angel-filled rooms at the Merry Cherub.

For all the fun and frivolity, make no mistake, while the events and legends and traditions are great fun, the heart and soul of this town lie in the generous people who live there. Especially the local knitting club, a group of town matriarchs who not only give advice and counsel, they're also mischievous matchmakers. Each year this group organizes and decorates the Angel Tree for those less fortunate and spends their Christmas Eve delivering food and gifts and well wishes to those in need, embodying the true spirit of Christmas—unconditional love.

Enjoy your stay.

CARRIE

CHAPTER ONE

Carrie MacGregor hated Christmas.

She despised the endless smiles and constant cheeriness, the forced ho-ho-ho-ing. She loathed the cheesiness of tinsel and blinking multicolored lights and plywood Santa Claus cutouts decorating every lawn in Twilight, Texas. She dreaded the commercialization of gift-giving, the continual overeating, the ubiquitous music, and the stressful push-pull of relatives' unrealistic expectations.

Yes, okay, she too was a Christmas cliché—the obligatory Grinch. Every family had one. Bah-humbug.

Her only goal for the next six weeks was to get from Thanksgiving to New Year's Day as quietly as possible. No fuss. No tears. No drama. No memories. She refused to dwell on what the holidays represented to her—lost love, dashed hopes, a broken heart.

Breathe. Put one foot in front of the other. Take it day-by-day.

Funny, she sounded just like her dad, Floyd, an AA member who had been clean-and-sober for four years, with only one accidental fall off the wagon. That was something to be grateful for, at least.

Right now, it was Thursday. A week before Thanksgiving, and tonight was the last meeting of the year for the Sweethearts' Knitting Club. The members of the club would be here soon. She had the refreshments laid out in the community room at the new Yarn Barn.

Her older sister, Flynn, had originally started the yarn shop, but Carrie had taken over the business after the first store on the town square had burned down three years ago. She'd reestablished it in the shopping center on the bluff overlooking Lake Twilight. She was damn proud of herself, only twenty-five years old and running her own successful business. Especially when, not so very long ago, she'd been engaging in self-destructive activities. Grief could make a girl do crazy things.

Carrie paused a moment from unpacking a box of yarn that had just arrived on the UPS truck, a skein of red and green alpaca yarn clutched in her hand. Through the big plate glass window, she gazed out at the lake. A sailboat swooped gracefully by, reminding her of the time Mark had taken her sailing.

For a split second, Mark's handsome face popped into her mind, but she squelched the image of him as quickly as it materialized. *No fuss. No tears. No drama. No memories.* That was her holiday mantra.

A knock on the door announced the arrival of the first members of the Sweethearts' Knitting Club. Ten minutes early, but Carrie didn't mind. The lively group of knitters would keep her darker thoughts at bay. She abandoned the box of yarn and went to greet them.

She opened the door to four of the six knitting club members who stood there with containers clutched in their arms. "What's all this?"

"Surprise!" they exclaimed in unison.

"We know how tough Christmas is for you." Sixty-something Patsy Cross sailed over the threshold, a golden garland trailing from the cardboard box she carried. After more than forty years, she and her high school sweetheart, Sheriff Hondo Crouch, were finally getting married this Christmas Eve. Lately, the normally no-nonsense businesswoman had grown quite giddy.

"We're going to decorate the Yarn Barn!" added plump Belinda Murphey, a relentless optimist who ran the local matchmaking service. She was in her forties, long married with five kids. She wore a blue-and-white Frosty the Snowman stockinet-stitched sweater.

Carrie forced herself not to roll her eyes. "Please, you don't have to do that."

"We *want* to do it," cocoa-skinned Marva Bullock assured her. Marva was the principal of Twilight High, and in the course of her job had punished

Carrie more times than she cared to remember. "You've worked so hard rebuilding the Yarn Barn and creating a cozy place for us to meet. You deserve this."

"Besides." Elderly Dotty Mae, who smelled of peppermint schnapps and mentholatum, patted her on the shoulder. "We promised your mama we'd look after you. She knew that dying on Christmas would forever mar your holiday."

Her mother's death five years before from the lingering disease of amyotrophic lateral sclerosis was only part of why Carrie hated Christmas. Mark Leland was the other half of the equation.

Forget about him. Ancient history. Old news.

Kind of hard to do, though, when she was in a room filled with women who had married—or in Patsy's case was about to marry—their high school sweethearts.

You and Mark weren't sweethearts, you were just hot and horny.

"We're not going to knit?" Carrie asked, scrambling to think of a way to circumvent the decorating.

"Nope," Belinda sang out, and then scratched at a crusty white patch on her sweater. "My kids had a food fight at the dinner table. Looks like I took mashed taters to the ta-tas. Oh well, we'll pretend it's just snow." Belinda laughed. She had a thing for alliteration. All her children's names started with K's. "Like the Kardashians," she was fond of saying. "Patsy, I just thought of something. Do you realize you're going to be Patsy Calloway Cross Crouch?"

"Let's not bring that up again." Patsy started

plucking the pieces of a nativity scene from the box she'd settled onto the refreshment table next to the crudités. Lamb, donkey, baby Jesus. She paused long enough to snag a purple radish from the platter, swish it in ranch dressing and pop it into her mouth.

"You really don't have to do this," Carrie said. "I can handle my own decorating."

Marva wagged a chiding finger. "You're not fooling us. We know you won't do it if left to your own devices."

"Well, yes, that's sort of the point."

Dotty Mae reached up to pinch her cheek. "You live in Twilight, dear. It's your moral obligation to uphold Christmas tradition."

"Is it too late to move?"

"Far too late." Dotty Mae reached into her box and produced a twelve-inch-tall cardboard gingerbread man and woman. "You're indigenous."

All around Carrie, the ladies were stringing lights and positioning figurines and hanging stockings. Taking over her shop. Four surrogate mothers doing what mothers did—butting in.

"Doesn't anyone want to knit? I got a fresh yarn shipment in today," Carrie enticed, making Vanna White motions at her new display.

Before anyone could answer, the door opened and Raylene Pringle flounced in. Ever since her high school sweetheart and husband of thirty-five years had left her last Christmas, she'd been as down in the dumps about the holidays as Carrie. Everyone had been tiptoeing around Raylene since her split with Earl. No one knew how to take her anymore.

She'd stopped dying her hair, which was once Miss Clairol platinum blonde, but was now steel gray, and she'd quit wearing her famous short shirts. She had on baggy blue jeans, cowboy boots, and a faded black Rolling Stones T-shirt with a big red tongue sticking out at everyone.

Carrie breathed a sigh of relief. At last, an ally.

"I'm here," Raylene drawled. "What the hell do you want me to do?"

"Help us set up the Christmas tree," Marva said brightly.

"Not a Christmas tree, too." Carrie groaned.

"It's not for you." Patsy spread green felt on the floor in front of the window facing the parking lot. "It's for your customers."

"We need some music," Belinda said, and the next thing Carrie knew, Dean Martin was singing over the store's sound system about how cold it was outside. Hard to buy into when it was a balmy sixty-two degrees in North Central Texas.

"Got anything to drink?" Raylene asked.

"There's coffee, fruit punch, and iced tea." Carrie moved to the refreshment table.

"Let me rephrase. Have you got anything *substantial* to drink?"

"I think Jesse might have left a beer in the back of the fridge during the Halloween party," Carrie said, referring to her brother-in-law who was also Patsy's nephew. Halloween. Now that was a holiday. Costumes. Tricks and treats. Goblins. Ghouls. There was nothing sentimental about Halloween.

"Thank God for Jesse." Raylene sauntered over

to the dorm-sized refrigerator that Carrie stored behind the checkout counter. She fished around until she found the long-neck bottle of Lone Star and twisted off the cap.

"Terri just pulled into the parking lot," Patsy called out as she sorted green plastic tree limbs by size.

"What is she bringing?" Carrie muttered. "Santa himself?"

"Don't be grouchy, Grinch." Belinda smiled and ruffled Carrie's hair as she passed Dotty Mae a handful of candy canes.

"I'm not fourteen," Carrie protested. "And I'm not Flynn."

"We know." Marva opened a bag of potato chips. "*You* can knit."

Even though Carrie's older sister couldn't knit, the group had made her an honorary lifetime member of the Sweethearts' Knitting Club. Everyone in town loved Flynn. She was one of those magnanimous people, who always put others first, herself second. Carrie, on the other hand, was selfish and ornery and stubborn. The wild-child MacGregor. If she and her sister were ever cast in a remake of *Gone With the Wind,* Flynn would be Melanie and Carrie would have to play Scarlet. The sassy heroine everyone loved to hate.

"Don't try so hard to be Scrooge," Patsy said. "Jesse called and told me what you did for them."

"Who me?" Carrie glanced away. "I didn't do anything."

"If not you, then what little fairy sneaked over to

their house, cleaned up and left dinner in the refrigerator?" Patsy asked.

"Dunno, maybe Tinkerbelle?"

Okay, yes, she'd done it, but only because Flynn had sounded so exhausted when she'd talked to her last night. Flynn was in her last year of college, getting her teaching certificate in elementary education and eight months pregnant with her first baby. Jesse helped out as much as he could, but besides running his own motorcycle shop, he was working a second job at Home Depot to get health insurance, pay Flynn's tuition and put away extra money for the baby.

The door burst open and dark-haired Terri Longoria—the final member of the Sweethearts' Knitting Club—rushed inside, eyes sparkling. Terri ran Hot Legs Gym and looked the part. Toned. Firm. Athletic. She appeared half a decade younger than her forty years.

"Guess what!" Terri exclaimed.

"What?" obliged the other ladies.

"Remember when I was on *Fear Nothing*?"

Several years ago, Terri had appeared on a reality show where she was required to gulp down a bucket of earthworms. She'd fearlessly dived in, eaten the wriggly lunch in two minutes flat and won ten thousand dollars for her efforts. On the evening that the show aired, the entire town of Twilight had been glued to their television sets cheering on one of their own. Ever since then Terri had become something of a local celebrity.

"Please tell us you're not going to eat earthworms

again." Belinda looked worried. "I about gagged watching you do that on TV."

Terri waved a hand. "Although there was some talk about me returning for an All-Stars show, *Fear Nothing* got cancelled last season."

"Oh, thank goodness," Dotty Mae said. "I know you enjoyed it, but that show was uncivilized."

"So what's the big news?" Marva asked, handing Patsy the Christmas tree stand.

"I'm on Burt Mernit's mailing list," Terri bragged.

"Who's Burt Mernit?" Raylene took a pull off her beer.

"He created *Fear Nothing* and a bunch of other reality shows," Terri explained. "He's got a new show that debuts in January, but they've already been filming episodes for the last several weeks. It's sort of like *MythBusters* but with the focus on fables, legend and folklore."

"And you're going to be on that show?" Patsy guessed.

Carrie retreated to the corner. She contemplated slipping out the back door and abandoning the knitters to their busybody decorating but dismissed that thought. She had to be here to make sure they didn't go nuts with the Christmas cheer. She glanced around the room. Far too late for that. Sighing, she poured herself a cup of fruit punch.

"Nope. Not me." Terri grinned and danced around the room in time to "Jingle Bell Rock."

"I'll bite," Marva said. "Who *is* going to be on the show?"

"All of us." Terri clapped her hands. "The entire town of Twilight."

"What do you mean?" Patsy straightened, narrowed her eyes. "All of us?"

Twilight lived and died by its legends. The town that claimed a resident population of six thousand had been founded on the Brazos River in 1875. To keep a steady influx of cash pouring into the community, a cottage industry had sprung up around the prevailing town legend. According to lore, two teenage sweethearts were separated during the Civil War. Jon Grant had been a soldier for the North; Rebekka Nash, a sweet Southern belle. Circumstances tore them asunder, but they never stopped loving each other. Fifteen years later, they met again at twilight on the banks of the Brazos in the exact same spot where the town now stood.

In the early 1900s a statue in the lovers' honor had been erected in the park near the town square. Rumor had it that if you threw a penny into the fountain at Sweetheart Park, you would be forever reunited with your high school sweetheart and live happily-ever-after. Whether it was true or not, the legend did indeed bring in the tourists. In 1910, the *Fort Worth Star-Telegram* nicknamed Twilight "Sweetheart Town," and there'd been a steady influx of romance-related tourism ever since.

Carrie had grown up with the fairy tale, but she didn't believe in it. For one thing, she was a cynic. For another, she'd thrown countless pennies into that damned fountain and Mark Leland had never returned. Never wrote. Never called. Never even accepted her friend request on Facebook.

"*Fact or Fantasy* is coming to Twilight," Terri went on.

"To bust the myth of our town legends?" Marva looked alarmed.

"That's just it," Terri exclaimed, clearly not realizing the implications. If Twilight's myths were busted; bye-bye tourism dollars. "They won't bust us. We *know* the story of Jon and Rebekka is true."

"We do?" Dotty Mae blinked.

Oh crap. Carrie kneaded her forehead. The town was in deep trouble.

"That's not the best part," Terri said.

"If this is your idea of exciting news, I'm scared to ask what the best part is." Even perky Belinda shifted nervously.

"The host of the show is none other than a former Twilight denizen." Terri's smile went smug, and her eyes met Carrie's.

For no reason at all, goose bumps blanketed Carrie's arm, and her skin suddenly felt too tight. Her mouth went bone dry. She took a big swallow of punch and almost choked on it.

Belinda reached over and patted her on the back. "You okay, sweetie?"

Carrie nodded, set down the punch.

"Come on you guys, guess." Terri held her arms out in a ta-da gesture and rolled her eyes heavenward. "The host is a very handsome young man."

"Who used to live in Twilight?" Patsy's forehead wrinkled in a quizzical frown.

"Yes, ma'am."

"Could you give us a hint?" Belinda asked.

"He was once very special to someone in this room."

Raylene snorted. "Stop playing coy, Terri, who the hell is it?"

Terri made a drumroll noise with her tongue. "The new host of *Fact or Fiction* is none other than our very own Mark Leland."

Mark Leland?

Carrie stopped breathing. Six pairs of inquisitive eyes immediately shifted to stare at her. She felt at once dizzy and sick to her stomach.

Her Mark Leland? Coming back to Twilight? Not only coming back, but returning with a camera crew to bust the romantic myth that the town's economy thrived on.

The myth that said if you threw a penny into the fountain in Sweetheart Park that you would be married to your first love forever. The very same myth that she and Mark had already busted eight years ago when they'd had their impulsive Vegas wedding annulled.

Chapter Two

Twilight hadn't changed one bit in eight years.

That was a surprising sucker punch, even though Mark should have expected it, because he *had* changed. He'd changed a whole lot from the provincial farm kid who once sped his pickup truck around these quaint, meandering streets.

In his Brioni suit and A. Testoni shoes, his two-hundred-dollar haircut unruffled by the November breeze blowing across Lake Twilight, Mark stood on the front lawn of a Bed and Breakfast called The Merry Cherub. Back when Mark had lived in Twilight, the three-story Victorian had been a private residence. So okay, one thing had changed.

The bus that *Fact or Fantasy* had chartered at DFW Airport was parked curbside as his crew unloaded their gear. The show had reserved the entire third floor of The Merry Cherub for the three weeks they would be filming the "Romance of First Love" episode.

It was the episode he had inadvertently, and regrettably, triggered over dirty martinis at the Emmy Awards, when he'd told Burt Mernit about Twilight's legendary Jon and Rebekka, the fountain in Sweetheart Park and the enduring folklore of high-school sweethearts forever entwined.

Guests had come out of the establishment. Residents from the surrounding homes peeked through the curtains. Their audience stood on wide verandas, or paused on sidewalks, watching the goings-on with keen-eyed interest.

Eight years and he hadn't once come back. There'd been no need to return since his parents had moved away after he got a scholarship to Columbia University, buying their retirement home on the Texas Gulf Coast. There was nothing here that he'd left behind.

Except for Carrie.

At the thought of fiery Carrie MacGregor, who for forty-eight glorious hours (back when he had just turned nineteen and she was seventeen and a half) had been his wife, Mark's gut gave a strange squeeze. Blast from the past. He couldn't help wondering if she still lived in Twilight. If she did, he knew he'd run into her, and that thought tightened the squeeze.

He could have broken down and looked her up on the Internet, but for some reason he'd been reluctant to confirm her whereabouts. It felt too much like an invasion of her privacy. Too much like picking at an old scar.

Pasting the television smile on his face that he'd

been perfecting over the last five years in his meteoric rise from broadcast journalism intern to local L.A. news reporter to host of his own reality show, Mark turned and started up the sidewalk. He greeted the people on the front porch, pressed flesh, winked and charmed his way to the front door.

The proprietors of the Merry Cherub, a couple of married thirty-somethings named Jenny and Dean, ushered him inside. Jenny looked several months pregnant and kept her hand cradled lovingly around her distended belly.

The minute he stepped over the threshold, his mouth gaped. Everywhere he looked there were angels—angels on thick textured wallpaper, angel mobiles dangling from the ceiling, angels carved into the staircase banister and the crown molding. He doubted they had this many angels even in Heaven and every single one of the angels was grinning.

Hence the Merry Cherub. Now the B&B's name made total sense.

The crew, who trooped up the steps behind him, had similar reactions. There were gasps, chortles, and a few polite coughs.

Mark recovered quickly and dialed his surprise into the stunning dimpled grin that he knew had the power to send women into a swoon. "Beautiful place you've got here," he told Dean and Jenny smoothly.

Blushing prettily, Jenny led the way upstairs, while Dean helped the crew with their equipment. Mark's natural impulse was to roll up his sleeves and help with the bags as well, but he'd been coached in the finer points of looking like a star. His mentor was fond of saying, "Talent doesn't fetch or carry."

Mark was considered "the talent" of *Fact or Fiction*. The main draw. The future of the show rested on his shoulders. It was a heavy responsibility. Far better for him to look the part of successful host and ensure the crew members got to keep their jobs than to risk losing his authority by carrying a few bags. Still, it bothered him to ascend the steps empty-handed. This wasn't how he'd been raised. Letting others shoulder his burdens.

You can take the country boy to the city, but you can't take the country out of the man.

Jenny showed him to his suite. "The best in the house," she told him.

Angels had encroached even here. He resigned himself to an angel-filled three weeks. He was about to tip her, but when he reached into his pocket, a horrified look crossed her face and she raised her hands. "No tipping allowed at the Merry Cherub."

Feeling like a jackass, he stuck the twenty back in his pocket as she scooted out the door, tossing over her shoulder, "Dinner at seven. Homemade chicken pot pie."

She shut the door, leaving him all alone with the angels.

They wouldn't start shooting until tomorrow when the director, Iris Tobin, arrived. Until then, Mark was at loose ends. He walked to the French doors, threw them open and stepped out onto the balcony.

A bloom of autumn flowers decorated the wrought iron patio table. He stepped to the edge of the stone balustrade. To his right stretched Lake Twilight, simmering green-blue in the November afternoon. To his left lay the public street leading to a main thoroughfare that circled the town square. The street was framed with old-fashioned sidewalks and tall, elegant elms.

And that's when he saw her.

The tempestuous, gorgeous Carrie MacGregor, the woman who'd first stolen his heart way back in high school. She strode purposefully down the sidewalk, shoulders back, chin up, looking ready to tackle the world. She'd always been fearless like that—undaunted by obstacles, plowing straight ahead, letting nothing get in her way. Except for when his parents and her older sister conspired to break them apart.

The day was burned into his memory when they'd walked into his parents' home two days after Christmas, simple gold matching wedding bands on their ring fingers. Already the reality of what they'd done was starting to sink in. He didn't regret marrying Carrie, but facing his parents wasn't easy. They'd walked into the house, hand-in-hand, to find his parents and Flynn huddled around the kitchen table, the letter from Columbia lying open on the middle of the snowflake tablecloth and weighted down by a round Santa Claus salt shaker.

Don't blame it on Mom and Dad and Flynn. You were young, but plenty old enough to fight for her.

Yeah. There was the rub. He hadn't fought for her.

Carrie had taken one look at the letter and quickly sized up the situation. The first words out of her mouth were, "We made a big mistake."

What she blurted had shocked him because he'd been trying to figure out how he could be a freshman and provide for his young bride who had yet to finish high school. Everyone had discussed it. And Carrie had calmly suggested they should have the marriage annulled.

Mark had just sat there, letting it all unfold around him, feeling mournful, but also secretly a bit relieved and then guilty for that relief. He loved Carrie, but they were in over their heads. They'd allowed their hearts to overcome reason. He had graduated in December. Off-schedule, because when he'd been in seventh grade he'd contracted hepatitis A, missed three months of school and had to be held back a year. To compensate, he'd doubled up on classes in his senior year to finish at the Christmas holidays instead of the following May. With college looming and the thought of leaving Carrie behind weighing heavily on his mind, he'd hatched the idea of a Vegas wedding.

And so the wedding had been annulled.

He'd packed up for college. He'd promised to email. Promised he'd come back for her once he'd graduated.

He had not.

Carrie stopped on the corner, waiting for the light to change. She was dressed in blue jeans, comfortable sneakers and a bright yellow sweater that accentuated the auburn streaks in her soft brown hair.

The light changed and she took a step off the curb just as a zippy black Camaro darted through a red light at the intersection.

Mark's heart vaulted into his throat and he cried out a warning. "Carrie!"

She halted just in the nick of time as the car sped past her.

Relief pushed out fear, leaving his knees weak, shaky. If he hadn't called to her . . . He didn't even want to think about what could have happened.

She stepped back onto the curb, tossed her head, and glanced up over her shoulder.

Their eyes met.

He saw instant recognition dawn on her face. Her eyes were bluer than ever, her silky hair pulled back in a ponytail, no makeup on her face. But she didn't need makeup. Carrie was a natural beauty.

"Hold it," he called, suddenly freaked out that she would disappear on him. "Stay right there. I'm coming down."

He tore from his room and scrambled down the stairs. Several guests, including members of his crew were in the parlor. They stared at him as he flew out the front door. His heart was a piston, slamming hard and quick.

In six ground-eating strides he cut catty-corner across the Merry Cherub's lawn to find her still standing on the corner, a sardonic arch to one eyebrow, arms folded over her chest. Once he was there, he felt tongue-tied and stupid.

"Carrie," he mumbled, jamming his hands in his pants pockets. He realized he was breathing only from the top part of his lungs, short and tight, yet he couldn't seem to make himself haul in a deep breath.

She raked a sharp gaze over him, from the top of his head, down the length of his suit, to the tips of his shoes polished to a high sheen. He was very aware of how different he looked from the last time she'd seen him. Back then he'd dressed just as she dressed now—comfortable, homey, authentic.

Authentic? What did that mean?

"I suppose I should thank you," she said, cool as an ice water shower. "I was almost Camaro road kill."

He tried out his grin, hoping to win a smile from her in return, but no dice. Her blue eyes drilled through him like a spike. His smile stumbled, faltered.

"Thanks for the save." She turned her back and started walking away, but in the opposite direction of where she'd been headed before. Was she that rattled? Or had she simply changed her mind about where she was going?

He took off after her. "That's all I get after eight years?"

She stopped, her shoulders stiffening, and she sliced him with that razor gaze of hers. "That's all you deserve," she sassed.

Okay, he asked for that, but his blood was racing through his veins. He kept smiling.

She never budged, her mouth pulled in a taut, disapproving line. Ah, Carrie. How could she be even more beautiful now than she'd been before?

"You can go on about your rat killing." She waved a hand.

He hadn't heard that colloquial term since he'd left Texas. He'd done his best to scrub his accent and vocabulary of Texasisms. "I just wanted to make sure you were all right."

"Fine. Perfect. Hale and hearty. Gotta get back to work. See ya." She stalked off, ponytail swishing.

He sprinted after her, knowing he looked pretty damn silly in his fancy suit and shoes, chasing after her as autumn leaves swirled around them. "Can't you just stop and talk to me a minute?"

She chuffed out a sigh, sank her hands on her hips and turned to him. "What? What do you want from me?"

It was a legitimate question. What *did* he want from her?

She looked ferocious. Like she could rip his head off at the neck. Was she mad at him? Still? After all this time? Why should she still be mad, especially when she was the one who was the first to say they'd made a big mistake?

Why hadn't he called her?

Yeah, well, and say what? Sorry I bailed on you when opportunity knocked? Sorry I've changed and I'm not the country boy you once loved?

"We have nothing to discuss. We knew each other a long time ago."

"Can we at least be civil?" he asked.

She eyed him suspiciously.

"How's your folks?" he asked, trying for polite conversation.

"Mom died five years ago on Christmas Eve," she said dispassionately.

Immediately, he felt like a giant shitheel. He had not known. "Carrie. I'm so sorry."

"Appreciate the condolence card you sent." Her sarcasm was a knife to his heart.

He toed the ground, getting his shoes dusty. This was a mistake, trying to talk to her, but he didn't turn away. "How's your dad?" he asked softly.

"Clean and sober, thanks for asking." More sarcasm.

"What about the twins?"

"My brothers are in their senior years at Texas Tech."

"I can't believe it. Little Noah and Joel about to graduate college?"

"It *has* been eight years."

"And Flynn?"

"Happily married and expecting a baby."

"That's great news." He paused. "What about you, Carrie? Did you ever get married again?" He was stricken by the idea that he was too late, that she was already married. His gaze darted to her ring finger. Bare.

"Did you?" Her eyes narrowed.

"No."

"Me either. Once bitten, twice shy."

He swallowed, tried to think of the right thing to say.

"Listen, I've got things to do." She shifted her weight but did not meet his gaze.

"I'm going to be in town for three weeks, filming a show. Maybe we could get—"

"I know all about your show. Yay for you. In the

future, if I see you coming, I'll be sure to head in the opposite direction. Like now." She turned and started walking again.

"You didn't used to hold grudges," he called out, feeling unexpectedly desperate to keep her engaged in conversation. What was that all about? Why did he care?

Face it. You blew the best thing that ever happened to you.

It was a reality he'd spent eight years running from. He'd tucked her into the recesses of his mind. In the mental file, marked FOOLHARDY YOUTHFUL MISTAKES. From time to time, usually when he was feeling nostalgic or lonely, he'd trot out the memory file. Not often, but every once in a while when he found himself wondering, *What if?*

But now that he was here, looking at her, seeing how she'd bloomed into an amazingly beautiful woman, one thought dominated his brain.

You were a fool to let her slip through your fingers.

He remembered the salty sweet taste of her lips, like a big scoop of vanilla ice cream drizzled with caramel and topped with chopped nuts, and he had a compelling urge to taste them again.

She whirled on her heels and came marching back, wagging a finger at him. "Don't you believe for one single minute, Mark Leland, that I've had the time or inclination to think of you even once. God, what an ego! You think I've been sitting here pining away for your return?"

"A guy can hope."

"Look, yes you were a hottie in high school and

I was smitten enough to run off to Vegas with you, but it was just one dumb weekend out of my life."

One dumb weekend? She'd *married* him.

"Time marches on and you—" She waved a hand, curled her upper lip. "You became a sellout. Once upon a time you wanted to be a novelist. How in the hell did you end up hosting some silly reality show? The way I see it, you did me a huge favor. I dodged a bullet when you left. Thank you. I owe you my undying gratitude."

A sellout? She thought he was a sellout? He didn't know why that staggered him, but it did. "You're going to deny that you were in love with me?"

She opened her mouth as if she was about to hit him with a humdinger of a zinger, but she then snapped it shut. He dropped the smile that he'd been hanging onto. It was his default mode, and he just let it go. It felt scary, shucking off Mark Leland, TV personality, letting the well-constructed mask slip, if only for a second.

Narrowing her eyes, she stepped closer. So close the tips of her sneakers were almost touching the ends of his toes. He could smell her. Fragrant as the summer memories of time spent on her family's porch swing, all ripe honeysuckle and peaches and lovesick teens. Her scent had not changed. It was still the same honest, melodious aroma. She smelled of home.

Every impulse in his body pushed him to grab her up in his arms and kiss her until neither one of them could breathe.

"I was in love with an image of you. The person

I thought you were. Clearly, I was delusional. The person I knew would never, ever come back to wreck his hometown for personal gain."

If she'd hauled off and punched him in the stomach he couldn't have been more shocked. He shook his head. "I'm not here to wreck Twilight."

"No?"

"This show is going to help the town. Bring in more business."

Her glare dissected him like a medical examiner's scalpel, clean and mean. "Ah, I get it now."

"Get what?"

"How you live with who you've become. You spin yourself beautiful lies and then fall for them. Lying is one thing, believing your own bullshit is something else."

A brackish taste filled his mouth, and he felt immediately defensive. Who was she to judge? The woman who'd stayed in the same small town all her life. The woman who told *him* their marriage was a mistake. "What's wrong with who I've become?"

"If you have to ask, you're even more clueless than I thought." Tart. That tongue of hers.

He should have just let it go. There was absolutely no reason to continue the conversation. He had changed. He no longer belonged here, and she was wrapped in the cocoon of Twilight and couldn't see beyond the narrow confines of her insular little world. This is what he would have been like if he'd stayed.

But he couldn't help thinking about all he'd missed. Waking up beside her every morning, making love to her every night. Wistful. Whenever he looked at those lush lips, stared into her saucy blue eyes, he felt an unexpected yearning for what he'd let slip through his fingers.

"Wake-up call, Leland. Your show is going to destroy Twilight," she said. "Not boost business."

"How do you figure?" He leaned in toward her until their noses were almost touching. Alarm flared in her eyes, but she held her ground. She'd always been brave. It was one of the things he'd most admired about her.

"*Fact or Fantasy* is about busting myths and legends, right?" She notched up her chin.

"So?"

"What do you think is going to happen when you bust the very myth this town is founded on?"

"How do you know I'm not going to prove the myth true?" he murmured.

"Because," she said, darting out the tip of her pink tongue to moisten her lips. The gesture caused something to shift below his belt. "The myth says if you toss a penny into the fountain, you'll be forever reunited with your high school sweetheart and live happily ever after."

"You tossed a penny into the fountain?" His pulse was revving like the engine of his Cobra running full throttle on the open road. He could feel blood throbbing through his entire body.

"Once, long ago. When I was young and stupid and believing in a ridiculous legend."

"Carrie." Her name came out of him like a sigh. He remembered his longing for her, because it hit him anew. This yearning. A slap to the face—shocking.

"So you see, Mark. The legend is *total* crap, because there's no way in hell that you and I will ever, not ever in your wildest dreams, be reunited, much less live happily-ever-after."

"Okay," he said, feeling sick to his stomach.

"But if you ever felt anything at all for me, you have to make me a promise."

"What's that?"

"You cannot tell anyone about us. You cannot use our love affair to disabuse the sweetheart myth. You can't capitalize on our failure to line your pockets. Especially when doing so will put Twilight's livelihood in jeopardy."

"All right," he said.

"Promise me." Desperate sincerity shone in her eyes.

"I promise," he assured.

Her shoulders sagged visibly. "Thank you. If you keep your promise, then everything is square between us."

"I'll keep it," he said, mainly because he wasn't any more eager than she was for the world to find out exactly how much he'd let her down.

Chapter Three

Two days after her run-in with Mark, Carrie was at the Yarn Barn scowling at the cheery Christmas decorations that the knitting club had put up, but she wasn't glaring at the ornaments as much as she was the current situation. Seeing Mark again had shaken her more than she'd anticipated.

"Chill," said Renee, the high school girl who worked for Carrie on the weekends. "You're gonna pace a hole in the floor."

Carrie stood in front of the window looking out across the shopping center parking lot, realizing for the first time that she had been prowling like a cat outside a mouse hole. She crossed her arms over her chest.

"What's got you so worked up?" Renee asked, looking up for the first time that morning from the cell phone where she'd been engrossed in a game of Angry Birds.

"Nothing. I'm not worked up."

"Uh-huh," Renee said. "Sure you're not." The girl reminded Carrie far too much of her smart-mouthed self at that age.

"Don't you have work to do?"

Renee shrugged, shoved a strand of purple hair from her forehead. "I already put away all the stock."

Ever since Mark and his stupid reality show had come to town, business had slacked off. It seemed everyone would rather gawk and follow the film crew around town than shop for yarn.

Okay, she was cranky. She hadn't slept well the last two nights, but it had nothing to do with Mark Leland and those pesky sex dreams she'd been having. "Not at all."

"What did you say?" Renee asked.

Great. Now she was muttering under her breath. "Stop whacking pigs and knit something," Carrie told her.

With a long-suffering eye roll perfected to an art form by sixteen-year-olds the world over, Renee turned off her cell phone and picked up the basket-weave scarf she'd been working on.

The truth was Carrie was rattled. She thought she'd braced herself for seeing Mark again, but one look in those chocolate brown eyes and she'd known she was in trouble. All the old feelings had come rushing back, stronger than ever. Why? Because she thought she was long over him.

No love like your first love, Flynn was fond of saying ever since she and Jesse got back together. In fact, it was something irritating that all the ladies of the Sweethearts Knitting Club said from time to time with smug, knowing smiles on their faces.

Bah-freaking-humbug.

So much for her goal of getting through the holidays as smoothly as possible. Just as she was about to turn away from the window, she saw a bus pull into the parking lot. She recognized it immediately. It was the vehicle *Fact or Fantasy* had rented to haul the crew around.

It wasn't as if she could miss it. A parade of cars followed behind, including a red convertible, packed with young women holding a banner that read: *We Love You Mark.*

What a cluster circus. Carrie borrowed one of Renee's eye rolls. The bus door opened and Mark got out, along with a willow-branch thin middle-aged woman in stern, red-framed square glasses. They started in her direction, the film crew and entourage following behind.

For one panicked moment, Carrie thought they were coming into the Yarn Barn, then she realized with relief they were headed to her brother-in-law's motorcycle shop located on the other side of her building.

She was not the least bit curious about what was going on over there, but she pressed her nose against the window and craned her neck just in time to see Mark's backside looking unnecessarily spectacular in a pair of tailored suit pants.

Humph. She preferred him in jeans. That's how she remembered him. Rugged, scruff of beard,

Levi's clinging to his hard muscled butt. Not this smooth, shaved, sophisticated man. Columbia and L.A. had remade him into someone she did not recognize. It was inevitable, she supposed. Why then, did she feel like she'd lost something significant?

You didn't lose a single thing. Forget him. Sell some yarn.

Except there were no customers to sell yarn to; they were all over at Jesse's. A bulky bodyguard positioned himself at the door of the motorcycle shop after the film crew had gone inside. He held up his hand like a stop sign at the spectators mobbing around the front of the store.

"What's going on over there?" Renee asked.

"Who knows? Who cares? Watch the shop, I'll be right back."

"Huh?" Renee blinked.

But Carrie was already out the back exit and creeping down the alley that connected the Yarn Barn to the motorcycle shop. The wind blew off the lake, whipping through her denim skirt. She shivered.

What the hell are you doing? Go back to your shop. Forget Mark.

Quietly, she opened the rear door to Jesse's store and found herself surrounded by motorcycles in various stages of repair. Jesse not only sold new machines but repaired old ones as well.

The sound of voices in the showroom drew her in that direction. She crept to the door that led out into the shop and placed her hand on the knob. Flynn hadn't said a word about Jesse being interviewed on *Fact or Fantasy*. Maybe her sister didn't know.

Carefully, she pushed the door open a crack. The hinges squeaked. She cringed. The last thing she wanted was to get caught spying on Mark. If he caught her spying, he might think she cared. She didn't care.

Well, not much.

But she was curious. Cautiously, she put her eye to the slit and peered into the showroom.

Jesse was standing at the counter, his back to her, a sprocket in one hand, and a red grease rag in the other. Mark stood in front of Jesse glancing at note cards in his hand. The camera crew was setting up.

A woman carrying a makeup tray flitted around the two men. "Mr. Calloway," she said. "Can I put a dusting of powder on your cheeks so you don't shine on camera?"

Jesse shifted uncomfortably. "Never wore makeup in my life. Not gonna start now."

The makeup girl shot a glance toward Mark.

"It's okay, Ladonna," he assured her. "We can work magic in editing."

Ladonna smiled and turned her makeup brush on Mark's cheeks.

Carrie opened the door wide enough to ease through. She tiptoed closer, using various shelving to stay hidden.

"Ready?" a cameraman asked Mark.

Mark tapped his finger against a tiny microphone pinned to his lapel. "Testing."

The sound guy gave him a thumbs-up.

"Roll it," the thin woman in the red glasses ordered.

The camera honed in on Mark, who dissolved into a toothy dimpled grin. The same grin that used to turn Carrie's knees to rubber. Oh, who the hell was she kidding? Her knees were still wiggly as Jell-O.

Mark was so cool and self-possessed. Totally in control. He'd always been something of a cocky guy, but this was a whole new level of self-confidence.

Her heart thumped crazily. He is so out of her league—tall, cutting-edge hairstyle, striking brown eyes. He was perfect for television. No wonder he'd given up on the idea of writing a novel. He'd made choices that led him to the top of his field. He'd changed. While she . . . well, she was still in Twilight wasn't she? Running a yarn store and living with her father.

Mark's voice rang out, authoritative and clear. "Our investigation into the sweetheart legend has led us to an infamous resident of Twilight, Texas. Jesse Calloway was a bad boy incarcerated for ten years. But the love of his high school sweetheart, Flynn MacGregor, tamed his wild ways."

Jesse's scowl deepened. "That's not how the story goes."

Mark made a cutting motion with his hand across his neck. "We talked about this, Jesse. Casting you as the tamed outlaw is the angle we're pursuing. It's all about that marketing hook. Redeemed by love. That's the story."

"I was wrongly imprisoned for a crime I didn't commit," Jesse said. "Are you gonna mention that?"

Her brother-in-law's life had been hard indeed.

Carrie felt sorry for Jesse and wondered why he was doing this interview.

"We'll mention that in the wrap-up, but for the thrust of the story we're going with the outlaw tamed," Mark said.

"I don't think I want to do this after all," Jesse grumbled.

"If you don't complete the interview, Mr. Calloway," the woman in the red glasses said in her rapid-fire East-Coast staccato, "you won't get the thousand dollars."

Ah, that explained why Jesse was doing this. He was getting paid for his story. More money for his growing family.

The front door opened, and the bodyguard ushered Flynn in while blocking the chattering horde outside the store. Her sister's normally curly brown hair had been pulled into a French braid. She looked beautiful, a glowing mother-to-be awaiting the birth of her first child.

Carrie sidled around the rack of tires for a better look, ducking behind a cardboard Santa and its tray of holiday-sale wrenches.

No one noticed her, so she edged even closer.

"I'm so sorry I'm late," Flynn said.

"No problem. We're just glad you could make it. What's the story of the town's most famous lovebirds if only one of the birds ends up on camera," said the uber-thin woman. She held out her hand to Flynn. "I'm Iris Tobin, the director of *Fact or Fantasy*."

"Nice to meet you." Flynn smiled.

"When's the little one due?" Iris asked.

"Christmas Eve."

"Oh, seriously? That's so adorable. We must include pictures of the baby in a little epilogue when this episode airs early next year."

"We'll see." Flynn pursed her lips.

Her sister was a people-pleaser, but she was also cautious. Carrie admired her for not immediately agreeing to Iris's request to film the baby.

"Do you know what you're having?" Iris asked.

Flynn shook her head. "We wanted to be surprised."

The makeup artist bustled around Flynn, touching up her face.

A few minutes later, they started filming again. Mark was very much in control as he coaxed Flynn and Jesse into the story of their romance.

It was a touching tale, one that epitomized the town legend. As long as Mark stuck to couples like Flynn and Jesse, the sweetheart legend would bear itself out, and Twilight's reputation would be safe. But this show challenged popular myths. Sooner or later, someone was bound to unearth her connection to Mark and bust the sweetheart myth wide open. So far everyone had been keeping quiet about their relationship, but of course it was to the town's best interest for their failed love affair to be kept under wraps.

Carrie anxiously gnawed her thumbnail. It was unnerving to think that the town's fate weighed on her shoulders. But he had promised not to reveal their past relationship. Would he keep his promise? Once upon a time, his word had been golden. But now? Who knew? He'd changed so much.

She leaned forward, her gaze trained on Mark. He was impressive. Even in his polished persona, he exuded a raw magnetism that was impossible to deny. Honestly, she was taken aback by how handsome he'd become. He'd been good-looking before, but now he was breathtaking. Damn him.

Mesmerized by her former husband's accomplished performance, she didn't notice at first that the cardboard Santa had started swaying. When she realized what was happening, she put out a hand to steady the wavering display. Santa was lighter than she anticipated, the metal tray of wrenches balanced on his extended cardboard hands heavier than they should have been. Instead of helping things, her touch pushed Santa over the edge.

Carrie felt him slipping away. She scrambled, actively grabbing for the toppling effigy. Making noise. Drawing attention. *Crap!* Santa bucked backward. Wrenches flew into the air, clattering to the ground around her.

Iris Tobin yelled at her. "Who are you? Get out of here immediately. This is a closed shoot."

"Um . . . I . . ." Chagrined, Carrie dropped to her knees and started picking up the scattered wrenches, unable to look at anyone. Way to go, MacGregor.

"Stop that. Leave the mess. Get out. Who left the back door unlocked?" Iris Tobin snapped. "Ladonna, you were supposed to make sure the back door was locked. We can't have gawkers stumbling around and ruining our shoot."

"Mellow out, Iris," Mark said, a sharp edge in his voice. "You're acting like a bitch."

The director glared, nostrils flaring and she clapped her hands. "Olig!" She motioned for the bodyguard. "Escort this person out."

Carrie stood, preparing to run before the hulking bodyguard could get to her, cheeks blazing a hundred and twenty degrees worth of shame. Why, oh why hadn't she stayed put in the Yarn Barn?

Mark stepped between Carrie and Iris. "She stays," he said, his tone low and dangerous. "This is Flynn's sister, Carrie. She owns the yarn store next door."

"What? Are we inviting in everyone's family now?" Iris groused. "Should I call my mother? Send her a plane ticket?"

Mark ignored her sarcasm.

"I'm going," Carrie said. "I shouldn't have been here."

"Well what do you know?" Iris said. "We agree on something."

Mark reached out, took her hand. Carrie was aware that everyone was watching them. Could they see how his touch unraveled her? Did it show on her face that her stomach was in tumult and her heart, oh her stupid heart, was melting?

"You belong here," he said firmly and threw Iris a don't-make-an-issue-of-this glare. Still holding onto

Carrie's hand, he took her behind the counter, retrieved a stool and carried it to one side of the cameras. "You can sit here."

This was a bad idea. She wished she could slink off, but now that he'd made a big deal of it she had to stay. She perched on the stool. Mark gave her shoulder a squeeze, then moved back to take his place in front of the camera. Jesse smiled at her. Flynn gave her a little wave.

Unhappy Iris Tobin folded her arms over her chest. "Places everyone. Let's start again from the top."

The crew zipped about, doing their jobs.

Across the room Mark's eyes met her gaze. No, not just met hers. His gaze devoured her. When he gave her a conspiratorial wink, all the air rushed from her lungs and caused her nipples to bead. What was he doing? Was he trying to rattle her? And why was her shoulder still tingling from where he'd touched it?

Unable to fight back against his long, lingering stare, she clenched her eyes closed, hauled in a deep slow breath as a stunning realization smacked her.

Dammit. No matter how much she wished it was not true, she was still crazy about the man.

Chapter Four

"This is no good," Iris said on the day before Thanksgiving as she and Mark sat in his suite at The Merry Cherub reviewing the footage they'd shot so far. Delicious smells from the kitchen of the B&B drifted upstairs—apples, cinnamon, cornbread, pumpkin, nutmeg.

The rest of the crew had left, taking the bus back to DFW Airport to catch flights home for the holiday. They would all be back by Monday to continue shooting the "Romance of First Love" episode.

Iris stubbed out her cigarette in a china saucer that Jenny had brought on a tray with tea and cookies to the suite, and got to her feet.

"What do you mean no good? There are some wonderful stories here. Heartwarming. Touching." Mark waved away the smoke. "There's the story of Patsy and Hondo, loving each other since they were teens and finally just now getting married. There's the story of Sarah and Travis Walker, two polar opposites no one ever thought would end up together. There's Jesse and Flynn, whose love withstood Jesse's ten-year incarceration. There's Caitlyn Marsh and Gideon Garza. Not even death could keep them apart."

"Fluff. Feel-good pap." Iris shook her head.

Personally, he thought the interviews were the best work of his career. He was smooth on camera. His jokes were witty. He'd been prepping for this big break his entire life. Well, that wasn't entirely true. Initially, he'd wanted to be a journalist by day, a novelist by night, but with technology changing the landscape of journalism, his college advisors had quickly steered him toward television and away from print journalism.

Over the course of the past several days, the crew had gone around town filming the town square, the statue of Jon and Rebekka in a passionate embrace in Sweetheart Park, and the Sweetheart Tree, an ancient oak where lovers had carved their names since the town's inception.

All the stories they'd researched were happy ones. High school sweethearts who'd thrown pennies into the fountain and married their first loves. Sure, many of the couples, like Jesse and Flynn, had overcome a lot of obstacles on their way back to each other, but the truth was, for all their searching, they hadn't yet found any high school sweethearts that admitted tossing coins into the fountain who were not happily married to each other.

Except for you and Carrie.

And he was determined to keep that a secret from Iris. He'd made Carrie a sworn promise.

"We aren't busting anything." Iris scowled. "We're confirming this stupid myth. Where's the controversy? Where's the conflict? That's what is going to have viewers tuning in. Conflict. Not happy people with smug, sappy smiles on their faces."

Irritating as Iris could be, she was right. Ever since his talk with Carrie on the afternoon that he'd arrived, Mark had been tiptoeing around any whiff of controversy. He actively sought out couples that epitomized the legend. He wanted to spare Carrie any embarrassment or pain.

Come on. Be honest. It's not just about Carrie. You don't want anyone finding out about your annulled marriage because you don't want to look like a failure.

Okay, maybe not. But it wasn't because he was ashamed of her. Rather, he was ashamed of himself and the way he'd treated her. He was able to hide his guilt in L.A. Forget about what he'd done. But now that he was back in Twilight, remorse pole-axed him every time he saw her.

And she seemed to be everywhere. Eating lunch at The Funny Farm restaurant on the square at the same time he and the crew had walked in. Sauntering past The Merry Cherub twice a day on her way to and from work. Spying on them at the shoot in Jesse Calloway's motorcycle shop. He smiled. Damn, but she'd looked so cute, knocking over wrenches and pissing off Iris.

He glanced at his watch. She should be coming by right about now. He moved to the French doors.

"It's too soft, too pretty, too perfect." Iris followed him out onto the balcony. "We need to find those high school sweethearts who hate each other's guts. The ones who've gotten divorced. The ones who threw pennies into the fountain and found only busted dreams. They're here. You know they have to be here. We've gotta start kicking over rocks. It's clear the citizens have circled the wagons and are feeding us pablum. But you're an ace reporter. It's the main reason Burt hired you for this gig. Well, that and the damned dimples."

Right on schedule, here came Carrie heading down the street. Today she wore one of those round skirts that whirled and twirled as she walked. Red plaid, that skirt. Black tights. Black ankle boots, a perfectly crafted white cable knit sweater molded over glorious breasts. Mark knew first-hand just how glorious. She looked the epitome of autumn.

Mark took a deep breath. Imagined he could smell her sweet perfume. Carrie. No other woman had ever smelled like her.

"There's got to be at least one couple who did not live happily ever after," Iris harped.

Yeah, he thought, and they're closer than you think.

Iris tilted her head. "What about you, Leland? You grew up in this town. What ever happened to your high school sweetheart?"

"Didn't have one," he fibbed.

"You expect me to believe that? You of the lady-killing smile."

"I didn't say I didn't have girlfriends. Just no one special." The lie was acid on his tongue, but he couldn't tell the truth. He had to protect Carrie.

His secret was so transparent. Everyone who'd lived in Twilight eight years ago knew the story of what had happened between him and Carrie. Their impulsive Vegas marriage had made the front page of the lifestyle section of the Twilight paper, just as their subsequent annulment had. Small towns thrived on gossip, and sooner or later Iris was bound to find out about him and Carrie. In fact, he was mildly surprised it hadn't already come to light.

Then he realized the town had a vested interest in keeping their myths alive. Of course they would stay mum on the topic of his history with Carrie. And if their relationship was found out, Carrie could always deny that she'd ever thrown a penny into the fountain. No penny thrown, no myth set in motion.

He watched Carrie stroll closer, her steps springy and self-confident. She was almost underneath the balcony now. He held his breath. Willed her to look up.

She just kept on walking.

"I'm sending out a mole," Iris said. "Someone to hang out at the local hot spots, put their ear to the ground for gossip."

"Hey, maybe the myth is true." He shrugged. "It could be a self-fulfilling prophecy. These couples go into marriage with their high school sweethearts thinking that they are with their soul mates and it will last forever, and so it does. It's kind of sweet when you think about it."

Iris made a face and pushed her glasses up on her nose. "Don't be a dolt. The myth is total bullshit. All romantic stories are bullshit."

"Burned by love, huh?" he observed wryly.

"Everyone has been burned by love," Iris declared. "In one way or another. Every single human being on the face of the earth."

Angry much? Mark raised his palms. "Gotcha."

He leaned over the edge of the balcony, watching Carrie walk away. Her auburn hair tumbled provocatively down her shoulders. And the way those hips swayed. My. My. *Those hips could have been exclusively yours, but you threw them away.* Yes, yes. Stupid in hindsight.

Carrie turned the corner, disappeared from view. Bye-bye, Beautiful.

"You used to live in this town." Iris narrowed her eyes. "You should be the mole."

"They don't trust me. I'm the enemy, remember."

"It may take you a little time to win them over, but you've got the looks and the charm. Someone is bound to blab."

"Why can't we just roll with the idea that the myth is true? In all the other *Fact or Fantasy* episodes, we've proven every one of the legends were fantasies. Why not have one episode where fact wins?"

"Because the sweetheart legend is not a fact! Besides, I don't want to perpetuate this crap. Somewhere in this town the love of someone's life has broken their heart and you're going to find them." Iris shook a bony finger at him.

"Okay, boss."

"So go." She flapped a hand at him.

"Go where?"

"Go out and find the lovelorn. I suggest you try the local bar."

"Now?"

"Can you think of a better time? We only have two weeks left and we're losing four days of filming because of Thanksgiving."

"Are you flying home for the holiday?" Mark asked.

"What for?"

"Celebration, family, that sort of thing."

Iris snorted. "I have no time for that stuff. It's maudlin and mawkish."

"You don't have to act tough all the time."

"Look who's talking? Why aren't *you* going to have Thanksgiving with your family?"

"My parents are on a cruise for their thirty-fifth wedding anniversary."

"Lucky you. Now go. Head to the local bar. Do your job and when you get back, I want this sweetheart myth busted wide open."

Carrie wasn't much of a drinker. Because of her father's history with alcohol, she tended to stay away from the stuff, but she'd had a stressful week with Mark in town, plus she and her father were hosting Thanksgiving dinner the next day and she needed to decompress before gearing up for the celebration.

She climbed on a stool at the Horny Toad Tavern, hooked her boot heels over the top rungs and ordered a beer. The jukebox was playing "Blue Christmas," perfectly suiting her gloomy mood. Go Elvis. Raylene was behind the bar looking as glum as Carrie felt.

"What'll you have, honey?"

"Beer will do."

"Any particular kind?"

"Whatever is on tap."

Raylene poured up a mug, slid it over to Carrie, and then trailed off to wait on other customers.

Carrie sucked foam off the beer, and a pleasant burning sensation tickled her nose. She swiveled around to survey the crowded room. On the dance floor, couples were boot-scooting, dancing cheek-to-cheek. A cluster of mistletoe dangled from the strobe light over the dance floor. Every now and then some of the couples bussed lips.

Bah-humbug.

This town *was* too damn romantic for its own good. The ornery Grinch in her wanted to see the legend busted, but she was a Twilightite to the core. She couldn't disrespect her home.

It occurred to her that she would be the only single person at the Thanksgiving dinner table. Her brothers, Noah and Joel, were bringing their girlfriends home from college. Flynn had Jesse, and even her dad was dating again. Barbara Duffy, the public librarian.

That was okay. No problem. She didn't need a date. Didn't want one, really.

It occurred to her then that she hadn't had a serious relationship since Mark. Oh, she'd had boyfriends. Plenty of them, in fact. But not a single one she considered a keeper. Why not? Did she purposely pick inappropriate guys because she was secretly holding out hope that there was some truth to the legend of Jon and Rebekka? Some dumb indoctrinated belief that pennies flung into a fountain could somehow reshape the future?

Mark *is* back in town.

No. Stop. Don't even toy with that dangerous idea.

"Is this seat taken?"

She didn't have to look over to see who had just spoken to her in that bone-vibrating bass. She'd recognize it anywhere. Her hand tightened around the beer mug, and deep inside something foolish was happening to her body—a fine quivering, a smooth warmth, a delicious strum of energy. Carrie wasn't even going to acknowledge that she was turned on. No way. Mark Leland did not hold that kind of power over her.

"Yep," she said, not glancing his way as she took another draw from her beer.

He acted as if she'd said, "Yep, have a seat."

She wouldn't glance over because even as he pulled out the neighboring bar stool and sat down, she was fighting a highly stupid urge to grab him by the arm, drag him onto the dance floor underneath the mistletoe, and kiss him until she forgot that eight years and the distance from L.A. to Twilight stretched between them.

Dammit! She thought she'd beaten this attraction. Snuffed it out. Stamped it down. Gotten rid of any pesky desire she'd once felt for him. Apparently, she had not. Finally, unable to stand it, she darted a quick glance his way.

Big mistake.

He'd shed the high-dollar suit and shoes and instead wore faded jeans, a western shirt, and cowboy boots. There, in the shadows from the neon bar lights, he could have been nineteen again. He possessed deep brown eyes a girl could bathe in. Dimples that her index finger ached to caress. He was long and lanky and sexy as sin.

Stay strong.

There was no backtracking. No repeating the past. What was done was done. Hmm, how many more tired adages could she drag out to convince herself that it was well and truly O.V.E.R. between them?

Raylene came over. "What'll you have, Mark?"

"Beer will do."

"Slummin', huh?" Carrie couldn't resist the dig. "Beer is quite a comedown from Dom Perignon."

Another guy might have taken offense, considered that putting up with her barbed tongue wasn't worth the effort, but Mark just laughed. "Actually, Dom Perignon is way overrated."

"Aha, so you have drunk Dom."

"I have," he said mildly.

"You know what, I'm happy for you," she said, finding that she meant it. "You got everything you ever wanted."

"Not everything." His voice deepened.

Carrie darted a glance his way, saw dark emotion in his eyes. Was it regret?

"I wouldn't blame you for hating me forever," Mark said.

"I don't hate you." She splayed both palms against the smooth wood of the bar. *I still love you, you clueless nimrod.*

But there was no way in hell she would ever tell him that. She'd only quietly admitted it to herself right that very moment. She would always love him in a way, she supposed. Her first love. Her high school sweetheart. But so what? There were ninety thousand reasons they could never be together. She'd just have to live with the hole in her heart until one day when she found a new love who had the power to wipe Mark Leland from her memory.

At that moment, the music shifted on the jukebox, going from Christmas melodies to The Rolling Stones playing "Memory Motel." Okay, what joker put that song on?

"That means a lot to me," he murmured. Then he moved his hand ever so slightly and lightly touched her right thumb with the pinkie finger of his left hand.

Barely there, but that tiny touch lit her up like the Fourth of July sky. *Move your hand!* But instead of jerking away—instead, oh instead—she curled her thumb around his finger. Instantly, a brick of tears log-jammed her throat.

Do not cry! Under no circumstances are you to cry.

Mark's hand covered hers and he leaned closer. "Dance with me, Carrie."

It was a terrible idea. She opened her mouth to tell him no, but he was already off his stool, her hand clasped in his, dragging her toward the dance floor.

And just like that, she allowed herself to be led.

He slipped his arms around her, his gaze locked on her face. "What's wrong?" he murmured.

He could read her so well. Even after all those years. His gentle voice prodded, urging her to tell him everything. The tears were in her mouth now, salty and so close to slipping down her cheeks. She would not let him know how much he affected her.

"You mean besides the fact you highjacked me into dancing with you?" she sassed and gulped down the tears. There. She'd won.

"Uh-huh." His grip tightened around her waist as he two-stepped her around the other dancers. He moved with instinctive grace, never once taking his eyes off her face.

"I don't want to dance with you."

"I know." He pulled her closer still. "You can tell me anything, Carrie. I want you to know that."

Oh, yes. Just open her mouth and say, I love you. How well would that really go over?

He guided her head to his shoulder, and like a fool she just kept it resting there, breathing in the manly scent of his cologne.

Her stomach gave a shaky, vulnerable quiver. He was so much more than he once was. Masculine as ever, but now all the rough edges were polished off. He was on a whole different plane. A Hollywood big wheel. She was only Carrie MacGregor from Twilight. But Mark? He was a star.

From the jukebox, Chris Issak was singing "Wicked Games." She had to agree with the lyrics.

She did not want to fall in love, but it was far too late. She'd fallen for him in high school, and no matter what she told herself to the contrary she'd never really gotten over him.

"Do you remember when we danced like this at the nightclub in Caesar's Palace?" he whispered in her ear.

Carrie remembered all too well. She lifted her head from his shoulder, stared into his eyes. "That was a very long time ago."

He cupped her chin in his hand, his thumb sliding over her jaw, his gaze hooked on her mouth. She could almost taste him. The way he used to taste, once upon a time. Did he still taste the same?

"Carrie," he said softly, her name rolling off his tongue like a prayer.

As if he really, truly cared about her.

She stopped moving in the middle of the dance floor and rooted her feet, causing him to have to stop, too. "This was a really bad idea."

"So is this," he said. "But I'm doing it anyway."

Then there, underneath the mistletoe on Thanksgiving Eve, her former husband kissed her.

Chapter Five

Mark closed his mouth over Carrie's delectable lips and the circuit board of his brain lit up. At last she was in his arms once more. Illogically, it felt as if he'd been holding his breath for eight long years, and finally he could breathe again.

Dimly, he was aware of a smattering of applause, the sound of the jukebox changing, and then came John Mayer singing *their* song. "Your Body is a Wonderland."

Meddlesome, small-town folks. A guy had to love them. People you knew. People you could trust. People who had your back no matter what. The kind of people he had not found since he'd left Twilight in his rearview mirror. How much he had willingly given up for success.

His people.

Her sweet mouth turned salty, and Carrie gave a little shiver. Her shoulders trembled as if she was crying. Carrie? Crying? On another woman, maybe, but this was tough, sassy, tart-mouthed Carrie MacGregor. He'd never seen her cry. She was a rock.

Slowly, he peeled his mouth from hers. "Carrie, are you crying?"

She smacked a palm against his chest, pushed back. "Screw you."

Yeah, well, that thought had been primary in his mind since he'd looked over that balcony and seen her on the street. "Sweetheart, I didn't mean to make you cry."

"I'm not crying!" She swiped at her eyes. "Don't for one minute think you have that kind of power over me, Mark Leland." Her cheeks flushed.

Around them the other couples had stopped dancing. They were drawing an audience.

"Babe, I'm so sorry," he said. It was inadequate. Too little, too late. He knew it.

"If you're really sorry, then get me the hell out of here."

"What do you mean?" Mark asked.

"Do you want to be with me or not?"

She didn't have to ask twice. He took her hand and pulled her toward the exit, ignoring the hoots and catcalls from the bar patrons.

But once he had her outside, he didn't know what to do with her. He'd walked over here from the B&B.

Carrie seemed to understand his dilemma. She pulled car keys from her pocket and tossed them to him. "You drive."

"Where should we go?"

"Use your imagination."

Was this right? Did she want what he thought she

wanted? Should he take her where they used to go? The fishing pier beside the old Twilight Bridge that spanned the Brazos River not far from the house where Carrie grew up.

She climbed into the passenger side of a white VW bug. "You coming?"

Oh yeah, baby. You betcha. His breath slipped out in hot, excited exhalations as he climbed into the front seat and fumbled with the side latch, sliding the seat back far enough to accommodate his long legs. He was so hot and bothered by the thought of being with Carrie again that he couldn't think straight and for a moment got turned around. He took off in the wrong direction and had to make a U-turn.

He reached across the seat, found her hand, and squeezed it. "Are you sure about this?"

"Shut up and drive, before I change my mind."

He pushed his foot down hard on the accelerator, bulleting the VW past the Twilight city limits.

Carrie clung tight to his hand. He looked over at her. God, he couldn't believe it. He was going to be with her again. His heart kicked against his chest wall.

It seemed to take forever to get to the Brazos River, but in reality it was only a few minutes. Neither of them spoke. The moon was just coming up as he turned down the road leading to the old wooden suspension bridge.

Except the old bridge was no longer there. In its place stood a nice new stone footbridge.

"What happened to the bridge?" he asked.

"Long story." Carrie waved a hand.

"It's all changed." He felt confused by this new development. Disoriented.

"A lot of things have changed. You've been away a long time."

It was true. He'd changed as much as the bridge. "I know," he said huskily.

They sat there in silence, and for a minute he thought she was going to call the whole thing off. He fully expected it. This was not a smart thing to do. He opened his mouth to say so but never got the words out.

"The old pier is still there," she whispered. They'd made good use of that pier more than once. "There's a blanket in the back seat."

She opened the door and got out. He reached over the back seat, found the blanket and joined her in the darkness.

The river flowed lazily toward Lake Twilight, moonlight glinting off the smooth surface. The air was cool and damp, but not uncomfortably so. Carrie trailed out toward the bridge and Mark rushed to keep up with her. He took her hand and guided her down the sloping embankment to the water. A vapor security light mounted on the side of the bridge shone a misty gray light.

How many times had they come down to the water like this, hand-in-hand?

Carrie wore snug-fitting blue jeans that showed off her slender, curvy hips, a white T-shirt, tweed blazer, and cowboy boots. They could have been teenagers again, sneaking off to be alone.

Beside the bridge, a wooden fishing pier extended into the water. Their boots clattered against the sturdy cedar. They'd jumped naked off this pier more times than he could count. But that had been in the hot summer months. Not in the chill of November.

She took the blanket from his arms and bent to spread it out on an area of the pier that was cloaked in the shadow of the bridge. When she straightened, Mark pulled her close to him, felt the rapid thudding in her heart, and realized his heart was pounding just as hard and fast.

They stood looking at each other in a silence as long as the new bridge, as wide as the years that separated them. Her hair had started to curl in the humidity. She smelled so good. He loved the way her body felt molded against his. As if she belonged there. As if he belonged to her.

He wanted her. Oh yeah. He was harder than he'd ever been and he had no doubt that she could feel the strength of his desire, but he was content for the time being just to stand there savoring the moment.

Her hand crept between them, her fingers crawling up to stroke the hollow of his throat, as if she couldn't believe they were together again, her gaze locked with his. They breathed in the same air.

It wasn't just him. She was feeling it too!

The magic. The past rushing to meld with the future. The truth of the sweetheart legend. He and Carrie. Meant to be together forever. It startled Mark how much he wanted it to be true. Was there a way to reconcile his old life with the new one?

Carrie went up on her toes.

Mark lowered his head.

They met in the middle. A mutual kiss.

He reached for her hands, laced their fingers together. She arched her back, pushed against him, her breasts pressing into his chest. He had to have her.

Her teeth parted inviting him in.

That ripped his control. He darted his tongue between those teasing teeth, kissed her with every ounce of passion that had been gathering in him since he'd returned to Twilight.

There were so many reasons they should not be doing this. They hadn't talked about the future. Hadn't discussed their expectations. But the desire was too raw, too insistent for talk. Only action would serve. He had to act. Had to make her his once again. Had to correct the mistakes he'd made. Had to make amends, and the best way he knew how to do that was with his body.

No two ways about it. They were going to make love. Right now. Right here on this same pier where they'd made love several times before in the blush of their wide-eyed youth.

He kissed her until they were both shaky and clinging to each other. The kiss was hot and hard and full of everything he felt for her. All the feelings he'd tried to bury, tried to ignore and deny. Carrie! To have her in his arms again. Bliss.

He hungered for her in a way he had never hungered for another. His blood ran like lava, rising and surging, pushing through his body, down into his groin. Hell, he was lost. Gone.

There was nothing on the earth for him but her. The sound of her soft little sighs, the feel of her tender flesh, the taste of her. Damn, but she tasted like victory. Sweet and hard-won.

They fit. She curved into his planes. This was meant to be. They'd been high school sweethearts, and on his way to college he'd stop to throw a penny into the Sweetheart Fountain and make the happily-ever-after wish. Hoping against hope to reclaim her one day. Giving their future over to fate. Surrendering to a force beyond them.

The power of fated first love.

The kissing went on and on, and he never wanted it to end, but Carrie finally pulled her lips away. She was panting, her eyes filled with a lusty sheen. He knew his eyes reflected the same.

He tracked his hand down her spine, stopping at that sweet curve just above her fabulous ass. She was so slender. Delicate. But her fragility was an illusion. She was strong, both mentally and physically. In high school she'd played slow-pitch softball. The star of the team. He used to go to her games and cheer her on, just as she'd been in the bleachers when he'd quarterbacked Twilight to the district championships. She'd been so tough when her mother had been diagnosed with ALS and her father then sank into alcoholism. He remembered everything about her. The long talks they'd had. The way she swore she was never going to let her family's troubles define her. He admired her so damn much.

The air between them quivered with expectant

energy. All it would take was the crook of a smile and he'd be all in.

"Mark." She reached out to touch his cheek. "Are you really here or am I dreaming again?"

She'd been dreaming of him? The same way he'd dreamed of her. Why had he fought so hard to forget her?

Hell, how could he stop when the woman he loved was looking at him like he was her wildest fantasy come to life?

"Mark," she whispered. "Make love to me."

That was his Carrie. Direct. Honest. It was a damn slippery slope, and he was tumbling head over heels down it.

Carrie convinced herself it *was* all a dream. Being here again with Mark. In the same place where she had first given him her virginity. It had to be a dream.

But here he was, so very real when she put out a hand to touch him, big and warm and masculine. Her stomach jumped, and her knees wobbled. She felt knocked off kilter, and she couldn't trust this feeling.

It was dangerous, especially if this was not a dream.

Whenever she was around him, her brains turned to mush, and she was seventeen again and madly in love.

She wanted him with a bone-deep hunger. She needed him, and Carrie had never needed anyone.

Flynn often scolded her because she didn't like taking help from people. She was independent and proud. Always had been.

Which was why she'd said they made a mistake when they returned from Vegas. Dumping him so that he didn't have to dump her. She'd been too damn proud to admit how much she needed him. Neediness was not attractive, and yet here she was. Needing him all over again.

Except this was worse than before, because this time she knew better. Knew he was going to go right back to L.A. when this was all over. Right back to his smooth, shiny life. A life she could never be part of. The same issue that had broken them up before was still there. It had not disappeared. They had conflicting goals, valued different things.

But for this one beautiful moment in time, she did not care. All she wanted was to feel him inside her again.

Later. She could pick up the pieces later.

She shrugged out of her jacket.

Mark did the same.

She reached for the buttons of her blouse.

He kicked off his cowboy boots.

God, he looked amazing in his cowboy clothes. Just the way she remembered him. Texas boy. She knew that wasn't who he was anymore, but it's how she liked him best. He was a chameleon. He had an amazing ability to fit in wherever he went. She was envious of his skill.

He cocked his head, looking both inquisitive and devastatingly sexy. "You sure?"

"Shh. You are ruining the dream." If he kept talking, she'd change her mind, and if she changed her mind, she knew she'd kick herself for it later. This might not be forever after, but it didn't have to be. For right now was enough. It had to be enough because just like before, she refused to be a weight around his ankle.

He unsnapped the cuffs of his western shirt. She grinned and slipped off her boots. The wooden planks of the pier felt cool and familiar beneath her feet. Let it be. Just let this be whatever it is. Doesn't need a label. Don't need a name. Go for it. No regrets.

Wasn't that exactly how you ended up in Vegas married by an Elvis impersonator?

The thought stopped Carrie in her tracks. She'd always been impulsive. Too driven by emotion. In her head, she took a page from Flynn's cautious playbook and tallied all the reasons why this was a bad idea, all the ways this could hurt them both. Yet her heart overrode her brain. Who cared? She had him here now. She could pick up the pieces later. Right?

"What is it?" Mark murmured, instantly attuned to her shift in mood.

"Too late," she said. "It's too late for this."

"You're running scared."

"Yeah," she said. "And rightly so. This isn't going to lead anywhere but trouble for us both."

"Carrie." He reached out to her, and she took a step back, suddenly feeling the cold. "It's all right."

He moved closer, cupped her chin in his palm, raised her face and kissed her again. Long, slow, soulful.

Carrie melted. All resistance fled. This was Mark, and they were together again. Even if only for the briefest moment in time.

At that moment a swathe of light swung over the bridge, and a vehicle pulled up to the boat ramp, catching them in the blinding headlamps.

They sprang apart, scrambled for their clothes.

The car door opened, shut—once, twice—but the engine was still running. "Carrie?" Flynn's voice drifted on the night air.

Two people appeared at the top of the embankment, her sister and her brother-in-law. She couldn't see their faces in the shadows, but she heard Jesse's throaty chuckle.

Carrie stomped her feet into her boots while simultaneously threading her arms through her blazer. She sprinted up the embankment ahead of Mark.

"Yes?" she gasped when she reached the top.

"You told Dad you'd be home by seven to start Thanksgiving dinner preparations. He tried calling your cell, but you didn't answer. He got worried and called us. We were just headed into Twilight to look for you when Jesse spotted your car."

"I'm fine. I must have forgotten my phone at the Yarn Barn," Carrie said, feeling irritated. That was one bad thing about living in a small town with your family. It was next to impossible to sneak off for a little hanky-panky. She speared a hand through her hair, tossed back the errant strands falling into her eyes. "What time is it?"

"Nine o'clock," Jesse supplied.

Damn, she would be up until after midnight making fruit salad and cornbread for tomorrow's stuffing. She and Dad had offered to host the holiday meal this year since Flynn was so pregnant. Her father was frying the turkey, and the rest of the guests were bringing the remaining side dishes.

"Is that Mark?" Flynn asked, peering over Carrie's shoulder, one hand resting on her distended belly. "Hello, Mark."

Carrie felt Mark come up behind her. He stood so close she could feel his warm breath fanning the hairs at the top of her head.

"Flynn, Jesse." Mark's voice exuded his dimpled grin. She didn't have to see his face to know that he was smiling from ear to ear.

"We didn't mean to interrupt anything," Jesse said, "but you know how worried your sister gets."

"You didn't interrupt anything. Absolutely nothing at all." Carrie stepped away from Mark and his distracting body heat. "We were just talking."

"Uh-huh." Jesse's eyes narrowed knowingly.

"What are you doing for Thanksgiving?" Flynn asked Mark.

No, no, do *not* invite him to Thanksgiving dinner.

"I had planned on having dinner at The Merry Cherub," Mark answered.

"Jenny does put on a delicious spread," Carrie said. "You'll enjoy it."

"Oh, you have to come to dinner with us," Flynn said, and then turned to Carrie. "For shame, I can't believe you didn't invite Mark to Thanksgiving dinner."

Was her sister really that clueless? Carrie hadn't wanted Mark at Thanksgiving dinner because, well, when you invited a date to Thanksgiving that meant something special, and she did not want to send that message.

"Why, thank you for that generous offer, Flynn." Mark flicked a mocking gaze over Carrie. "I accept. When and where?"

"The old family place. You remember where it is. We're eating around five-ish."

"I'll be there."

"Great. We'll see you then."

Super. Terrific. Now she was going to have to spend Thanksgiving in the same house with her former husband whom she was still in love with.

Carrie jammed her hands in her pockets and swallowed hard. Here we go again.

Chapter Six

The MacGregor house hadn't changed a bit since Mark had last set foot in it. There was a fresh coat of paint and new draperies in the living room, but that was pretty well the extent of the changes. It made him feel both sad and soothed. It was comforting to know that some things never changed. But it made him realize how out of step he was with this world he'd once been a part of. A world he'd been so anxious to leave behind.

Why? Had it been merely the restlessness of youth? What had made him long for the trappings of external success? And why, now that he'd achieved everything he'd set out to achieve—fame, fortune, a fast car, a big house in the L.A. hills, gorgeous women on his arm whenever he wanted them there—did it seem so empty compared with the rich friendships and strong family ties going on right here in this modest home?

There was something comforting about consistency. Inside this bustling kitchen, he felt a connection to his roots, and the beautiful young woman lighting the candles at the holiday table had a whole lot to do with it.

Carrie.

She entranced him. He couldn't stop watching her. The graceful way she moved. The way the candle glow caught her hair and brought out the auburn highlights. The saucy little butterfly tattoo on the inside of her wrist. She was exquisite.

Watching her with her family made his heart feel too big for his chest. Her younger twin brothers, Noah and Joel, teasingly pulled her hair and trash-talked. Carrie handed it right back to them, telling her brothers' girlfriends about all their naughty antics.

Carrie's father, Floyd, had brought a date as well. Barbara, the local librarian. They were in the early stages of their relationship, casting coy glances at each other from time to time, but clearly love was in the air.

Flynn and Jesse canoodled in the corner, sharing stolen kisses, murmuring to each other. Occasionally, Jesse would touch his wife's belly and stare at her with wonder, as if he couldn't believe he'd married the love of his life and they were about to have a baby.

I want that, Mark thought. I want that, and I want it with Carrie.

It was a stunning realization.

Immediately, his self-preservation instincts tried

to backtrack. Whoa, slow down. You live in L.A. That's where your job is, and Carrie's whole life is here. Her business. Her family. Long-distance relationships never work. You know that.

Except he couldn't reconcile what he knew with what he *felt*. Longing. Desire. Need. Such desperate, hungry need for her.

He could give up hosting *Fact or Fantasy*. He'd lucked into the job. It wasn't anything he'd actively sought out, and he realized now that he enjoyed it for the attention more than anything else. Honestly, he was a bit embarrassed to be hosting a reality show, but the notoriety had gone to his head.

You used to want to be a novelist.

Wistful, he remembered the old dream. It was a specter of the old Mark. The same Mark who'd married Carrie.

It could be the new Mark. Doing what you love. Being with the woman you loved. Finding the real you. Exchange the rat race for the simple life. Back in Twilight. Back in Carrie's arms.

Are you nuts? Give up everything for a woman who might not even want you back? Yes, you've still got chemistry, but there's a lot of water underneath that bridge.

Maybe, maybe, but he had to try. He would never forgive himself if he didn't try. Since coming back to his hometown, everything had changed for him. The thought of returning to his life in L.A held no appeal. Odd, since he'd stayed away from Twilight because it represented everything he'd lost—but now, this was where his future lay.

Carrie glanced up at him. He winked at her. Her cheeks pinked and she ducked her head again.

"Can I do anything to help?" he asked.

"Put the rolls on the table." She pushed a wicker basket of fresh homemade yeast rolls that Barbara had brought as her contribution to the meal into his hands. In the exchange, her knuckles brushed lightly against his fingers and sent a flood of goose bumps spreading over his body.

Unbelievable! No woman had ever generated that kind of reaction in him. Even after all this time, she had the power to light his fire like no other.

The meal was sumptuous, and after dinner everyone pitched in to help clean up the kitchen. Noah and Joel scraped scraps into a big pan for the compost heap. The giggling girlfriends, Amber and Ashley (Mark couldn't keep straight which was which) carried the dishes to the sink, where Carrie was drawing up hot water. Jesse took out the garbage, while Flynn put the leftovers in Tupperware containers. Barbara grabbed the broom and started sweeping up crumbs. Floyd went outside to take care of the turkey fryer.

"What can I do?" Mark asked, wanting to be treated like part of the family.

"Dry dishes," Carrie said. "But you're going to need an apron so you don't get that fine suit wet."

He'd worn a suit in concession to the holiday. Over the years, he'd developed the habit of overdressing, because he figured it was better to be overdressed than underdressed, but all the other men were in jeans and western shirts and cowboy boots.

He slipped out of his suit jacket and hung it over the back of a kitchen chair and rolled up his sleeves.

Carrie came up behind him, dropped a frilly blue gingham bib apron over his head and then reached around his waist to gather the strings and tie them.

Mark had to shut his eyes to fight off his body's reaction to her touch and he was suddenly grateful to have the apron as camouflage for his stirring erection. Damn! The woman turned him inside out without even trying to be sexy.

They stood at the sink together. Her washing, him drying, occasionally bumping elbows, while all around them her family laughed and joked. Soap bubbles floated in the air along with the citrusy aroma of lemon-scented detergent.

As an only child, he'd never had this kind of family camaraderie. He remembered how much he'd enjoyed the MacGregors, although back then Carrie's mother had been really sick and the laughter had been muted. The family seemed to have overcome its loss and grief and took joy in simply being together. Mark was jealous of the easiness of their lives.

The elaborate holiday celebrations he threw in Hollywood paled in comparison. Once in a while his parents came to L.A., but mostly they took a holiday cruise, just as they'd done this year. His family had never been very traditional in that regard. Maybe because there had only been the three of them. He usually threw lavish catered events, his house filled with movers and shakers, but when he got right down to it, there were only a handful of people he could call true friends. His line of work attracted status-seekers and hangers-on.

Once the house was spick-and-span, Noah and Joel and their girlfriends announced they were going to the movies. Barbara invited Floyd back to her place to watch the football game. Flynn yawned, put her hands to her back, stretched and said she was really tired. Jesse jumped up to get her coat, and within ten minutes, the house was empty except for him and Carrie.

He couldn't help feeling her family had orchestrated the whole thing in order to give them some time alone. Carrie looked uneasy.

"Well," she said once everyone was gone. "Well."

"We're all alone."

"So it seems."

They were standing in the big farmhouse kitchen on opposite sides of the table.

"Do you want me to go?" he asked, his chest tightening up, terrified that she was going to say yes.

She didn't answer, didn't meet his gaze, busied herself with dusting a nonexistent crumb from the table with the hem of her apron. He still had on that silly gingham apron she'd tied around his waist.

"Carrie?"

Finally, she raised her chin. "What are we doing, Mark?"

"I don't know," he said honestly. "The only thing I know is that I want you."

"It's not that simple, is it?" Her eyes turned murky. Her bottom lip quivered so slightly he barely noticed it. She let out a long sigh and he couldn't stand being so far away from her.

He ripped off the apron and stalked across the kitchen toward her. She let out a little squeak of surprise, but she did not run. Of course she wouldn't run. Carrie MacGregor was the bravest woman he'd ever known.

Without another word, without another thought, Mark bent and scooped her off her feet. She felt so good in his arms. The best thing in the entire world. He asked her only one question. "Are you still sleeping in the same bedroom?"

In Mark's arms, Carrie felt incredibly cherished.

Don't fall for it. Won't last. Can't last.

"Carrie," he murmured. "My sweet, Carrie." He nibbled her earlobe as he slowly undressed her. "I've missed you so much."

He'd been her first lover. The template she'd used to gauge all lovers against since, and no one had ever measured up to him. She wanted so much to believe they could have a happy ending. That the silly sweetheart legend was indeed true.

They were lying naked together, face-to-face on her bed, peering deeply into each other's eyes. The air between them smelled of Thanksgiving.

Mark's mouth found hers with unerring accuracy.

The minute their lips touched, Carrie's body bloomed like a parched desert flower opening to the rain. Their excited tongues greeted each other. They kissed and kissed and kissed. They were sublime kisses of hope and reunion.

They melted into each other, the past merging with the future. They knew each other's bodies so well. Every touch, taste, sound, and smell was forever carved into them.

Carrie murmured a low sound of pleasure and wrapped an arm around his waist. Mark's fingers tangled in her hair, his touch hot and fierce. They were like two tuning forks vibrating at the same intense frequency.

She traced the landscape of his face, her fingertips exalting in the recognizable ridges and planes—the apples of his cheek, the hollow beneath, the scruff of his hard jaw, the softness of his earlobe. She felt the shape of him. His head, his neck, his sturdy shoulders.

Time.

So much time had slipped away from them.

The time they'd lost, never to recover.

But they were here now. Touching and tasting. Drunk on each other.

He gently rolled her onto her back, looked deeply into her eyes.

Bridged. Transcended. What they'd lost was within their grasp. How did they keep it from slipping away again?

She still loved him. More than ever before. The time apart added a melancholy richness to their joining, a sad loveliness that hadn't existed before. She allowed herself to ride the river of pleasure, to surf the tide of hope.

Dangerous. It was so dangerous to hope.

His tongue swept her up in the oblivion of pure bliss. A special bliss she believed she would never again experience. Sweeter now.

He ran hot palms up her bare belly. She arched her back, moaned a soft encouragement. Never mind the danger. Never mind her hopeful heart that was taking such a chance. She had to have him. Could not live without feeling him move inside her one more time.

Prickles of expectancy rippled from the base of Carrie's neck, rolled across her face, over her scalp, slipped along her shoulder blades, trickled down her belly to the spot where she burned for him.

His muscular thighs pressing against her soft ones. His erection hard against her pelvis. Hard and throbbing and big. She'd forgotten exactly how big he was.

He dipped his head and his mouth found the tip of her hardening nipple. Carrie inhaled sharply at the delicious shock of his warm, moist mouth on her tender breast. She sighed against the magical fusion of electricity and chemistry.

The stubble of his beard scratched provocatively along her chest as his mouth shifted, seeking to find her other aching nipple. The brilliant sensation sent a set of delectable chills shivering down her spine.

He sucked gently on her aching nipple. She wriggled her hips against him and smiled when her movements pulled a shuddery groan from his mouth. Lifting his head, he went for her lips again.

This was so beautiful. So wonderful. To be held

in his arms once more. A maelstrom of emotions swirled in her—jumbled and nonsensical. All the lies she told herself—how she was long over him, how she didn't care that he'd never come home—lies that built hard calluses over the scars of her heart, dissolved into the truth. She still loved him and always would.

"Carrie?" he asked and pulled back.

That's when she realized she was crying. Dammit! Last night she'd managed to fight off the tears, but now without her even knowing it, the maelstrom streamed salty down her face.

"Babe, what's wrong?"

She shook her head, unable to speak. Unable to believe she was crying. She wasn't a crier. Hadn't cried one tear since her mother had died. Why was she crying now? Oh, dammit, she was going to ruin the moment. A moment she could never get back.

"Not," she managed to squeak. "Crying."

"Ah, babe." He kissed the wetness from her cheeks and she could see a glimmer of tears shining in *his* eyes. "I know, Babe. I know."

Carrie started giggling then. Laughing through the tears. She was happy. Right now she was one hundred percent utterly happy. Nothing at all to cry about. She slipped her arms around his neck, pulled his head down for a long soul-stirring kiss.

Her skin quivered beneath the heat of his fingertips. They were both panting and desperate. Her mind was oblivious to anything but this man. He was all around her, lighting fire to her senses. His spicy cologne filled her nose. His quick breathing swept over her ears. The feel of his hard body clouded all objective reasoning. Passion ignited her blood, snatching her up a thick swell of sensation.

She had to have him or die. Damn the consequences.

That same thinking got you married in Vegas at the age of seventeen and broken up two days later.

Apparently she was still as hopelessly addicted to him now as she had been back then. What was this magnetic power he had that made her forget all common sense?

He kept kissing her, doing devilish things with his tongue. She'd missed this so much. He licked a sizzling trail down her throat, going back to tease her nipples. She sucked in a deep breath and forgot everything but the feel of his tongue against her skin.

"Hold on," he whispered.

She had a brief moment to catch her breath, while he hopped off the bed, found his pants, extracted a condom and was back beside her, rolling it on. He stroked her again, building the fire until she begged him to take her.

Slowly, in measured increments, he entered her body, and once he was all the way in they drew in a single breath. Together again. Velvet and steel.

"Mark." She moaned.

He moved inside her in a lazy rhythm. Heat spiraled out from her solar plexus, engulfed her. In and out. In and out. Such control. That was new. Back in the day, he'd been Johnny on the spot and jackrabbit quick. She admired his new skills. Maturity had its pluses.

On and on he went, making slow sweet love to her until she was on the edge of crazy.

He cooed her name. "You are so damn beautiful."

She closed her eyes, absorbed his words, lapped up the exquisiteness of what was happening. Then she felt his body stiffen and realized he was close.

But so was she. The whirlpool started deep inside her and rose and swirled.

"Open your eyes," he whispered. "I want to see inside you when you come."

She opened her eyes, bit down on her bottom lip as she looked up at him. His gaze was completely latched on hers. She felt herself falling, and she couldn't get her breath. It was so beautiful.

Amazing.

Her body tensed just as his jerked. She wrapped her legs around him, pulled him in as deeply inside her as he could go. In one brilliant squeeze, they came together. Rolling and tumbling and clutching each other.

Mark collapsed against her chest, their bodies slick with lovemaking. Their hearts slamming together in perfect timpani. He buried his face in her hair.

Carrie had never felt as vulnerable as she did in the moment of completion, but at the same time, she felt stronger than she'd ever felt in her life.

This was beyond her. Beyond them. This wasn't just lust. Not just chemistry. Not even just love. They were bonded. Meant to be. The sweetheart legend said so.

They were indeed each other's one true love.

Chapter Seven

Mark lay beside Carrie, gently drawing circles on her back with a lazy index finger. Her face was buried in a pillow, her cute naked butt on display. He could look at her all day and never tire of the view. His heart floated in his chest, free and easy. It had been a very long time since he'd felt this young. This happy.

Awesome. She was completely awesome.

He cradled the back of his head in his palms, crossed his ankles and grinned up at the ceiling.

"Got any more condoms?" she mumbled from the pillow.

"You betcha." He shot off the bed, scrambled for his pants, and in less than ten seconds had the condom on. "C'mon, cowgirl," he said. "Your turn to ride."

He pulled her astraddle his waist. She ducked her head to kiss him, her auburn curls trailing over his face. He couldn't believe how long he'd been without this. Without Carrie.

She eased herself down on him.

He hissed in his breath.

Carrie giggled.

"I love to hear you laugh," he murmured and slid his hand down her spine to cup her shapely buttocks. "This is the only way to fly."

"Buckle your seatbelt, Hotshot." She giggled again and he could feel the sound roll from her into him. Her joy was his joy. "I'm in control now."

"Oh, yeah?" He reached up a hand, ran his fingers over her smiling lips.

"Yeah." She moved upward.

He grabbed her around the waist, held her in place, his erection swelling inside of her. "Sure about that?"

"Hey, you're depriving yourself as much as you're depriving me by calling a halt to the pump action."

"Good point." He chuckled and let go of her.

"Hmm," she murmured, an expression of pure feel-good pleasure crossing her face. God he loved seeing her like this, sassy, willing, gleeful.

She quickened the tempo of her movements, and soon enough they were rocketing to a whole new sphere of sensation.

Hot and heavy, they flew through the storm of unquenchable desire and finally hit the clouds together. Slowly, they drifted down, arms and legs entwined.

"We weren't this good before," she observed in a sleepy voice.

"Nope." His eyes were closed, and he was too tired to say much more. She'd wrung him out like the proverbial dishrag.

"We were just kids. What did we know about sex? You were my first lover."

The tone in her voice had him tensing up. He opened one eye, turned his head, looked over at her. "I know," he said softly. "You were my first too."

She was quiet a moment. "Really? You never told me that."

"I was embarrassed. Nineteen-year-old virgin. I thought I was expected to have all the moves."

"No wonder we were lousy at it." She laughed.

"We weren't lousy. Just quick."

"But we're better now."

"Much better," he agreed. Then his mind crowded with thoughts of why they were better. Years apart. Years with other lovers. His head suddenly hurt. He reached up to massage his temple.

"Maybe we should get together every eight years and do this again just to see how much more we improve with age," she said.

This jolted him. Was she seeing this as nothing more than a one-time thing? Her tone was so lighthearted. Uncommitted.

Did she honestly not have any idea that he was still in love with her? Even though he'd only recently realized it himself. Maybe she honestly thought this was just scratching a familiar itch. Oh God, what if she wasn't feeling the same way he was?

She didn't say anything for the longest time, and he was starting to panic when she took a deep breath and said, "I sent you a Facebook friend request."

"You did? When?"

"A couple of years ago. You ignored my request."

"Carrie, honey, I don't run my Facebook page. I have an assistant that does my social media."

"Oh," she said. "I thought you didn't want to be friends."

It killed him that she thought that about him. Cut him right in two.

Downstairs, the front door opened, then slammed shut, followed by the sound of four voices.

"Crap!" Carrie exclaimed. "The twins and their girlfriends are back. You've got to get out of here."

"As if your brothers aren't intent on getting their girlfriends in the sack?" he said, partly relieved that they came home before he had to explain how he'd turned his life over to assistants, agents, and managers. There was time enough for that later.

She hopped out of bed. "I'm the responsible one in the family."

"Since when?" He laughed, delighting in watching her bend over naked and scoop up his clothes from the floor, her gorgeous tits bouncing as she moved.

"Since you went away."

There it was. The accusation he'd been waiting for since he'd come back to Twilight. Their separation had been mutual. Or at least that's what he'd told himself. It was the only way he could live with having left her. After all, she was the one who told him to go, the first one to voice doubts about their impulsive marriage.

But only after she learned you got the scholarship.

She stuffed his clothes into his hands. "Get dressed."

"Seriously? You're throwing me out?" He tugged on his boxer briefs.

She was getting dressed, too, pulling on her jeans, not bothering with underwear, zipping them up. She reached for a T-shirt, tugged it over her head.

He jammed his arms into his shirt, raked his hand through his hair. "Where's my shoes?"

The comforter had gotten tossed to the floor in their sexy adventures. She lifted it up, located his shoes. "A. Testoni. Wow, don't these shoes cost like a thousand dollars or more?"

"I'm surprised you know that," he said, buttoning up his shirt.

"What? Country hicks can't read fashion magazines?"

"I'm sorry, Carrie. I didn't mean it like it sounded. It's that you're so real, so grounded. Why would you care about stuff like that?"

She didn't acknowledge his apology. He had sounded like a spoiled rich twerp. Why had he said that?

"Why do you care?" she asked.

He looked her in the eyes. "I've been asking myself the same thing. Who needs a twelve-hundred-dollar pair of shoes?"

"Apparently you do." She padded to the window, opened it, and pushed out the screen. "Go out this way."

"Feels like old times," he joked, trying to smooth things over.

"Mark," she said. "Nothing is the same. No sense living in the past. You are who you are. It's okay."

He paused on the windowsill. One leg inside, one leg outside. That was when Mark realized there could be no spanning two worlds. He was either in or he was out.

Mark owned shoes that cost over a thousand dollars, and he thought she was such a dumb country hick she wouldn't recognize designer footwear when she saw it.

Somehow, recognizing that he owned shoes that cost more than the monthly rent on the Yarn Barn brought Carrie's silly little fantasy into perspective.

After they'd made love she'd started letting herself think foolish thoughts she had no business thinking, that the sweetheart legend just might be true, that they could have their happily-ever-after ending. She'd known all along it was a fairytale. Why hadn't she stuck to her guns? Why had she let her heart start to hope?

He orbited a completely different solar system from her quiet existence here in Twilight. He had assistants that ran his Facebook page. Probably tweeted for him too. She might be a Christmas Scrooge, but ultimately, Carrie *was* happy here. She loved living in a small town. Loved being near her family. Loved running a yarn store. Loved entertaining the gossipy knitters. This was where she belonged. She had no need for shoes that cost a thousand dollars. Or a life in the Hollywood hills. Not that Mark had asked her to share his life.

The shoes are just an excuse. You're scared. The

same way you were scared when Mark got the scholarship to Columbia and rocketed far away from you. He got what he wanted. So did you. You just want different things. It's as simple as that.

These same thoughts had been running through her head on a continuous loop since she'd thrown Mark out of her bedroom on Thanksgiving Day. She'd half hoped that he would call, but he hadn't. Good, she told herself. Great. Perfect. That's the way she wanted it.

The whole rest of the miserable weekend, she'd groused and complained as her father and Barbara and her twin brothers and their girlfriends put up a tree and decorated the house. Carrie had refused to participate. Bah-humbug. Believing in fantasies got you nothing but heartache.

It was Sunday evening, and she was rushing to The Horny Toad Tavern for a meeting of the First Love Cookie Club. Most of the members of the Christmas cookie club, who also belonged to the Sweethearts Knitting Club, were meeting in the back room of the bar to plan the annual cookie-swap party. Even though Carrie was not a member of the cookie club—she was too grinchy for that—Patsy had phoned and asked her to drop by.

She drove past The Merry Cherub, and her heart gave an odd little hop, but she made herself stare straight ahead and not search the B&B for any sign of Mark.

When she arrived at the Horny Toad, Christine Noble, the owner of the Twilight Bakery, was passing out cookie samples to the group.

"Taste this," Christine said and put a cookie in her hand.

"What is it?"

"Just taste."

Carrie popped the cookie into her mouth. Creamy, sweet goodness flooded her mouth. She tasted walnuts, cranberries, and white chocolate. "Mmm."

"Is that not the best cookie ever?"

"Pretty awesome." She nodded. Everything Christine baked was awesome.

"Have a seat." Patsy sat at one end of the table and waved to the empty chair at the other end.

Feeling a bit unsettled, Carrie scooted around the others and plopped down. "I can't stay long."

"This is important, or we wouldn't have bothered you," said Emma Cheek. She was a diminutive, red-haired actress, married to the local veterinarian. Her sleeping four-month-old daughter, Lauren, lay cradled in her arms. Emma had given up life in Hollywood to move back to Twilight and marry Sam, although she still acted in Texas-based projects.

Carrie's sense of unease increased. "What's this about?"

"Raylene," Marva supplied.

That's when Carrie realized that Raylene was not in the meeting.

"Has something happened to her?" Carrie reached for another one of those delicious cranberry cookies. She might not like Christmas, but the cookies were divine. And snacking kept her mind off Mark. Sort of.

"We're afraid something is about to happen to

her," Emma said. "Considering that the director of *Fact or Fantasy* is going around town offering money to anyone who can refute the sweetheart legend."

"Any takers?" Carrie asked.

She still wondered why Mark hadn't told Iris Tobin about their love affair. He had the ability to bust the myth wide open with just one sentence to his boss. But he hadn't spoken of it. Why not? Seems like it would make for great TV. That's what he cared about, right? Money, ratings, success, expensive shoes. And yet, he'd obviously said nothing. Was it because he'd promised her he'd stay mum on the topic? Or was there another reason?

Hope lifted Carrie's heart.

Stop it. No hoping. If you don't get your hopes up you won't get hurt.

Except she already had gotten her hopes up. Had already gotten hurt, but to keep Mark from knowing, she'd hurt him first. Just as she had eight years ago.

"Someone spilled the news about Raylene and Earl," Belinda said quietly. "Iris came here looking for her, but luckily she and Dotty Mae went up to the Indian casino in Oklahoma to play bingo over the Thanksgiving weekend. They're due home late tonight."

"So why call me?" Carrie asked.

"We were hoping you could talk to Mark," Patsy said. "Get him to call her off Raylene. She's suffered so much over her breakup with Earl. Over her dark secret coming out. You wouldn't think it by her sassy mouth, but Raylene really does have a soft heart."

Raylene's husband had left her after he'd discovered that Raylene had kept quiet about a secret daughter for thirty-five years. Her husband had felt totally betrayed by her lack of trust in him. They'd had a huge fight, and Earl had left Twilight the Christmas before and no one had seen or heard from him since.

"I don't have any pull with Mark."

The women around the table exchanged knowing glances. What? Had everyone in town found out about their Thanksgiving tryst?

"If this gets on TV I don't know what's going to happen to Raylene." Marva sighed.

"Not to mention what it will mean for Twilight's tourism business." Terri shook her head. "Our myth busted on national television."

"It'll kill Ray if she's responsible for that." Patsy clucked her tongue.

Carrie inhaled audibly. If she intervened, it would mean seeing Mark again, but how could she not try to stop this? Not only for Raylene's sake but also for Twilight. "I'll see what I can do."

Patsy looked relieved. She got up to place a grateful hand on Carrie's shoulder. "You have no idea how much we appreciate you."

Chapter Eight

It was almost ten o'clock when Carrie walked into the lobby of the Merry Cherub. Jenny and Dean would be locking the doors soon. Jenny was behind the reception desk when Carrie entered.

"Merry Christmas," Jenny greeted her.

Carrie forced a smile and returned her greeting. "I'm here to see Iris Tobin."

"I'm not sure she's in her room," Jenny said. "Let me just—"

At that moment, Iris Tobin came out of the parlor. "What can I do for you, Ms. . . ." She trailed off. "I'm sorry, I've forgotten your name."

"Carrie MacGregor."

"Ah yes, the one who knocked over the wrenches in the motorcycle shop."

"That would be me. Small-town klutz."

An awkward silence stretched between them. Jenny considerately disappeared into the back room behind the reception desk.

"What was it you wanted to see me about?" Iris asked.

Carrie hauled in a deep breath. This was it. Her bid to save Raylene by throwing herself under the bus. She drew herself up tall. "I heard that you've been out digging up dirt on people in order to refute the sweetheart legend."

Iris spread her hands. "I didn't want to stoop this low, but everyone in town was so adamant that the silly myth is true. And Mark was completely useless." She shook her head. "He kept telling me the legend is true."

He had? Carrie knotted her fingers together.

"But there is no such thing as true love. Out of all the high school sweethearts in town, statistically *someone* had to be divorced or broken up."

"You couldn't find any Twilight high school sweethearts who weren't happily married *except* Raylene Pringle, could you?"

"This is the most closemouthed small town." Iris crossed her arms over her chest. "Truly remarkable. Most small towns are hotbeds of gossip."

"Oh, we gossip plenty, but the reality is, many people in this town have found happiness with their high school sweethearts. Raylene and Earl included. They'll get back together. They were meant to be."

Iris sniffed. "You're seriously delusional. Raylene Pringle and her husband are not living happily ever after. The myth is busted."

Carrie touched her lip to the tip of her tongue. "What would it take for you to leave Raylene alone?"

"There's not much you could say to get me to

drop that line of inquiry." Iris was cold as a winter graveyard.

"What if I told you I could give you plenty of information to disprove the sweetheart legend? A story featuring a young couple instead of a forty-year-old love affair that's weathered a lot of ups and downs."

Iris cocked her head, looked intrigued. "I'm listening."

She was walking on hot coals here, but it was necessary. Not just to save Raylene, but to make sure Mark went back to where he belonged. He was Hollywood material. Things hadn't changed between them. He lived a life that she could never be part of. It was no different from eight years ago, when she'd seen that scholarship letter from Columbia tucked under the Santa Claus saltshaker on his parents' kitchen table. She couldn't allow him to throw away everything he'd accomplished. Besides, Raylene had been through enough. Carrie was tough. She would survive this, and so would Twilight.

"Mark and I were high school sweethearts," she confessed to Iris. "We ran away to Vegas and got married on Christmas Day, the month he graduated from high school."

Iris's eyes glowed. "Seriously? You're divorced?"

"The marriage was annulled after forty-eight hours."

"You did not live happily-ever-after." Iris rubbed her palms gleefully.

"That's your busted myth, and the host of your show is caught right in the middle."

"I love it!"

"You'll leave Raylene alone?"

"Meet me in my suite tomorrow afternoon for an on-camera interview, and it's a deal."

The following morning, Mark knocked on the door of Iris's suite. She'd called him the night before just as he was getting ready for bed and told him she had a surprise interview with someone who was prepared to blow the lid off the sweetheart legend and give them the ratings scoop they were hoping for, but she refused to tell him who it was.

After Carrie had kicked him out of her bedroom window, Mark had been hurt at first, then he'd experienced a moment of total clarity. Because he'd finally put two and two together. She was afraid that if she let herself love him, he'd hurt her again. His tough little Carrie was far more vulnerable than he'd realized.

He'd given it a lot of thought, and then on Saturday he'd made his move. He'd called his real estate agent and told him to list his house for sale. Then he called Burt Mernit and told him this episode of *Fact or Fantasy* would be his last and he wanted out of his contract no matter what it cost. Last, he called his manager and asked him to find a literary agent. He was writing a novel about his experiences in Hollywood. When he finally was able to tell Carrie he was moving back to Texas, he wanted it a done deal. She would no longer be able to argue that his life was in L.A.

On Sunday, he'd borrowed a motorcycle from

Jesse and driven to Fort Worth to shop for the perfect engagement ring. He'd spent the remainder of the day worrying about how and when to pop the question.

Apprehension tickled the back of his neck when Iris answered the door with a triumphant grin on her face. A bi-fold screen had been set up, creating a backdrop setting for the filming, and he could only see a shadow of the mystery person sitting on the other side of the screen.

"Come on in," Iris said, stepping aside.

LaDonna rushed him over to a makeup chair in front of a vanity, and tied a bib around his neck so she wouldn't get makeup on his clothes. He twisted around, trying to see who was behind the screen, but LaDonna took hold of his head. "Face forward, squirmy worm."

"Who is it?" he murmured as Iris directed the camera crew in their setup.

"You'll see soon enough. Be still." Ladonna tucked on his ear.

"Why is everyone acting so enigmatic?"

"You know Iris. How she likes to make a deal out of everything."

Mark certainly wasn't going to miss Iris. She was a terror to work for. He just wanted to get his interview over, so he could go tell Carrie he loved her and was moving to Twilight. Then he'd go down on one knee and tell her what he should have told her eight years ago. That she was the love of his life and he was never going to let her go.

"Iris," he called, "where's my questions?"

"They're on the teleprompter," she said, coming over to stand next to him, a sly smile on her face.

Something was up. Mark didn't trust Iris when she was happy. "I don't get to see the questions first?"

"It would give away the identity of our guest."

"I'm going to find out who it is as soon as I step in front of that screen. What's the big secret?"

"You'll see." Iris chuckled.

The hairs on the back of Mark's neck lifted. Who on earth could it be? Obviously, it was some muckraker set to make trouble for Twilight.

"You done?" he asked LaDonna. Without waiting for an answer, he pulled the bib from around his neck. Enough of this nonsense. He stalked around the screen.

And stopped in his tracks.

Carrie.

Sitting in the interview chair. Looking pale and nervous.

For one split second his blood ran completely cold. She was giving an interview? She was here to bust the sweetheart myth using their relationship of love gone wrong?

Staggered, he could do nothing but stare at her.

"Surprise," Iris whispered in his ear.

"Carrie," Mark said, ignoring Iris. "What are you doing here?"

"Giving us an exclusive interview," Iris supplied, throwing an arm around his shoulder. "Won't this make for sensational television?" She turned to the cameraman. "Randal, did you get a shot of the look on Mark's face when he saw Carrie?"

From behind the camera, Randal made the "okay" sign. Mark had been so startled to see Carrie that he hadn't even noticed the camera was recording. Some newsman he was.

You're not a newsman anymore. You've been co-opted into a smiling boob. If he harbored any lingering doubts about leaving *Fact or Fantasy*, they completely evaporated. He'd already asked Burt Mernit to be let out of his contract; he didn't have to stay here and do this.

"Have a seat, Mark," Iris said. "I'm conducting today's interview. Oh and in case you're thinking of refusing, I've talked to Burt. If you don't want to be sued for breach of contract, you'll give this interview."

The second she saw the stunned look of betrayal on Mark's face, Carrie knew that granting the interview was a big mistake, but there was no turning back now.

He sat in the chair behind her, his eyes burning into hers.

A poignant bleakness crept over her—bleak as a North Pole blizzard wind. She'd been here before, felt this before. When she'd lied about wanting out of their marriage. She'd been so young and foolish then. What was her excuse now?

"Carrie," said Iris, who was perched on a third chair in front of their two chairs. There were three cameras. One on her face, one on Mark's, one on Iris. "You and Mark Leland were high school sweethearts."

Carrie couldn't get her breath. The air in the room tasted stale. "I . . ." She swallowed, kept her gaze fixed on Iris so she didn't have to look at Mark. "Yes."

Iris shifted her attention to Mark. "And do you confirm this, Mark?"

"I do." *I do.* The same words he'd spoken at their wedding.

"High school sweethearts," Iris said directly into the camera. "In a town that romanticizes first love."

Iris returned to Carrie. "And you bought into the legend. To the point where you and Mark decided to run off to Vegas and get married when you were only seventeen. Is that correct?"

"It is." Oh God, this was a train wreck.

"But things did not end with a happily-ever-after for you, did they?"

Silently, Carrie shook her head. She felt like she was on trial. She didn't know it was going to be like this. She could feel the heat of Mark's stare on her, but she did not dare meet his eyes.

"Please speak up," Iris urged.

Carrie cleared her throat. "No, they did not."

"And why is that?"

"We were too young." She wasn't going to say anything more. It was the truth, and the rest of the details weren't anybody's business but hers and Mark's. "And the marriage was annulled."

"In the aftermath of your tattered marriage, did

you ever fling a penny into the Sweetheart Fountain and wish to be reunited with Mark?"

"I did," Carrie confirmed.

To the camera, Iris said, "The sweetheart legend claims that if you toss a penny into the fountain you will be reunited with your first love and be happily married for life."

"Yes."

"But the legend did not come true for you, unlike all the other people in your town who claim that it did. Why do you suppose that's the case?" Iris leaned forward, malicious delight in her eyes.

"Iris," Mark said, his voice hard as a stone. "You've made an erroneous assumption."

The woman snapped her gaze from Carrie, swiveled her head to face Mark. "And what is that, Mr. Leland?"

"That the course of true love runs smoothly. The sweetheart legend is based on Jon Grant and Rebekka Nash who were separated for fifteen long years. You're missing the entire point. Just because lovers are separated does not mean they stop loving each other. Sometimes circumstances are beyond their control." He shifted his gaze from Iris to Carrie. "Or sometimes, in the case of Carrie and me, love is the reason we were separated in the first place."

Iris looked miffed. "How do you mean?"

"Carrie loved me so much that she put my needs ahead of her own. She knew that if she didn't convince me to go, then I would not have taken the scholarship I'd been awarded to attend Columbia. I would not have gotten my degree. I would not have this job or the lifestyle that I do today. So she pretended our marriage was a silly mistake, and she did it because she loved me. Did it hurt? Hell, yeah. But I eventually came to realize why she'd done what she'd done. I also figured out just how much she loved me."

Iris rolled her eyes. "Pul-*lease*."

"She's doing the same thing right now. That's why she's on this show. Not to help you bust some myth, but because she's under the mistaken impression that I'm better off without her."

Carrie blinked. Her heart pulsed. Her throat tightened.

Mark stood up, came to stand right in front of her. "Carrie, my love, I'm on to you. I made a mistake by walking away the first time. I let my ego get the better of me. But I know what you're up to, and I'm not letting you get away with it. I belong here in Twilight with you. Coming home has shown me how much I've missed out on."

Her hands flew to her mouth. She couldn't speak. Not a word came out.

"I take full responsibility," he said. "I let my hurt keep me from contacting you, from coming back. But I'm here now. I want to make amends." Then he hitched up his pant leg and went down on his right knee.

Her heart pounded so hard she feared it would explode. She could hear the throb, throb, throbbing in her ears. Her entire body vibrated with the force of it.

Carrie looked down and saw a black velvet box clutched in his hand. He thumbed it open and the biggest diamond engagement ring she'd ever seen caught the light and sparkled.

"I told you when we got married the first time that one day I would buy you the kind of diamond ring you deserved." His voice quavered. "Here I am, keeping my promise. Carrie MacGregor, will you do me the honor of becoming my bride? This time forever and always?"

"Mark," she whispered. "Oh, Mark."

Then tears were flowing down her face, and she was out of the chair and into his arms and kissing his face all over. His eyelids, his nose, his cheeks, his chin.

Mark laughed and wrapped his arms around her, still on one knee. "Is that a yes?"

"Yes, yes, yes, yes." She slung her arms around his neck and squeezed so tightly they both had trouble drawing in breath.

He stood up, taking Carrie with him. Then with his arm around her waist, he turned to face Iris Tobin and the camera. "Looks like this is one myth that has just been confirmed. In Twilight, Texas, true love really does conquer all."

EPILOGUE

Carrie MacGregor loved Christmas.

She adored the carolers on the street corners, even though a couple of them were singing off-key. She treasured the artificial Douglas fir her friends had put up in the window of her shop for customers and the passing tourists to enjoy. She cherished the wreath hung from every intersection on the town square and The Sweetheart Tree in the park, hung with paper Christmas angels. She loved wassail and peppermint candy canes and popcorn garlands.

Yes, okay, she was a Christmas cliché—the fanatic who wasn't happy until everything was gift wrapped or covered in tinsel. Every family had one. Merry Christmas!

Her only goal for the next month was to enjoy every single minute of the holiday with her new fiancé. Yes, Carrie loved Christmas, but not half as much as she loved Mark.

They walked hand-in-hand through the town

square, taking in the annual Dickens-on-the-Square event. Street vendors sold food from carts—roasted chestnuts, turkey legs, spiced apple cider. Reenactors were dressed in Victorian garb from Beefeaters to English bobbies to Charles Dickens himself. The courthouse square hosted Santa's workshop and children ran giggling about. The air was cool. A right nice fifty degrees.

After the interview in which Mark proposed to Carrie on the camera, the *Fact or Fantasy* crew had packed up and left Twilight. They still had no idea whether Burt Mernit was going to run the episode or not. They didn't care. Mark was home to stay, and for once Carrie believed he was right where he was supposed to be.

With her.

He led her down the street to the walkway leading to Sweetheart Park. White twinkle lights decorated every tree in the park. They traveled along the wooden bridge spanning a narrow creek that was an offshoot of the Brazos, and they ended up in the middle of the park where the statue of Jon Grant and Rebekka Nash locked in a passionate embrace graced the flowing stone fountain.

"Got a penny?" Carrie asked.

Grinning, Mark fished in his pocket and produced a copper coin.

Carrie plucked it from her fingers, made a wish for a happy-ever-after love, and tossed it into the fountain. It hit with a merry splash.

"Do you have any idea how beautiful you look right now?" Mark murmured, drawing her close.

She nuzzled his neck. "You say the sweetest things."

"Only because they're true. I'm so sorry that it took me so long to get here."

"It doesn't matter," she said. "You're here at last."

"I had to come back." He smiled. "We were fated after all."

"Joined from the first time we laid eyes on each other in study hall."

"Linked for life."

"There's no escape."

"If this is prison," he said, "lock me up and throw away the key." Then Mark dipped his head and kissed her, proving once and for all that the sweetheart legend lived on . . .

Raylene

CHAPTER ONE

Down at the Horny Toad Tavern off Highway 377 in Twilight, Texas, Elvis Presley was singing, "Blue Christmas."

The jukebox music sounded tinny and faraway as it bled through the door into the crisp night air. Weather reports predicted temperatures would slide below freezing by morning, and listeners had been urged to bring in plants and pets. No holiday lights decorated the building as they had in previous years. Other than Elvis's mournful tune, the establishment gave no hint that Christmas was on the way. Only a few cars sat in the parking lot, sparse for a Saturday night, but most of the hamlet's denizens were out celebrating the annual Dickens on the Square.

In the thick of darkening shadows from the cedar copse rimming the outskirts of the parking lot, a silent figure in a red suit, long white beard, and shiny black boots waited, watching the back entrance of the tavern, hungry to catch a glimpse of one person in particular.

After an interminable half-hour, shortly before midnight, the rear door to the Horny Toad opened, hinges creaking in the cold and letting out the strain of the Eagles singing "Please Come Home for Christmas." The watcher tensed, heart pounding and windburned hands fisted inside the pockets of the Santa costume.

A woman appeared. Once upon a time she'd possessed beautiful blond hair, but now it had grown steely gray. The watcher's breath caught. She had stopped dying her hair.

She carried a black garbage bag, heavy with clanking bottles, and started toward the Dumpster, her movements graceful as always. Years ago she'd been a Dallas Cowboy cheerleader and she'd kept her slender, hourglass figure even into her sixth decade of life. But instead of the mini-skirts she usually favored because she had the most sensational legs of any woman in town no matter what their age, she wore oversized blue jeans and a gray wool sweater with a saggy hem.

The watcher's tongue moistened parched lips. Wishing. Wishing for so many things. Wishing, but unable to make those dreams come true. You couldn't turn back the clock, no matter how hard you might try. Redemption was so close and yet so far away.

The garbage bag made a muffled thumping sound when it landed in the Dumpster. The air smelled of juniper and wood smoke. She dusted her hands and turned toward the bar. Her breath came out in frosty puffs. The moonlight caught her face. Her eyes were worn thin, exhausted.

The watcher shifted in the darkness, gut twisting. *Don't go. Stay. Stay so I can see you for just a little while longer. One last time.*

She paused and looked out into the darkness, her face a portrait of abject bleakness.

A lump blocked the watcher's throat.

The woman shook her head, pushed open the door. Roy Orbison was singing "Pretty Paper." Sad songs. All sad Christmas songs. She stepped inside, the door snapping shut behind her.

A single chilly tear tracked down the watcher's cheek. Gone. Everything once loved and taken for granted was now forever gone.

"Last call," Raylene Pringle said, more out of habit than necessity. There was only one patron left in the Horny Toad on this lonely Saturday night, and he never drank more than a single glass of whiskey. "Have another one, Nate?"

"I'm good." Nate Deavers knocked back the last swallow of whiskey. Set the empty glass down on the bar.

For the past six months, he'd been coming into the bar almost every night. He arrived late, had one drink, and went home. Nate didn't talk much about himself, deflected questions by sitting alone on the far side of the bar beside the Benjamin Ficus. He was on the optimistic side of forty and very good-looking, with coal black hair lightly salted at the temples and peacock blue eyes. He was built like a Keith Black Hemi engine, big, strong, and quick. His biceps were the size of footballs. Raylene had once gotten a glimpse of a Navy SEAL Team Six emblem tattooed on his upper right arm, but she'd never dared asked him about it. He seemed a man who was waiting for something important to happen.

She poured herself a glass of Cabernet, sauntered over to the jukebox, and punched up "Blue Christmas."

"Twenty-seven," Nate said.

"Huh?" Raylene blinked.

"Number of times you've played that song since I've been here."

"If you're keeping count, then it's taking you too long to drink that glass of Jack."

"Probably right about that." He shrugged into his camo-green down jacket. He wore faded Levi's, a blue flannel shirt and black military boots.

A long moment passed. He just stood there. Not moving.

Raylene was not the type of woman who felt uneasy when she was alone in the room with a man, but a dangerous air lingered about this one. She squared her shoulders, stiffened her jaw the way she did when she had to throw drunks out of the bar.

"I don't normally ask a lot of questions," he said, "since I don't like answering them myself, but I'm going to ask anyway."

Great. He's going to ask about Earl. She braced herself, not wanting to discuss the husband who'd run out on her last Christmas after she told him the big bad secret she'd harbored for thirty-five years. Nate must have heard the gossip in town. Lord knows enough of that went on in Twilight.

Raylene swallowed hard, tasting the salt of regret. So many damn regrets. She and Earl had been sweethearts since the first grade, although they broke up and made up at least a dozen times before they'd finally made it to the altar. Most of it was due to Raylene's flirtatious nature, but she'd never—not once during any of their break-ups—stopped loving Earl. He was her rock. The anchor that kept her grounded. Without him, she was cut loose, unfettered. It was a horrible feeling. He'd always had her back, even when he was mad at her. Earl had been her first boyfriend, her first lover, her first everything.

Until last Christmas, when she'd confessed that during the final time they'd broken up (when Raylene was traveling with the Dallas Cowboys as a cheerleader) she'd gotten dead drunk one night in Vegas with Cowboy running back Lance Dugan and had woken up the next morning married to him. They'd immediately gotten the marriage annulled, but then Raylene had turned up pregnant. Lance's blueblood family had stepped in. They were horrified he'd gotten "trailer trash" like Raylene pregnant, but they wanted that grandchild. They'd offered her a quarter of a million dollars to come to New York to give birth and then let them adopt the baby. And, damn her hide, the poor girl who'd grown up wearing bible school hand-me-downs on the farthest side of the railroad tracks had taken the money and run.

The decision had haunted Raylene for thirty-five years. After the baby was born, she'd taken the Dugans' highfalutin' money, returned to Twilight and the love of her life. And when Earl had gotten down on one knee in front of the Sweetheart Fountain in Sweetheart Park and asked her to marry him, it was the happiest moment of her life.

She'd lied to Earl and told him she'd made the money modeling in New York. They wed and bought the Horny Toad so Earl could live out his dream of running his own bar. Ironically, shocker of shockers, his family struck oil on their property six months later. They were rich beyond their wildest dreams.

She and Earl had had a very good life. They'd had a son of their own, Earl Junior, although he was grown and gone. She had lots of friends. But in her heart, there remained an empty place for the baby she'd given away.

A daughter.

In the end, Earl left her not because she'd given her own child away for a quarter of a million dollars, but because she'd kept it a secret from him.

Raylene's eyes met Nate's. He settled a green John Deere cap on a head full of thick, dark hair. "What is it?" she asked.

"How come you haven't decorated for Christmas? Everyone else around here acts like this is Whoville. You're the only one in town without lights on your place."

Relieved at his question, she lifted one shoulder in a half-shrug. "I'm too old to be out climbing on a ladder hanging Christmas lights."

"I could hang them for you."

She gave a sharp, humorless laugh. "Why on earth would you do that?"

"You sort of remind me of my mother," he said.

"Oh that's something every woman wants to hear from a handsome man." But it was true. She was old enough to be Nate's mama. That was a depressing thought.

"My mama was a spitfire." He shifted, looked uncomfortable as if he wished he hadn't started this mess. "Just like you are. This time of year, I get to missing her. I'd consider it an honor to put up your Christmas decorations for you, Mrs. Pringle."

"Why not?" she said with an easy shrug. "But only if you let me pay you. You're going to have to go dig the lights out of the shed and untangle them. I had to take them down myself last year, and I dumped them all in a big box."

"You can pay me in trade," he said, nodding at the bottle of Jack Daniels behind the counter.

"Deal." Raylene set her wineglass on the jukebox and stuck out her palm.

Nate shook her hand. "I'll put the lights up for you next Wednesday. I'm off on Wednesdays and Thursdays."

She'd never asked him about his work, but somewhere she'd heard he worked for Devon Energy, keeping check on the numerous gas wells that had sprung up when the big oil companies decided it was worth their while to go after the Barnett Shale.

"Maybe that's exactly what I need," she mused. "A little Christmas cheer."

"Traditions are good," he said.

"Can I ask you a question, Nate?"

"If I can retain the option of not answering."

She laughed. "Deal."

Nate looked suspicious. "What's on your mind?"

"Have you ever been married?"

"No." His eyes clouded. He could shut off a conversation faster than a spigot.

"Do you like women?"

A smile flitted at the corner of his lips. "I do. Why?"

"I was just wondering why a guy like you is spending Saturday night alone in an empty bar."

"You're not trying to fix me up are you? I know how the ladies of your clubs like to meddle and make matches."

Raylene raised her arms. "Hands off. I promise."

He headed for the door. "You be careful going home, Mrs. Pringle."

"Thanks, Nate," she said, feeling oddly comforted. She followed him to the front door, bid him goodnight, and locked up behind him.

When she went behind the bar to finish cleaning up, her mind drifted back to Earl. She hadn't heard a word from him in a year. Not after he withdrew a quarter of a million dollars from their bank accounts. The significance of that amount was not lost on her. He was sending a message. He'd never been one to nurse a grudge, but her secret had been a bombshell. Now, not one word from him in twelve months. She worried and fretted and finally prayed. She'd started to fear he was dead. She hired a detective to find him, but it was like he'd dropped off the face of the earth.

Raylene was in limbo, waiting for the love of her life to return. How long could she live like this? Not knowing what had happened to him? The punishment he was dishing out was more than she could bear. Raylene had changed, and not for the better. Without Earl, she was only a shell of her former self.

You're gonna have to move on. It's clear he ain't coming back.

But that was just it. She didn't want to move on. She wanted Earl. Wanted things to be the way they used to be.

You can want in one hand and spit in the other and see which one fills up first. That was something her daddy used to say when she asked him for anything. Meaning that if she wanted something, she had to make it happen for herself. And for most of her life, she had done exactly that. But this was one desire that she had no control over.

"Earl," she whispered. "Where are you?"

For the last year she'd been caught in limbo. Unable to do even the simplest thing like dye her hair. The activities of daily life without Earl took too much effort. She'd made no decisions. Changed nothing. One of her waitresses had quit, and she hadn't even replaced her. Tonight it had been no big deal because the annual Christmas festival on the square had siphoned off her regular Saturday night customers, but usually she was run ragged waiting tables, pinch-hitting for the bartender, and doing all the back-office stuff, especially during the holidays.

Nate's remark about the Christmas lights brought it all home to her. She couldn't keep living in limbo. Time was marching on and it wasn't waiting on her. Earl might never come back.

That thought was a stab to her heart. She dropped her head in her hands. Sooner or later she was going to have to face the possibility of divorce.

But if Earl wanted a divorce, why didn't he just come home and ask for one? Could he really just stop loving her after all these years? Raylene felt sick to her stomach.

What if Earl was dead?

That was the horrible thought she couldn't shake. It was the only explanation she could come up with for why he hadn't come home. He was born and bred in Twilight. All his family lived here. But they all claimed he had not been in contact with any of them, either.

"Earl," she whimpered. "Please come home for Christmas."

She lifted her head and looked around. It felt so empty without Earl behind the bar. So lifeless. Nate was right. She needed to decorate for the holidays. Cheer this place up.

She also needed to hire someone, but the thought of going through interviews exhausted her. She worked more than sixty hours a week to keep her mind off Earl, but she needed time to heal. To think. To come to some kind of closure.

Yet what closure could there be without knowing what had happened to her husband?

Make a move. Do something. You've got to snap out of this.

With a heavy sigh, she got up, retrieved the glass of wine she'd left on the jukebox, and poured the remainder down the sink. She washed the glass and put it on the shelf. When she was done, she went to the office and took a faded Help Wanted sign from the desk drawer. She padded back to the front of the bar, pulled back the dusty red gingham curtains, and slipped the sign in the window.

There. She'd taken action. Forward motion. It wasn't much, but it was a start.

Symbolism. The last refuge of a desperate woman.

Chapter Two

On Sunday afternoon, Shannon Dugan sat in the plain white Chevy Malibu she'd rented at DFW Airport, staring at the front of the Horny Toad Tavern.

The place was a country-and-western bar built from rough-hewn cedar. The emblem of a giant horned frog decorated the center of the façade erected over the entrance. Weathered, knobbed pine resembling old west hitching posts served as railing.

A few pickup trucks were parked on an asphalt parking lot that needed resurfacing. The smell of popcorn, hickory smoke, and beer tinged the air. An old George Jones song leaked from the windows.

On the right side of the bar sat a pawnshop. On the left was a barbecue restaurant. Behind all three establishments lay gently rolling land heavy with juniper, mesquite, and cedar trees.

So this was it. The place her birth mother had bought with the money she'd gotten after she'd sold Shannon to her grandparents.

She drew in a deep breath, clutched the steering wheel tightly, and for one serious moment considered turning the Chevy around and catching the next flight back to New York. How easy it would be to flee. It had taken her a year to work up the courage to come here.

Of course, she'd found out about Raylene at the very same time she'd discovered her husband of six months was a con man who had taken her for three million dollars.

The sour taste of shame and regret slipped over her tongue as she relived the past Christmas Eve in vivid detail. That was when her lawyer had called to tell her that the check she'd written him for settling her grandfather's estate had bounced. At first, she'd assumed it was simply some banking glitch, and she'd assured the lawyer that she would get it straightened out.

But the banks had already closed, and there wasn't anyone she could talk to until after the holiday. She'd gone online to monitor her main checking account only to find it overdrawn. As was her savings account. She immediately checked on her money market account. It too had been drained. Later, she discovered that the gold kept in her safe deposit box had been cleaned out as well.

Panicked, thinking they were victims of identity theft, she'd put out a call to Peter who'd said he was going out shopping for her Christmas gifts. He was spontaneously boyish that way. Waiting until the last minute to do everything. Although Shannon didn't complain about that because Peter's impulsive, fun-loving nature was what had attracted her to him from the moment her best friend Charlotte had brought him to the country club as a mixed-doubles partner for her. He'd been a classmate of Charlotte's late brother when he'd attended school at Oxford.

Peter Clark was so different from her—chatty where she was quiet, daring where she was conservative, flashy where she was drab. Peter had drawn her like a magnet, mainly because she'd grown up in an austere household with older people determined that they would not make the mistakes with their granddaughter that they'd made with their morally lax son. Shannon had the strictest upbringing of anyone she knew, but she was obedient by nature. Rebellion never crossed her mind.

When Peter asked her out, it was so unexpected that a man like him would be interested in a bookish woman like her that she suspected it was for her money. Shannon was unaccustomed to intriguing, good-looking men courting her, but after having him checked out by a private detective and learning he came from a wealthy background himself, she went out with him. What she had not known at the time was that his real name was Owen Cleary and he'd stolen Peter Clark's identity.

Peter proposed on their fourth date, and she found herself saying yes. After so many years of nursing her ailing grandparents, it felt good to do all the things other women got to do when they were in their teens and twenties.

The wedding had been lavish. Her grandfather insisted on it, even though his health was rapidly failing. Her grandmother had died the previous year, and all the fight had gone out of him. He was dwindling before her eyes.

Life had been good with Peter. He was fun and an exciting lover. Yet there were warning signs she'd chosen to ignore, blissful in her cocoon of false happiness. He never seemed to have any money. "Tied up in investments," he'd say.

Whenever she asked him about his past, or his family, he shook his head, told her he was alone in the world and it hurt too much to talk about his past. She backed off. What else could she do? And she hoped for the day when he felt comfortable enough to confide in her.

Then her grandfather's condition had worsened and she'd been by his bedside until the end on Thanksgiving Day. Peter had been solicitous. Taking care of paying the bills—or so she thought. Telling her that she should stay at her grandfather's house on Long Island and not worry at all about coming home to their condo in the city until everything was wrapped up. He'd been kind and considerate, and she'd stupidly told herself she had the best husband in the whole world.

So it wasn't until midnight on Christmas Eve that she finally realized Peter was not coming back. Nor was he going to answer her repeated texts and phone calls, because he was the one who'd absconded with her money. She had other monies, of course. The house, investments, some rental properties, treasury bonds, but her net worth and cash flow had taken a crippling blow. Ultimately, however, what hurt the most were his betrayal and the fact that she'd been so desperate for love and attention that she'd let down her guard. How stupid. How gullible. What a terrible judge of character.

In the midst of all this, a knock sounded at the door of her grandfather's house. An armed security guard stood there with a disheveled man in his sixties.

"I found him cruising the neighborhood, Mrs. Clark," the security guard said. "He claims he has something important to tell you. Do you know this man? Should I call the police?"

She blinked at the rumpled man, thinking he might have some connection to Peter. "Who are you?" she'd demanded, all traces of her well-bred civility gone.

"Name's Earl Pringle," the man had said. "And I've got sumpin' important to tell you about your real mother."

"My mother died when I was a baby."

Earl shook his head. "No, ma'am. She didn't. She's alive and well and living in Twilight, Texas."

A car horn honking on the highway jerked Shannon back to the present. It had taken her a year to make her way here. She'd had a lot to deal with. Her grandfather's passing. Being robbed by her husband and made a fool of. Pinning down her father and asking him if Earl Pringle's story was true. Learning that it was indeed.

She wasn't going to leave until she'd done what she'd come here to do. Confront her birth mother.

But how to go about it? It wasn't a topic that rolled

easily off the tongue. She'd planned an entire speech. Rehearsed it on the plane. But now that she was here, all the scenarios she envisioned had vanished. For one thing, she wasn't a confronter. Her grandparents had stoically kept negative feelings bottled up tight and had expected her to do the same. Her father, Lance, had a sunny, easygoing disposition whenever he was around. She had no training in the art of verbal aikido.

But she had to have answers. Had to hear her mother's side of the story.

Her breathing was coming out thin and reedy. Her stomach knotted. What to do? What to do?

And that's when she saw it.

The Help Wanted sign in the window.

Dear Earl,

Raylene paused, pen in her hand, and stared down at the yellow legal notepad. Her nephew Travis's new bride Sarah was a writer, and during the First Love Cookie Club meeting this morning, she'd suggested Raylene write a letter to Earl and tell him how she felt. It had sounded like a good idea at the time, but now that she was doing it, the words simply wouldn't come.

It might work for writers, but this letter-writing nonsense wasn't for former Dallas Cowboys cheerleaders turned bar owners. Raylene yanked out the piece of paper, crumbled it into a tight ball, and banked it off the wall above the trashcan. It dropped right in.

"She shoots, she scores."

"What did you say, boss?"

Raylene was startled to see her main bartender, Chap Hyndman, standing at the partially opened door. "Nothing," she mumbled, stuffing the pad and pen in the desk drawer with her stack of Word Find anagram puzzles. "What did you want?"

"There's a lady here," Chap said. "Asking about a job."

"A job?" Raylene blinked.

"You put a Help Wanted sign in the window."

"Oh, yeah." She'd forgotten about that. "Well, send her on in."

"Okay." Chap nodded and moved off.

Raylene heard him talking to someone in the hallway. A minute later, a woman appeared at the door. Raylene waved her inside. "C'mon, have a seat, shut the door behind you or that busybody bartender will eavesdrop."

The woman hesitated. Raylene's eyes met hers and instant gooseflesh carpeted her arms.

Someone just walked over your grave. It was something her grandmamma used to say. Raylene never really understood what the saying meant. How could someone walk over your grave if you weren't dead yet?

The woman stepped inside the office, closed the door.

Raylene shook off the weird feeling, got to her feet, extended her hand. "Name's Raylene Pringle," she said.

The woman accepted her hand. Surprisingly, she had a strong handshake. From the size of her, skinny as a tentative stray cat, Raylene was expecting a limp fish handshake. Not only was her handshake solid, but she looked Raylene squarely in the eyes.

"My name is Shannon . . ." She paused for a fraction of a second before saying, "Nagud."

"Nagud? That's a new one on me," Raylene said. "What nationality is it?"

The woman shrugged. "Does it matter?"

Raylene held up both palms.

"Nope."

The woman glanced around the office, sizing it up. Her gaze fell on a picture of Raylene back in the seventies in her Dallas Cowboys cheerleader uniform surrounded by several grinning football players. One of whom was Lance Dugan.

Suddenly it occurred to her that she should never have displayed that picture. It had been up there for years, the picture that she and Lance were in together. In the office she shared with Earl. *Used* to share. She'd been damned insensitive. Raylene suppressed an impulse to yank it off the wall and throw it into the trash along with the wadded-up letter she could not write.

"Have a seat." Raylene waved at the Naugahyde couch and inspected Shannon Nagud more closely.

She wasn't young, but neither was she quite yet middle-aged. Early- to mid-thirties. Near the same age Raylene's daughter would be. She was a little taller than Raylene's five-foot-six, with dark brown hair and a heart-shaped face. She had killer legs. Almost as good as Raylene's own. A simple gray wool sheath dress clung to her skinny frame, and a single strand of pearls encircled her long, elegant neck. She moved like Grace Kelly. Above it all. Smooth and cool. Emotionally untouchable. Certainly not cocktail waitress material where big tits and a ribald sense of humor garnered the most tips. No, this one belonged in a quiet, dignified work environment. A museum curator or boutique shop owner. Somewhere serene and clean and distant.

For no reason at all, Raylene thought of her ex-mother-in-law, Kathryn Dugan. The woman who'd come into the hospital in upstate New York and written out a check for two hundred and fifty thousand dollars, only hours after Raylene had given birth to the daughter she never got a chance to see. Back in those days, they knocked your ass out when you had a baby. "I've booked you a flight on Braniff to DFW for tomorrow morning," Kathryn said. "Be on it and don't ever contact us again."

For thirty-five years Raylene had stuck to her promise. The past Christmas, though, she'd broken that vow, and she'd paid a heavy price. The familiar squeeze of shame, remorse, and disappointment rolled through her. Life didn't give you second chances. There were no do-overs. You screwed up when you were young, and it haunted you for the rest of your life.

"The bartender had me fill out an application." Shannon reached into her chic Burberry purse. It was not a knockoff. Raylene puckered her lips. How could an out-of-work cocktail waitress afford a Burberry purse?

Shannon passed the application to her. "I didn't fully fill it out."

Raylene raised an eyebrow. The only boxes that were filled in on the form were Shannon's name and cell phone number. No address. No previous work experience. "Is this some kind of a joke?"

"I have to be honest with you, Mrs. Pringle." She cleared her throat and an uncertain expression flitted over her face.

The way she said it sent a spark of warning up Raylene's spine. There was something decidedly unusual about this woman. For a fraction of a second, she almost told her to leave, but her curiosity got the better of her. "I'm intrigued. You've got five minutes to explain yourself."

"I didn't fill out the address portion because I'm new in town, and I don't yet have a residence." Shannon paused. "I was wondering if you could suggest a place?"

Raylene thought about the apartment upstairs over the bar. Earl had converted the space for Earl Junior to get him out of the house when he turned twenty-one, with the idea being that E.J. would help his father run the Horny Toad. As with most expectations when it came to your kids, things hadn't turned out the way they'd planned, but she and Earl had used the apartment as rental income for several years. After the previous tenant had left in August to go back to college, Raylene hadn't bothered renting it out. She'd been happy to be shed of the hassle. It was hard keeping things up without Earl.

Instead of answering Shannon's question, Raylene asked, "Why'd you come to Twilight?"

Shannon held her gaze with unnerving steadiness. "It seems like a fairytale town."

"Looks can be deceiving."

"Yes." Shannon's gaze turned into a full-on stare. "Yes, they can."

Unnerved, Raylene lowered her eyes to the form. "You didn't put anything down under previous employment."

"I've never worked as a cocktail waitress before."

Helen Keller could have figured that out. "Where *have* you worked?"

Shannon shook her head. "Is that really important? It has no bearing on the position I'm applying for."

Red flags flew. There was something very fishy about Shannon Nagud. Raylene shook her head and stood up. "I'm sorry, but I need an experienced cocktail waitress."

Shannon got to her feet as well. "Mrs. Pringle, I'm asking you to take a chance on me. I need a job very badly. In fact, I'm desperate."

Raylene's gaze went to the pearls, then dropped to the Burberry purse.

"I know it doesn't look that way, but . . ." She paused and her cool faltered. For one fraction of a second, she looked so utterly vulnerable that her expression tore at Raylene's crusty old heart.

"I didn't want to tell you my dark secret."

Empathy flooded Raylene. From one person who'd held onto a dark secret to another. She reached out and briefly touched the younger woman's shoulder. "What is it?"

Shannon dipped her head. "I'm so ashamed."

You're not a therapist, Raylene. Show her the door. You don't need to get mixed up in her drama. "We've all made mistakes we regret."

Shannon raised her head, that piercing stare was back. "Have you?"

An instant lump blocked Raylene's throat. She nodded.

"I did a very stupid thing," Shannon said. "I was lonely and I fell in love with the wrong guy. He turned out to be a con man. Took me for my inheritance."

"That rotten shitbag," Raylene said, wondering why she had such an impulse to rally behind this woman.

A wry smile pulled tightly at Shannon's mouth. "To say the least."

Raylene kneaded her forehead. *Don't do it. Don't do it.* "Ever done any kind of waitressing?"

"No, but I'm a fast learner."

She knew she was going to regret it. Mentally, she was already calculating how much broken beer mugs were going to cost her until Shannon got the hang of balancing drinks on a tray. Her wrists did look strong. As if she played a lot of tennis or lifted dumbbells. Maybe she wouldn't be as bad as Raylene feared.

"You can't expect the same salary as an experienced waitress."

An emotion that Raylene could not identify lit

Shannon's eyes. It wasn't quite excitement, nor was it relief or even hope, rather it was more a nervous anticipation.

"No, no," Shannon said, "of course not." Raylene low-balled her on the salary.

Shannon nodded. "That's fine."

Hmm, she didn't even try to bargain. Another cause for concern. Was she that desperate? The woman with the Burberry purse. "You're on two weeks probation."

"I would expect that."

"There's a loft apartment upstairs. With a side entrance," Raylene said, feeling a bit bad for low-balling her. "You're welcome to stay there rent-free until you can find other accommodations."

Shannon looked surprised. "That's very generous of you."

Raylene shrugged. "It's empty. No skin off my teeth. You'll have to clean it yourself."

"Yes, surely. Thank you for this opportunity."

"Get settled in, and I'll introduce you around."

"I'll go get my suitcase. Thank you again, Mrs. Pringle."

"Thank me by doing a good job."

"You won't regret hiring me," Shannon promised, hurrying toward the door.

"We'll see about that," Raylene mumbled. She was a lunatic for hiring an unproven cocktail waitress. Something just wasn't right about Shannon Nagud.

CHAPTER THREE

"What in God's name are you doing?" Shannon stared at herself in the dusty bureau mirror.

She stood in the middle of the tiny apartment above the bar, still in heels and pearls, a bottle of Windex in one hand, and a page of newspaper in the other. Raylene had given her a plastic carrier filled with cleaning supplies and told her to "have at it."

She'd come here to confront her birth mother, and instead she now had a job and a place to stay in a Texas town she'd never heard of until a year ago. She squirted glass cleaner on the mirror and, using a circular motion, rubbed it with the newspaper. Shannon stared into her own tawny eyes, so similar in color to her father's.

Honestly, she had no idea what she was doing. But for the first time in a year, she felt as if she'd taken control of her life instead of being rocked by circumstances.

What? You're a cocktail waitress now? How long do you plan on staying here?

"I don't know," she said.

She was an art history major who'd given up her art gallery job in Soho to nurse her grandparents the last three years of their lives. A true trust-fund baby who'd never really had to work a day in her life.

When she'd walked into the bar on the pretext of looking for a job, she'd thought she would size up Raylene and then make up her mind about what to do next. Apparently, that meant rolling with the punches and accepting the job she never in a million years thought Raylene would offer. In the back of her mind was a voice that whispered, "Here's your chance to get to know your mother."

Was that what she really wanted? That was the thing. At thirty-five, she still didn't know her own mind or what she truly wanted. She'd even studied art history at her grandmother's suggestion. A genteel field of study fit for a Dugan. The best part had been studying in Italy. The downside had been that her grandparents had rented a villa in Florence so they could keep a close eye on her—although she had managed a short-lived clandestine romance with a wild-haired French artist who taught her a great deal about the human form. She was painfully aware that she'd been raised in an ivory tower; thirty-five, and just the last few years really feeling the sharp teeth of life.

Shannon set the Windex on the bureau, walked across the braided rug covering the knotted pine floor, and sank down on the full-sized bed covered with a friendly homemade quilt. It was getting dark outside, the purple blue fingers of dusk darkening to navy.

From downstairs, the jukebox played Christmas carols. Maybe the truth was that she didn't want to be alone for the holidays. Grandfather was gone. Her father was spending the entire month of December in Aspen with his new girlfriend, who was six years younger than Shannon. Her friends all had their own families. She had nowhere to be and no one to be with.

Maybe she should stay here until Christmas Day and drop the bombshell on Raylene then.

That's a bit cruel, don't you think?

What was cruel was Raylene running out on her when she was a baby.

Shannon blew out her breath, leaned back, and stared at the ceiling. After that mess with Peter, she'd found it difficult to make a decision and stick with it, terrified that she would make another huge mistake.

She remembered then what Raylene had said to her, recalled the haunted look in her eyes. *We've all made mistakes we regret.* Had she been talking about abandoning her child?

A knock sounded on the door.

"Come in," she said, sitting up.

Raylene stepped inside. She wore blue jeans and cowboy boots and had her gray hair pulled into a ponytail. She glanced around the room. "Doesn't take you long to clean up."

"I'm a hard worker," Shannon said, lifting her

chin proudly. She'd hired on to be a cocktail waitress, and that's what she was going to do.

Raylene tilted her head, studied Shannon for a long moment. "Come on downstairs," she said. "Chap made a pot of stew for the bar menu. Might as well go meet everyone."

Nate had just tossed a handful of pistachios in his mouth and was busy chewing when through the side window he caught sight of a gorgeous pair of legs descending the outside stairs. His throat worked, but for a moment, he couldn't swallow. All he could do was stare. By the time the owner of those spectacular legs appeared in profile in the window, he was already a goner.

He swiveled his head, eyes beaded on the front door. It creaked open, and Raylene sauntered in. A slender brunette in a gray dress and matching high-heeled shoes that looked like they came from Paris or Rome, followed her.

Holy smokes! Who was this?

She wasn't young, but neither was she old. Just the right age. Maybe three or four years younger than he was. Although with all he'd seen and done, Nate felt a lot older than his thirty-eight years.

The bar was quieter than usual, although a rowdy college-aged crowd was in the back room playing pool. The wide-screen TV was turned to the football game, and several regulars sat at the bar eating stew and watching the Cowboys and the Dolphins seesaw back and forth across the gridiron. An older couple sat at a table near the empty dance floor, holding hands over their drinks and gazing into each other's eyes.

Nate liked the Horny Toad. It was family owned and operated, a hangout for locals. Few tourists ventured in, so the prices were lower than the flashier bars near the Lake Twilight marina. He also came here because it was better than drinking alone in his cabin. He allowed himself only one drink a night. He'd almost gotten into serious trouble with alcohol when he'd first returned from Afghanistan, trying to drown the terrible memories. He didn't want to go down that road again. Since moving to Twilight, he'd been able to stick to his one-drink policy, and the nightmares had faded. The town turned out to be just the tonic his ragged soul needed. This afternoon, he'd even ordered a beer instead of his usual whiskey. He took a big swallow to wash down the pistachios.

Raylene guided the woman behind the bar, and Nate had to quell an impulse to stand up to acknowledge her presence.

"Fellas," Raylene addressed the men at the bar. "I want you to meet Shannon. She's our new cocktail waitress. I trust you'll all take it easy on her while she learns the ropes. She narrowed her gaze at one patron who was notorious for pinching waitresses on the fanny. "I'm talking to you, Snake."

"Who, me?" Snake asked, trying to look innocent.

"If he grabs your ass," Raylene said to Shannon, "haul off and slap the fire out of him."

Snake reached up and rubbed his cheek as if he'd already been slapped.

"Have a seat," Raylene told Shannon. "And I'll get us some stew."

"I can get it," Shannon said.

"Don't worry." Raylene waved a hand as she pushed through the double doors leading to the small kitchen where they prepared a small bar menu. "You'll be waiting on me soon enough."

Shannon looked a bit stricken to find herself alone at the bar with a dozen guys giving her the once-over. Up close, she wasn't drop-dead gorgeous. Her nose was slightly crooked, her complexion was pale, and her lips were a bit too wide. But she had high cheekbones, a mass of sexy dark hair that swayed over her shoulders when she moved, and those world-class legs.

Nate's entire body tensed, which both unnerved and irritated him. It had been a very long time since he'd had such an instant sexual attraction to anyone.

She glanced around for a place to sit. There were two vacant spots. One beside Snake and one beside Nate. Snake patted the stool next to him.

Shannon didn't look Snake's way. Instead, her intriguing golden brown eyes met his, and Nate found himself smiling at her like some damned schoolboy.

"May I sit here, Mr. . . . ?"

"Nate," he said, holding out his hand, surprised by how hopeful he felt. "Nate Deavers."

"Shannon." She returned his smile and took his hand.

A snap of static electricity crackled between them. Just normal, static discharge. Happened all the time in the winter months. So why did it feel like a nuclear reactor had gone off in his hand?

"Oh." Her eyes widened. "Oh." She jerked her hand back, ran it down her side. He couldn't help tracking her palm as it ran over her hips. "Sorry about that. Must be the wool dress."

"I'm not."

She looked puzzled. "Not what?"

"Sorry about the zap or the wool dress. It looks good on you." *And so do those killer shoes.*

Her high cheekbones colored instantly, and she dropped her gaze.

Subtle, Deavers. Real subtle.

Nate wasn't a flirt. Not usually. He'd had his moments in the past, but by and large he didn't say things like that. Now he was coming across like a douche. What was he trying to do? Scare her over next to Snake?

But no, she climbed up on the stool beside him. She sat up straight, perfect posture, legs crossed demurely at the ankles, hands stacked on top of the bar.

Nate's heart thumped weirdly.

Everyone was still staring at her, some with lusty gazes. The new girl in town. He felt an absurd urge to blacken a few eyes. Raylene came backward through the double doors carrying two steaming bowls of stew. She sat one bowl in front of Shannon and another on the bar in front of the stool beside Snake.

"Keep your hands to yourself," Raylene warned, shaking a finger under Snake's nose before coming around to the other side of the bar and taking the last open spot.

"Hey, I'd never pinch you. Earl's my best friend."

At the mention of Earl's name, everyone fell silent. Nate didn't know the full history, but Chap, the bartender, had told him that Raylene's husband had left her the past Christmas and no one had seen or heard from him since.

"Could someone pass the pepper?" Shannon asked brightly, as if looking for something to break the tension. She hadn't even tasted her stew yet.

The pepper grinder was sitting in front of Nate. He passed it to her. Their hands touched again.

Zap!

"Oh," she exclaimed a second time, then laughed nervously.

"Guess we better stop touching each other," Nate said.

"Good idea." She plucked a thin napkin from the dispenser on the bar and spread it over her upper thighs. "Apparently, together we're combustible."

Her statement wasn't particularly provocative, but Nate's body lit up as if she'd just said something very naughty. His mind immediately filled with red-hot images. Those sexy legs of hers wrapped around his waist, their naked bodies drenched in sweat.

Nate ran a hand over his forehead.

She scooped her spoon backward in the steaming stew, and then brought it up. A lingering drop of juice fell into the bowl instead of in her lap. Perfect table manners.

Beside her, Nate felt like an ox. Big and uncouth and bumbling.

Shannon puckered her lush lips and blew across the stew to cool it.

Watching her, Nate just about fell off his chair.

God, she was incredible in an effortless way—refined, elegant, understated. She seemed completely unaware of her natural sexuality and the power she could have over a man if she chose to exercise it.

One of her delicate hands reached up to finger the strand of pearls at her neck. His gaze tracked her movements. A pale blue vein at the hollow of her throat fluttered with each pulse beat. Her short fingernails were filed into smooth half-moon shapes and polished with a pinky-white luminescent polish.

She slipped the spoonful of stew into her mouth and chewed slowly. Her jaw muscles moved in a hypnotic rhythm.

Mesmerized, Nate couldn't have looked away if someone had yelled "suicide bomber."

"Want something to drink?" Chap asked her.

She placed two fingers to her lips, smiled, swallowed, and said, "A glass of wat—no," she interrupted herself. "I got a new job today and a place to stay. A celebration is in order. What kind of wine do you have?"

"Red and white," Chap said, completely serious.

A quick frown furrowed her brow. "Maybe I'll have a beer. What do you recommend?"

A bemused expression crossed Chap's face, and he shot Raylene a where-in-the-hell-did-you-dig-this-one-up look. "We got Bud and Coors on tap. Or Lone Star long necks."

"I'll have that last one," she said. "The one with the long neck."

Snake chortled, and Raylene none-to-subtly jammed her elbow into his ribs. "Hey!" Snake protested, rubbing his flank. "Whyja do that?"

"Watch the game," Raylene told him.

Chap pulled a Lone Star from the cooler, twisted off the top, and slid it across the bar to her. Shannon took another napkin and ran it around the head of the bottle. She brought it to her lips, took a tiny sip, winced.

Seriously? Had the woman never drunk a beer before? At her age?

Now, besides being sexually aroused by this pretty stranger, Nate was completely intrigued.

She stroked her slender fingers, with the pearly nail polish, up and down the long hard neck of the smooth glass bottle. On any other woman, Nate would have assumed the action was a come-on, a flirtatious gesture, but Shannon seemed unaware of the effect she was having on him.

He couldn't stop looking at her. It was disturbing how much he wanted to stare at her. His mouth was dry. His gut knocked. He curled his hands into fists and forced his attention back to his mug of beer. Seconds later he was back for more, tracing his gaze over the swell of her breasts. Not big. But not small. Just the right size for fitting into the palm of a man's hands.

"Where are you from?" Chap asked her, tossing the bottle cap into the garbage.

"I was raised on the east coast," she said mildly.

"You don't sound like a Yankee." Chap polished the chrome with a bar towel. "More like a newscaster. Can't tell where you're from."

"Whatcha doin' in Texas?" Snake asked.

"Looking for a fresh start."

"Runnin' from the ghost of Christmas past, huh?"

"You might say that." Her fingers were still tracking up and down, up and down that cool glass bottle.

Her words got to Nate. She was here for the very same reason he'd moved to this town. To start over, forget the past.

"Well, with those dynamite legs, I'm glad you ran straight to Twilight," Nate blurted.

Shannon ducked her head, but not before he saw twin splotches of pink spread across her cheeks. Apparently compliments embarrassed her. Why? It's not like she was an inexperienced teenager. Better question: why was he so fascinated by her?

She reached for the pepper mill again, twisted it a few turns over her bowl. So, she liked things hot. She settled the grinder back on the bar, and he caught a whiff of her scent. Understated though she was, her fragrance packed a delightful punch. First there was the mild aroma of new linen, followed by a clean note of lemon, ending with just a crisp hint of evergreen. She smelled like soft sheets dried on the clothesline outside a summer cabin in the mountains.

"Cowboys got it on the ten-yard line, forty seconds left on the clock, fourth down," Snake hollered.

Every gaze at the bar—including Shannon's—riveted on the television screen overhead. "Run the ball, Romo."

"They're going for the flea flicker," Shannon said.

"What?" Snake craned his grizzled head to stare down the bar at her. "No way, sister."

"Would you care to make a wager?"

"Do you even know what a flea flicker is?"

"The Dolphins' new defensive line is a brick wall against fourth-down runs. The Cowboys' head coach is smart enough to know that. They need an unorthodox play to win this game. Fifty dollars says flea flicker."

"Make it a hundred and you've got a deal," Snake said.

"Fine by me if you want to throw your money away." Shannon shrugged.

"Shh, shh." Chap thumbed the remote to turn up the volume. "They're back from commercial."

"There's the snap," the announcer said. "Look, look!" His voice rose. "It's a flea flicker! And Smith catches it in the end zone. Cowboys win!"

"Just like the old days," Raylene said wistfully. "With Landry, Staubach, and Pearson."

"Dammit!" Snake cursed.

Several of the other men hooted and joked.

"Pay the woman," Raylene told Snake, sliding off her stool. "She out-strategized you."

"That was amazing." Nate grinned at Shannon.

"Don't be in awe." She canted her head. "When your father is—" She broke off suddenly, as Raylene passed behind her seat.

"Is what?" Nate prodded.

"A die-hard Cowboys fan," she finished, though he had a feeling that was not what she had intended to say.

He took in the bright sheen to her eyes. Was it from the money she'd just won from a disgruntled Snake or because she was hiding something? She was an unusual woman. Studying her, Nate felt his body stir. He didn't know what her agenda was, but she was cultured, smart, and unique. A breath of fresh air in a small town that could get stuck in its ways.

"I think I'm a die-hard Shannon fan," he murmured.

She looked startled, and then the slightest smile tipped her lips. "Are you flirting with me, Mr. Deavers?"

"Nate," he said. "Call me Nate."

He dropped his fingers to her hand and *snap!* Electricity. Shocking, that vigorous crackle.

Shannon pulled her hand away, scooted her stool back and picked up the bowl of stew she had not finished. Had she lost her appetite? Or had he crossed the line? Chased her off?

She started for the double doors behind the bars that led into the kitchen, a purposeful expression on her face as if she couldn't get away from him fast enough.

"Shannon."

She turned her head, looking frazzled, uncertain, cornered. "Orientation," she said. "Raylene's going to show me the ropes."

"Hold on a minute."

She stopped at the door.

Nate got up and walked toward her, with each step his heart thumping harder. He reached her.

She stood, frozen in place.

"You forgot this." He took Snake's hundred-dollar bill that she'd left behind on the bar in her rush to get away from him and slipped it into the pocket of her dress, his hand skimming over her hip in the process. "You earned it fair and square."

At his touch, her lips parted slightly, and an emotion Nate couldn't decipher flicked across her face. He was coming on too strong. He knew it and yet he couldn't seem to help himself.

"Thanks." Her voice came out in a husky rush.

Clearly, this woman had some mental baggage. *Hey, just like you do.* He would be smart to get away from her before he took advantage of her vulnerability, because right now he wanted to kiss her more than he wanted to breathe. If they didn't have an audience, he probably would kiss her. So much for his Navy SEAL self-control.

"I don't . . . I can't . . ." She didn't finish her sentence, but her golden-brown eyes rounded and her gaze shifted to his mouth. The tip of her tongue darted out to moisten her lips.

Was she thinking the same blasted thing he was thinking? Nate lowered his head.

She was standing between the bar and the kitchen, a bowl of half-consumed stew in her hand. Behind them sat a bar full of patrons, and he was seriously thinking about kissing her?

Timing, Deavers. Timing.

Yeah, well, his timing mechanism was screwed up. He hadn't allowed himself to feel anything for so long, he thought he'd forgotten how. So why this woman? Why now? Was it because he was lonesome, and the spirit of Christmas was moving him to do things he wouldn't ordinarily do, like volunteering to put holiday lights on the Horny Toad for Raylene?

Nate leaned in closer. She peered into his eyes.

"Shannon?" Raylene called from the kitchen.

She jumped back. "Duty calls."

She spun around too quickly, apparently forgetting how close she was to the door, and ran smack dab into it. The bowl of stew slipped from her hand and crashed to the floor.

"Oh no," she exclaimed, and bent to pick up the shattered pieces of the earthenware bowl.

"Broken dishes come out of your paycheck," Raylene hollered.

"Good thing you're good at hustling football plays." Nate squatted to help her.

"I've got this," she said. "Please, go back to the bar."

"I can't help feeling responsible."

"It's not your fault. Go. Please. Leave me alone and we'll get along just fine."

Chapter Four

For the next two days, Shannon learned the ins and outs of cocktail waitressing. She had a great memory, so she had no trouble remembering who ordered what drinks. The difficult part was standing on her feet all day. Yes, she was fit, spending hours a week on the treadmill at the gym, but that kind of exercise was far different from standing on hard floors for eight hours at a stretch.

Hard work prevented Shannon from dwelling too much on that devastatingly handsome Nate Deavers. She could have sworn that for a minute there, before she'd dropped that bowl of stew, he'd been about to kiss her.

Even more alarming, she'd been about to let him.

Which distressed her. A great deal. Hadn't she learned anything about fast-paced romance from her disastrous relationship with Peter?

He's not like Peter, whispered an unruly voice at

the back of her brain. *In fact, he's the exact opposite of your con-man ex.*

Peter had taken care with his appearance, a true metrosexual. He was suave, sophisticated, and articulate. By contrast, Nate was all guy. Big and strong. Rough around the edges. A man of few words. When he'd tucked that one-hundred-dollar bill into her pocket, the heat of his fingers burning straight through her clothes, she'd come completely unraveled.

Luckily, Nate did not come into the bar on either Monday or Tuesday. By the wee hours of Wednesday morning, when she fell exhausted into bed, Shannon had convinced herself that the physical attraction between them was nothing more than an aberration that would quickly pass.

She awoke at nine a.m. on Wednesday. Normally, she got up before dawn and enjoyed the quiet of the morning with a cup of coffee and a slice of whole-wheat toast. But when you worked in a bar and stayed up past two a.m., sleeping late simply followed.

Feeling self-indulgent, Shannon contemplated rolling over and going back to sleep for another hour. But then she heard an odd tapping noise outside her window.

She got up, wearing nothing more than the thin cotton nightshirt she slept in, and went to investigate. She pulled back the curtain and found herself peering into Nate Deavers's face.

Startled, a high thin screech escaped her lips. She

plastered a hand over her mouth. Her pulse raced, pumping blood lickety-split through her body.

He had a hammer in one hand, a string of Christmas lights strung over his neck, and a guilty grin on his face. "Sorry, I didn't mean to scare you," he said, the window glass between them muffling his apology.

Irritated, she raised the window. "What in the hell are you doing?"

He raised the strand of twinkle lights. "Puttin' up Christmas decorations."

"While I'm trying to sleep?"

"It's nine a.m."

"I work in a bar. I don't get into bed until almost three."

"I waited as long as I could. This project is going to take hours."

"Poor you."

"Come help me," he invited. "Seeing as how you're wide awake." He looked so charming with a dark brown curl flopped boyishly over his forehead.

"And why would I do that?"

"Because you feel sorry for me?"

She folded her arms over her chest, remembering belatedly that she was bra-less. "But I don't."

He gave her a sad face. "I'm up here on a ladder, no one to hand a fresh strand of lights up to me when I'm ready for them. I have to climb all the way back down and get them for myself."

"You live such a hard life."

His devilish eyes met hers. "You have no idea how hard."

Shannon had never been one to pick up quickly on flirtatious clues, but the fire in his gaze blistered her to the bone. Flustered, she snatched the curtains closed, heard his deep chuckle. She'd never been around such an earthy man.

She got dressed in blue jeans and a long-sleeved blue sweater and sneakers. After pulling her hair into a ponytail, she stepped out onto the landing. On the ground below was an elaborate six-foot plywood rendition of Santa's sleigh and eight reindeer, but instead of a regular Santa at the helm, the caricature of a purple horned frog in a Santa suit guided the sleigh.

"What are you going to do with Santa's sleigh?" she asked, leaning over the railing to see Nate at the top of the ladder against the side of the building.

"Put it on top of the roof."

"By yourself?"

"See why I need help?"

"Fine." She blew out a breath. "I'd hate to have to hose your broken body off the parking lot."

"I knew you'd see it my way."

She couldn't help smiling. What was it about this guy she found so charming? He had none of Peter's slick, sophisticated ways.

Precisely.

Listen, she lectured herself as she clambered down the stairs. You are not getting involved with anyone. So there's a little chemistry here. So you're enjoying flirting with him. Big deal. It doesn't mean a darned thing.

She rounded the bottom of the stairs, walked over

to the ten-foot metal ladder and peered up. Up the rungs, up the long, lean legs of Nate Deavers. Stared up at the most spectacular butt she'd ever seen in a pair of snug-fitting blue jeans. She put up a hand to shield her eyes, more to focus exclusively on that butt than to block the sun.

He glanced down. "You made it."

"What do you want me to do?"

"Let me come down and I'll show you."

She stood back, and when he was on the ground, he turned to face her.

"Aw, you," he said. "You changed out of the Betty Boop shirt."

"It was a nightshirt. Of course I changed out of it."

"I like Betty Boop. She's feisty and cute."

"She's a cartoon."

"You surprised me with the Betty Boop shirt."

"In what way?"

"I had you pegged as a La Perla kind of woman."

Honestly, she did own some La Perla lingerie. "I'm surprised you know what that is."

"Just because I live in a small town doesn't make me ignorant."

"I never said it did."

"You can make it up to me by taking me to lunch."

"Make what up to you?"

"The stereotyping."

"Hey, you were stereotyping me with the Betty Boop remark."

His jaw pulled down at the same time his mouth pulled up. "Well, you do have a point. Okay, you convinced me with the validity of your argument. I'll take *you* to lunch."

"How about you have lunch on your own and I'll have lunch on my own."

"Now what would be the fun in that?" He grinned.

"You're a tease."

His eyes went somber. "Not usually, but there's something about you, Shannon, that makes me feel like teasing."

She placed a palm to her heart. "Oh, so this is my fault?"

His eyes twinkled invitingly. "I'm glad you realize that."

"I'm here to work. If you don't have something for me to do . . ."

"Yes, okay, we're being serious now." He pulled a rolled-up piece of paper from his back pocket and showed her the diagram of where he was going to put up the decorations. They set to work.

By lunch, they were more than halfway finished with their task.

"Thanks," he said. "With your help, that went much faster than I thought it would. But it's break time." He rubbed his palms together. "C'mon, I'll take you to my favorite lunch spot."

Shannon's shift didn't start until six, so she had the day to hang out with Nate if she wanted. The question was, did she want to? Before she could ponder the thought, Nate grabbed her elbow and guided her to an old red Chevy pickup truck.

She was surprised to find the inside of his pickup

spotless. She hadn't expected such cleanliness from a bachelor. At least she hoped he was a bachelor. It occurred to her for the first time that he might be married. He didn't wear a ring, and he flirted like a single man, but that didn't mean anything.

"Are you married?" she blurted.

An amused smile turned up the corner of his mouth. "No, are you?"

"Not anymore," she said resolutely.

"Bad breakup?"

"The worst."

"I would say that I'm sorry to hear that, but you know what?" He stopped the truck before merging from the parking lot onto the main thoroughfare and turned to look at her. "I'm glad the guy was a stupid chump, because otherwise you wouldn't be here with me now."

"He was a lot more than a chump." On their drive into town, Shannon told him briefly that her ex-husband had turned out to be a con man who'd drained her bank account. She almost slipped and told him about Earl Pringle's visit the previous Christmas and had to bite her tongue to keep the words from slipping out. She wasn't very adept at pretending to be something she wasn't.

"Ah," Nate said. "That explains it."

"Explains what?"

"Why you're so classy. You come from money."

"Not so much after Peter got hold of me."

"You're going to prosecute him, right?"

She shrugged. "That's what I've spent the last year trying to do, but he skipped the country."

Shame burned through her. "I was so dumb. Falling for his slick con."

"You weren't dumb. You were an open, loving person who got taken advantage of." Nate reached a hand over and placed it lightly on her knee. Immediately, static electricity snapped between them. "Damn," he said, pulling his hand away. "Is this going to happen every time I touch you?"

"It's the dry weather," she said.

"I think it's more than that." His voice was low, sultry.

Heart in her throat, leg still tingling from his touch, she cocked her head and shot him a sideways glance. His dark hair was swept back off his forehead, and his skin was deeply tanned. The faint sprinkles of gray at his temples declared him an experienced man. He was big and broad-shouldered, but he was pure muscle. A man who'd spent his life doing vigorous outdoor work.

She wondered what he did for a living but decided not to ask. That would have opened the door to him asking her questions, and if she wasn't careful she'd end up disclosing her true identity. She wasn't ready for that yet.

Nate pulled up to a tiny building scarcely more than a shack. Perched on the roof was a red-and-white wood sign proclaiming: The Lunch Box. The drive-through line was ten cars deep.

"This is your favorite lunch spot? A drive-through restaurant?"

"Nope, this is the place to come for the best burgers in the state. The spot is somewhere else." He turned in his seat to rake his gaze over her. "Please don't tell me you're a vegetarian."

"What if I said I was?"

"I'm afraid you'd be out of luck. I have no idea who serves the best tofu in town."

She grinned. "Relax, I'm a carnivore."

"Thank God," he said, rolling his eyes heavenward.

"That might have offended a vegetarian."

"If my preference for meat was a deal-breaker, I figured it was better to know now than after."

"After what?"

"After we start dating."

"Oh, is that right?"

"Yeah."

"I don't get a say in the matter?"

"Are you going to tell me that you're not intrigued by this startling electricity?"

She opened her mouth to deny she felt anything, but she couldn't do it. Just looking at him made her go warm and gooey inside. "Listen, Nate. I like you. You're a handsome man, but I told you about Peter—"

"The chump."

"—for a reason. It's only been a year. I'm still putting the pieces of my life back together."

His truck engine rumbled quietly as they waited in line at the drive-through, the keys on his chain swinging rhythmically. The sun beat through the windshield, heating the dash and warming up the inside of the truck in spite of the fifty-degree weather outside.

"I get it," he said. "You're scared. So am I. It's been a long time since I've felt this way. Hell, I wasn't ever really expecting to feel this way again, but I'm edging up on forty. Not getting any younger, and I've come to realize just how precious life is. When you find something great, you owe it to yourself to at least explore the possibility."

"There's a fine line between sweeping a girl off her feet and scaring the hell out of her," she whispered.

His smile widened into a grin. "How am I doing on the balancing act?"

She waggled her hand in a teeter-totter motion.

"I'm a straightforward guy. There's no hidden agenda with me. In fact, I hate secrets and especially in my intimate relationships."

The thought of an intimate relationship with Nate sent a thrill through her. *Hold on. Put on the brakes. This is too fast. Not only that but the man just said he hated secrets. And you're in no position to come clean. Not yet.*

"I think we'd enjoy hanging out with each other," he said. "I'm not asking for anything beyond that, but if you need more time, I understand." He took his hands off the steering wheel, held them up in a gesture of surrender. "Absolutely no pressure."

It was their turn at the drive-through window. Nate ordered two Lunch Box specials. He passed the white paper bag redolent with the smell of cooked onions over to her. Her mouth watered. A few minutes later, he pulled up at a public picnic area on a small bluff overlooking Lake Twilight.

They got out. The breeze rolling in off the lake made her shiver.

"Hold on," Nate said and sprinted back to the truck. He returned with a warm down jacket and draped it over her shoulders.

She poked her arms through the sleeves, laughing at how it swallowed her up. The jacket smelled of him. Manly. Woodsy. Authentic.

"You look cute as hell," he said. "Cosmopolitan woman gone native."

"Thanks." She chuckled. "I think."

They ate their burgers, sitting side by side, looking out at the lake. Waves lapped at the shore. Across the water, several piers had been decorated with wreaths and red plastic bows. The boats docked at the Marina bobbed jauntily.

They didn't speak, just enjoyed the food. It wasn't awkward at all. In fact, the silence was welcome. By nature, Shannon was quiet, introspective. Apparently, Nate was as well. One thing they had in common.

When they finished, they wiped juice from their fingers on blue-and-red napkins stenciled with The Lunch Box logo. Nate handed her cinnamon candy that had come in the bag and took the second one for himself. The cellophane crinkled between her fingers as she unwrapped the mint. The spicy taste enlivened her tongue.

"Would you like to take a walk?" Nate nodded at the serpentine walking path that ran beside the lake.

She could say *no*. Maybe she should say *no*. Instead, Shannon nodded. "I'd like that."

Round, fruitless pear trees had been planted along the path. Strands of Christmas lights had been wound around the trunks and woven through the limbs. At night, with the twinkle lights aglow, she imagined it looked quite festive.

They walked abreast, passing a row of park benches. Their shoes occasionally crunched on the fallen leaves the wind gusted across their path. Nate reached out and lightly bumped the side of his right hand against her left. An invitation?

Shannon caught her breath. She turned her hand outward, revealing her palm.

He made a noise of satisfaction, so soft she wondered if she'd imagined it. He pressed his palm against hers and interlaced their fingers. It was so easy, holding hands with him. Surprisingly intimate. She hadn't held hands with a man in years. Probably not since high school.

They reached a point where the path forked, one branch going on around the lake, the other branch leading to downtown Twilight. Nate paused, uncoupling their hands. Her heart did an odd little stumble. A fish jumped from the water, tail slapping as it fell back under the surface. A flock of small birds flew overhead. In the distance, holiday music played. *Have a Holly, Jolly Christmas.*

Shannon looked up into Nate's face. Maybe she would have a good Christmas this year.

"It's nice here," he said, as if reading her mind, and held her gaze with steady certainty.

Shannon itched to run her fingertips over the scruff of beard that had sprouted on his face since that morning. He lowered his eyelids halfway, giving him a sexy, sleep-rumpled appearance and exposing long, thick jet-black lashes. Staring at him, she felt a compelling clench deep inside her belly.

He lowered his head.

Shannon rolled her fingernails into her palms. The look in his eyes told her exactly what he was intending on doing. If she were smart, she'd turn and flee. But she'd married Peter, hadn't she? Proving she was not smart. Not smart at all. *Not all guys are con men. Not everyone wants to take advantage of you, and then abandon you.* But Peter had. Raylene had. Even her father, who would mainly show up to trot her out for publicity photos before disappearing again with the *femme du jour* on his arm.

She wasn't ready for this. Wasn't up to a man like Nate. It was easier to be suspicious and distrustful than to open her heart again and take a big risk.

Too bad, because he smelled so very good—provocative and appealing. She dug her fingernails deeper into her palms, felt the tiny pinches of pain. She was so aware of this big man. So utterly fascinated. Her body felt achy, twitchy, in a way she'd never quite experienced before.

His head dipped even lower, his cinnamon-scented breath warming her skin. His eyes were the color of cocoa beans, dark and deep. She wanted to sip him like coffee.

"Shannon," he murmured.

The way he spoke her name sent a throb of sexual hunger unfurling through her veins. Instead of turning and running away as a prudent woman would have done, she tilted her chin up to him.

A pulse of a minute passed. Then two. They were locked together, their gazes chained to each other.

"Nate," she whispered. "Nate."

His arm went around her waist, and he drew her close. A soft sigh slipped from her lips, quick and heady. His mouth barely touched hers, landing like a butterfly on a rose. Behind it, she could feel the masculine power he kept leashed. His tongue was warm and cinnamon tangy. He tasted like hope.

And that scared Shannon most of all.

Chapter Five

Nate heard music. Angels singing. Bells ringing. *Hallelujah.*

From the very moment he'd laid eyes on Shannon, he'd wanted her. But he'd been completely unprepared for the taste of her sweet little mouth. He'd meant just to brush his lips against hers, a promise of more to come.

But when she'd parted her lips and sunk against his chest, well, there was only so much a man could take. He cupped her chin in his palm and held her face still, while he fully explored that glorious mouth. Even through the down of his jacket, he could feel her trembling. She was scared.

Hell, he was scared, too.

When he finally broke the kiss and pulled back, her golden brown eyes had gone murky, and she gazed at him with a look of desire and confusion so intense he could feel it. Her body tensed in his arms, ready to bolt.

He couldn't blame her. He'd come on too strong. He should not have kissed her. It was too soon. He might have blown the whole thing. Scared her off for good.

Even so, he couldn't resist kissing her again.

The sweet moan of pleasure slipping from her lips cut straight through him. The next thing he knew, her fingers were threaded through his hair and she was pulling his head down in a kiss so blistering that if he was to strip off his clothes and jump into the lake, his heat would kill all the fish in the water.

After a long, hard, desperate kiss, she dragged her mouth away. Her chest was heaving, her eyes wide and her lips wet with his moisture.

They blinked at each other.

"Again!" she exclaimed.

Laughing, Nate kissed her a third time. He gently bit her bottom lip and then rolled his tongue over her upper lip. He placed a hand to the small of her back, pressing her tight against him. He kissed her chin, her throat, and he must have found an erogenous zone, because she gasped and clung to him. "God, you taste good."

"Cinnamon candy."

"I'm not talking about that. I'm talking about you. The taste of Shannon. Sweet and sexy. All woman."

Her laugh was nervous. Somewhere along the way, the band that had held her hair in a ponytail had come out, and the wind sent a fall of lush brunette locks dancing about her slender shoulders.

He ran two fingers over her cheeks. "I want you, Shannon."

She sucked in her breath, moved back. Nate released her immediately. Why had he said that? Dammit. He seemed to be saying and doing all the wrong things.

"This is . . . I can't . . ." She swallowed visibly. "Please take me back to the Horny Toad."

"I . . ." He cleared his throat. "Okay."

In silence, they headed back to his truck. This time, the quiet was anything but companionable. Nate had screwed up, and he could only pray the damage wasn't irreparable.

Two nights later, the Watcher waited. Standing sentinel in the juniper bushes. The Christmas lights from the roof of the Horny Toad blinked and twinkled in a rotating flash pattern.

The fact that Shannon Dugan was living in the upstairs apartment came as a surprise. What had gone on inside the bar the day she'd arrived? Had Raylene so quickly accepted the daughter she'd once left behind? And if so, why put her to work as a cocktail waitress and send her to live in that tiny loft apartment? And why had Shannon stayed?

Confused, the Watcher shifted in the darkness. The beard of the Santa costume was itchy, and the wind was especially cold. It was nearly midnight. Lots of cars in the parking lot. Probably many would stay until closing time. Another two hours spent in icy blackness.

But the Watcher didn't mind. It was the only way to see her. In the wee hours of the morning. From the shadows. Watching over her as she went to her car.

Sadness weighted lungs heavy with regret. Sorrow and longing and shame and remorse. So many things done wrong. So much lost. Time. Health. Youth.

It felt stupid now. This waiting. Watching. To what end? For what purpose? Best to just disappear for good. But the old heart beating beneath the red-and-white suit was reluctant to let go.

Useless. These impulses.

The Watcher tugged down the beard and ran a hand over the savage scar. The irregular edges of grafted skin were still achy and raw. Every look in a mirror revealed the monster.

No hope of a normal life. No hope of repairing the past. No hope of forgiveness or redemption.

No hope at all.

After the last patron left, Chap came to stand in the doorway of the office where Raylene sat paying bills. Not for the first time, she thought about selling the bar. But that would feel too much like giving up. Yet without Earl, the joy she'd once gotten from running and owning the bar was gone. It had been his dream, after all. She'd just been lucky enough to share it with him. Why not throw in the towel and walk away?

Why not?

Because she stupidly kept hoping against hope that somehow Earl would find his way back home.

"I'm about to head out," Chap said. "Shannon's already gone upstairs. Would you like me to walk you to your car?"

She glanced up from her computer. "I'll be here for a while, but thanks for the offer."

"Somebody's got to look out for you," Chap said. "Since Earl left."

"I can take care of myself." Raylene bristled, even though she knew Chap hadn't meant to get her dander up.

Chap raised his palms. "I know."

Her irritation boiled off, and she felt a small pinch of pain in the region of her heart. "Sorry. The holidays are getting to me."

"No need to explain. Goodnight, Ray. You be careful going home."

"Thanks, Chap. I do appreciate you."

He gave a slight smile and sauntered away, leaving Raylene to balance the books in peace. Except the minute he was gone, she dropped her head onto the desk and squeezed her eyes closed.

How long before the pain went away? How long before she stopped missing Earl? The main problem was that she'd had no closure. Had no idea if he was dead or alive. No way to make amends. She was frozen. Gridlocked.

Overhead, footsteps sounded. Shannon going about the business of getting ready for bed. She was quiet as a church mouse, but in the empty bar, late at night, Raylene could hear her moving about. Shannon had only been here a few days, but she was quickly catching on to her duties. Which surprised Raylene.

Shannon got along well with both the staff and the customers. She was pleasant, a hard worker, and she didn't stick her nose into anyone's business, but Raylene couldn't shake the feeling that the woman was hiding something. Then again, who was she to point fingers?

She liked Shannon. More than she expected to. She reminded Raylene of someone, but she couldn't put her finger on who it was. Sometimes, she caught Shannon watching her with an odd expression that unnerved her.

Raylene also hadn't missed the attraction arcing between her new waitress and Nate Deavers. That surprised her, too. In all the time he'd been coming into the Horny Toad, she'd never seen Nate flirt with anyone, and plenty of women had tried to snag his attention. She had often wondered why, but seeing the way his face lit up when Shannon walked into the room let her know that he'd simply been waiting for the right one to come along. A patient man who knew what he wanted and wasn't afraid to wait for it.

They made a good couple. Polished Shannon smoothed out Nate's rough edges. Nate's down-to-earth nature balanced Shannon's detachment. She was more open when she was around him. Smiled more. Even laughed occasionally.

Raylene had never been much of a matchmaker like her friend Belinda Murphey, but she enjoyed watching the romance bloom between her employee and her loyal customer.

Thinking about Shannon reminded Raylene that she needed to ask for her social security number, so she could pay her. Paychecks went out the following Friday.

Yawning, she rubbed her eyes. The bills could wait until morning. She logged off the computer, got up, stretched. The thought of going home to that big empty house had her wishing she had a cot in the corner to curl up on.

Raylene slipped on her coat and took her purse from the bottom desk drawer. She heard a sharp thump. Like the whap of a newspaper being tossed against a door or a bird flying headlong into a clear glass window.

Was someone knocking?

She paused, canted her head, but heard nothing else. She walked to the rear door. Hesitated. Was someone out there?

Never one to back down from trouble, Raylene crept forward. She pressed one eye to the peephole and stared out at the alley beyond. Empty. No one around. But someone could be hiding behind the Dumpster.

She waited a long moment, then thought briefly about calling Shannon and asking her to come down. But she didn't want to put the younger woman in jeopardy.

You're being an old fool, Raylene. Hell, you were probably just hearing things. Get the hell out of here and go home.

She might be old and foolish, but she wasn't stupid. Raylene took the Glock from the bottom of her purse and clutched it in her right hand. Heart skipping a beat, she eased the door open with her left hand while a litany of Clint Eastwoodisms rolled through her head.

Total silence greeted her.

A flurry of snowflakes drifted from the sky. They wouldn't stick. It had been too warm the last few days. None of the weather forecasters had predicted snow. But there in that quiet moment, the soft white falling looked like a miracle.

Raylene glanced down. On the back steps sat a pot of white poinsettias, the base of the pot wrapped in red foil.

All the air left her body.

"Earl," she whimpered. Tucking the Glock back into her purse, she bent to pick up the flowerpot.

She took the flowers inside and locked the door behind her. The bright foil crinkled as she set the plant onto her desk. Carefully, she dusted the melting snowflakes from the vibrant green leaves.

Raylene had always loved red poinsettias. Way back in high school, when she and Earl were dating hot and heavy, and they'd both been poor as church mice, he'd waited until Christmas Eve to buy her flowers, knowing they'd be cheaper. By then, only the white ones were left. When he'd given them to her, his eyes full of apology because he hadn't gotten her red poinsettias, she announced that she liked the white ones much better. And she had ever since. Now, whenever she saw white poinsettias, she automatically thought of Earl.

Gooseflesh spread over her body. Could Earl have left the poinsettias for her?

She bolted from the office, unlocked the back door and flung it open. "Earl!" She ran into the alley. "Earl, where are you?"

Nothing. No one. Dead quiet.

And a swirl of white snowflakes that would not stick.

On Saturday, Shannon came down to start her shift. She still couldn't get Nate out of her head. They'd come back from lunch and finished putting up the Christmas decorations, but the easy camaraderie they'd shared before had vanished.

Things had changed between them, and there was no going back. Yet she could not regret kissing him. He made her feel desirable, wanted.

Nate had come into the bar every night since, sitting where he always sat. Keeping his distance, saying very little, watching her cautiously. Space. He was giving her space.

She would glance up from delivering drinks to find his gaze on her. Sometimes he looked puzzled, as if trying to decipher why he was attracted to her, but at other times the expression on his face was so raw and hungry that her body heated instantly.

And when she lay in bed at night, the memory of his kisses haunted her. His taste was a tangy sweet memory that kept her awake long past the time she should have fallen asleep.

"Shannon," Raylene called from the office door. "Could you come in here a moment?"

Tying a bar apron around her waist, she stepped into Raylene's office. Anxiety gnawed at her and she couldn't help wondering if she'd screwed up somehow. She'd had a big learning curve, but she was trying her very best to be a great cocktail waitress. Honestly, it surprised her how hard she tried. Then again, Shannon never did anything in half measures, and that included screwing up.

"Is there a problem?" she asked, trying to keep her tone even and calm.

Raylene rearranged a pot of white poinsettias that was sitting on her desk, moving it off a book of anagram word-find puzzles. "No problem." She smiled. "In fact, you've been doing a great job."

"Thank you."

"The customers like you."

"I try to go out of my way to make sure they're happy."

"Your maturity makes up for your lack of experience. Those young girls I get in here as cocktail waitresses." Raylene shook her head. "Wild as March hares. Always running off with guys or getting pregnant. Undependable."

"No March madness here." She ran her hands down her thighs.

"Listen," Raylene said. "I need your social security number."

"What?" Shannon gulped. She'd been so wrapped up in Nate, so busy playing waitress that she'd forgotten she'd given a fake last name. She couldn't tell Raylene her social security number. Not unless she was ready to reveal who she really was.

"Your social. I need it in order to pay you."

"Mmm." Shannon moistened her lips. "Is there any way that you could pay me cash?"

Raylene narrowed her eyes. She didn't say anything for a long time. The clock on the wall ticked loudly. "Are you in some kind of trouble?"

"How about this," Shannon said. She simply could not bring herself to say, *hey, I'm your daughter.* Not yet. Not until she'd figured out how to handle the situation or what it was she really hoped to gain from confronting her mother. "Don't pay me until the end of the month."

"I thought you were broke."

"By allowing me to stay here rent-free and feeding me, all my current needs are being met."

"Something's going on," Raylene said, "but I'm not one to pry in other people's business. Folks got all kinds of reasons for keeping the secrets they keep. So, okay, I'll pay you in cash."

"Do you?" Shannon asked.

"Do I what?" Raylene looked wary.

"Have secrets."

Raylene's eyes met hers. "Everyone has secrets."

Shannon's heart rate quickened. This was the perfect time. Just come out and tell her. "I . . ." She blew out her breath. "Thank you for understanding."

"If you ever feel like unburdening yourself," Raylene said, "I'm a good listener."

"Same here." Shannon's breath was coming in rapid little puffs. "If there's anything you'd like to confess."

"Me?" Raylene flicked her gaze over Shannon's face. "What makes you think I have anything to confess?"

"Everyone's got secrets. You just said so yourself."

They stared at each other. Shannon didn't know

how long they would have stood there like that, before a woman's voice cut through the chain of their linked gazes.

"Well, hello, you must be Raylene's new cocktail waitress."

Shannon turned to see a woman about Raylene's age. Her body was fuller, her blond hair cut short and curled around her face. She extended her hand, came across the room. "Hello, I'm City Councilwoman Patsy Cross, soon to be Patsy Crouch, and I own the Teal Peacock. It's a boutique just off the town square. You ought to drop by sometime."

"Shannon Du . . . Nagud," she said, stumbling over the fake last name and shaking the older woman's hand.

"Patsy's getting married to her high school sweetheart on Christmas Day," Raylene explained. "How goes the wedding plans?"

"Craziness, but that's how wedding plans are, right?" Patsy blushed prettily as if she was all of sixteen instead of sixty. "Hondo and I took a long time getting here."

"That you did." Raylene caressed the white poinsettias.

"I just dropped by to tell you that we're moving the venue for the Christmas cookie swap. The roof of the Baptist church reception hall sprung a leak." To Shannon, Patsy said, "The First Love Cookie Club holds an annual Christmas cookie swap party. Women only. You should come." Then she cast a glance at Raylene. "Bring her with you to the party, Ray. The more the merrier."

"First Love Cookie Club?" Shannon asked.

Patsy waved a hand. "Our little local legend at work. Everyone in the First Love Cookie Club has been reunited with their first loves. Well, all except Christine Noble, but she's the local baker and her cookies are the best, so we made her an honorary member."

"And me, of course," Raylene muttered. "My first love flew the coop."

Patsy cleared her throat. "Earl will be back."

Raylene's eyes took on a wistful haze. "Maybe," she whispered so low that Shannon couldn't be sure she'd heard her.

"So anyway, the cookie swap party is going to be at Rinky-Tink's, next Friday night. It'll be our version of a send-off, since the ice cream parlor is closing up shop. One last hoorah. The end of an era." Patsy clicked her tongue. "Such a shame."

"A lot of things are falling by the wayside," Raylene said.

"Well, not the First Love Cookie Club, and not our traditions." Patsy placed a hand on Shannon's shoulder. "I do hope you'll come. It's always a pleasure to have visitors."

"I'll bring her," Raylene said.

Shannon slipped toward the door. The opportunity to confront Raylene had passed, but as she stepped into the hallway she heard Patsy Cross say, "Ray, that girl's legs look just like yours did at that age."

That's why she was really here, wasn't it? To catch hold of memories that she'd never known. To find her pattern. The imprint that had never taken.

The mother she never knew.

CHAPTER SIX

"Are we ever going to talk about what happened last Wednesday?" Nate murmured as Shannon sat the mug of beer in front of him when he came in that evening.

"Nothing to say." She put on a cheerful smile.

"Oh now that's where I disagree," he said. "I think we have a whole *lot* to talk about."

She shrugged, her heart thumping harder underneath her shirt. "I'm not . . . This isn't the time or place."

"I concur. That's why I'm asking you out."

"Nate, I don't know if that's such a good idea."

"Why not?"

"I've got a lot of things I'm dealing with in my life."

He shrugged. "So tell me about them. Maybe I can help."

What was the deal? Everyone wanted her to talk. People were inviting her to things . . .

Just like you're part of their community.

But she wasn't a part of their community. She was a fraud, and she could not forget that. It wasn't smart to start feeling comfortable here.

All she had to do was tell Raylene who she was, demand an explanation for why she'd abandoned her, and get the hell out of Twilight.

Except she did not want to leave Twilight, and it wasn't just because of Nate. Although the intriguing man with the dark eyes was certainly a contributing factor. Shannon liked it there. She liked the people. She liked the town. She even liked being a cocktail waitress. Apparently Raylene's blood did run through her veins.

In Twilight, she'd shed her previous life. Let go of old expectations. Become someone new and different. She felt free.

Don't grow accustomed to it. This is all a lie. It's not your life. You belong in New York. You were raised in a milieu of money and privilege. You don't belong here.

Yet, as long as she kept her mouth shut, she did belong.

It was only in that moment that Shannon realized how out-of-step she'd always felt in her life. From the time she was a small child, she always felt like an outsider in the world she grew up in. She thought it must have been because she had no mother, but now she knew it was more than that. She'd been searching for where she belonged, and, as strange as it sounded, Twilight felt like home.

Nate laid his hand over hers. "The town puts on an annual Christmas play. At the Twilight Playhouse. I thought you might like to go." He pulled two tickets from his front shirt pocket. "It's tomorrow night."

"I don't know if I can get off—"

"She can get off," Raylene said as she passed by on her way to the kitchen.

Nate's eyes brightened. "Your boss said you can go." He waggled the tickets. "I'll even treat you to dinner at The Funny Farm beforehand."

"The Funny Farm?"

"You'll see what I mean if you say *yes*."

"She'll go," Raylene told him on her return trip, a tray of cheesy nachos in her hand. The smell of cumin scented the air. "Shannon, go."

Shannon held up her hands. "Apparently it's been decided."

"Great." Nate grinned. "I'll pick you up at six. The show starts at seven-thirty."

A date. The last time she'd had a date, Peter had taken her out on a yacht with a private chef who'd served caviar, foie gras, pheasant under glass, and baked Alaska. He'd pulled out all the stops and she'd fallen for the grand seduction.

It'll be different this time. Nate's different. You're different.

She would take a small-town play and dinner at a place called The Funny Farm over an elaborate yacht cruise any day of the week. Especially with Nate as her date.

He winked, and Shannon thought, *I am in so much trouble.*

Dinner at The Funny Farm turned out to be . . . well . . . entertaining and quite a contrast to the elegant restaurants where Shannon normally dined. The place was cute and campy and over-the-top with a barnyard-themed dining area. The waitstaff wore aprons fashioned after straightjackets as a takeoff on the double meaning of funny farm. A pun. What fun.

Nate and Shannon teased and flirted over chicken fried steak with cream gravy, homemade yeast rolls, buttery mashed potatoes, string beans, sweet tea and banana pudding. He told her about his job monitoring numerous gas rigs in the county. Before that, he'd been a Navy SEAL. But when she'd asked him about that, Nate had shaken his head. "Ancient history. I've put the military behind me."

"You don't like talking about it."

"Not tonight. When we know each other better, we can talk about the dark stuff. Tonight, I just want to have a good time with you." He reached across the table to stroke her knuckles with his thumb sending delicious waves of heat rippling up her arm.

Afterward they went to see *Miracle on 34th Street* at the Twilight Playhouse. The lead actress, who reprised the Maureen O'Hara role, was a diminutive red-haired actress who'd recently made a big splash in Hollywood, but who had returned to Twilight to marry her high school sweetheart, a local veterinarian by the name of Sam Cheek. Nate whispered this scoop behind his playbill as the lights dimmed.

During the play, Nate reached over to take Shannon's hand and she did not pull away. She might be playing with fire, but it felt so good to hold hands in the dark with a sweet Christmas message playing out onstage. It was a fantasy. A cocoon she'd soon be leaving behind, but Shannon was determined to enjoy it for as long as it lasted. Soon enough reality would intrude. During intermission, they got Coca-Colas and struck up conversations with other theatergoers about Emma Cheek's fabulous performance.

Shannon drifted back to her seat in a sweet haze of happiness, Nate's arm linked through hers. The ending of the play cemented the feel-good endorphins pumping through her blood. As they left the theater, Nate turned to her. "It's not that late. Only ten o'clock. Would you like to go for a walk in Sweetheart Park?"

"In the dark? Is it safe?"

"For one thing," he said, "it's Twilight. For another thing, they've got the place lit up brighter than Arizona in August. C'mon. I'll show you."

He guided her down the street as they joined other couples strolling home from the play on the same circuitous route. A line of people snaked outside the door of a coffee shop. On the courthouse lawn, Santa's Workshop was just closing up.

"I'm surprised it's so busy this late on a Sunday night," she said. "I thought small towns rolled up the carpet at nightfall."

"Not Twilight. Not in December. Don't forget, this is a tourist town. And I've discovered Twilightites love their holiday celebrations."

"It's nice though, isn't it? Even if it is a bit hokey."

"It *is* nice," he said.

The pressure of his hand against her spine was both reassuring and disconcerting. Mainly because she kept imagining his hand slipping lower.

Nate was right. The park was incandescent with lights. In the trees, on the quaint wooden footbridges, wrapped around wire frame sculptures of reindeers and elves and snowmen and Santa Claus.

"I feel like I'm on a burlesque stage," Shannon said as they sauntered past oversized Christmas packages bedecked with blinking lights every color of the rainbow. She stopped and twirled, giddy with the moment. Which wasn't like her. Not at all. But Nate made her feel things she'd never felt before.

He gave her a puckish grin. "If you start stripping, can I watch?" His smile went from mischievous to downright wicked.

Her pulse quickened, and her knees weakened. She thought, *This is a beautiful man.*

"Or," he said, lowering his voice. "I could strip and you could watch. I believe in equality of the sexes."

"Maybe we could work out a tandem striptease."

He linked his arm through hers. "I like the way you think."

The warmth of his skin stirred her, and she found herself leaning into him. Their shoulders rubbed as they walked. A lovely romantic friction. She closed her eyes a moment, savoring the contact. It was silly to be so eager for his touch. Nate paused before a stone fountain depicting two embracing lovers in old western clothing. A plaque declared that it had a spot in the national registry of historic places. Beside it stood a sign proclaiming that if you threw a penny into Sweetheart Fountain, you would be reunited with your high school sweetheart and live happily-ever-after. The message was both silly and hopelessly romantic.

"Do you want to throw a penny into the fountain?" Nate asked.

"No."

"You don't have fond memories of your high school sweetheart?"

"I didn't have a high school sweetheart."

He pulled back, looked surprised. "Seriously? I find that very hard to believe."

"It's true."

"What? Were you home-schooled?"

Almost. Private school. "No. I was just quiet and shy and into my studies. Not the type of girl who turned guys' heads."

"I don't believe that for a second."

"I'm not a great beauty."

"Yes, you are." He cradled his palm against her cheek, looked deeply into her eyes. "Not in a flashy, obvious way, but you have a serene beauty. Calm, understated, comforting."

She swatted at him playfully. "You make me sound like house slippers."

"I'm mucking this up." Nate stepped back, stabbed fingers through his hair. "What I meant to say is that your beauty is natural. Real. You don't need makeup and short skirts to make you pretty, although . . ." His gaze flicked to her legs covered by her knee-length brown-and-cream plaid skirt. "I certainly wouldn't object if you strutted around in miniskirts. You've got the most awesome pair of legs I've ever seen."

The hot look of lust on his face excited and scared her. Scared her because she was feeling the same thing for him, and it was too much, too soon. She'd fallen too fast for Peter. She wasn't taking that roller-coaster ride again.

But Peter was conning you. Nate is sincere.

Could she really say that? She didn't know the man. Not really. Just because her heart skipped a beat whenever he walked into the room didn't mean anything. Her heart had led her astray before.

His callused palm reached for her hand again, and her resolve melted. The handholding thing got to her every time. A Navy SEAL. This man had been a Navy SEAL. He knew how to protect a woman. And yet, there was a dark side, too. Secrets kept. Covert deeds done in the course of defending his country from foreign enemies. Maybe that's why he'd told her he didn't like secrets. After a lifetime in the shadows, he wanted to live in the light. Nothing to hide. No ulterior motives to second-guess.

She turned to face him. She was about to comment on the extraordinary light display, when one look into his eyes froze her lips.

In unspoken consensus, they moved toward each other. He dropped her hand in order to raise both of his hands to sandwich her face between them.

"People are watching," she whispered.

"No one cares. This is Twilight. Land of love and romance." He kissed her gently, a simple brushing of their lips.

Shannon sighed softly. "I'm in so much trouble here."

"You are," he said huskily, "but so am I. Are you going to run off if I kiss you again?"

"I don't know," she answered honestly.

"I'm not that other guy. I'm not going to hurt you or take advantage of you."

"I know," she mumbled.

"But?"

"Nate, I'm afraid about where this is headed."

"Me, too, but I'm brave enough to find out."

"I'm not ready. I'm messed up. I'm conflicted. I'm—"

"Talking instead of listening to your heart." He tugged her snug against his chest and kissed her again, firmer, hotter, brooking no argument.

Helplessly, Shannon's eyes drifted closed. She fully surrendered to his kiss and the revved-up emotions pouring through her thick as honey. The man certainly knew how to use his lips. He tasted like a PayDay candy bar, both salty and sweet. She wanted to gobble him right up.

She planed her hands over his shoulders, his denim jacket heavy and rough underneath her palms. She breathed him in, the piney smell of the December evening mixing with his masculine cologne. Her thoughts were like a thousand-piece jigsaw puzzle tossed into the air. Fractured. Separate. Making love to Nate would be like fitting all those disjointed pieces together to form a pretty picture of a longed-for landscape.

His mouth took possession of hers hungrily, but

his grip loosened, letting her know she could back out at any moment if that was what she wanted. His kiss said the pieces of the puzzle could so easily be joined, if she just had the time and patience to put them together. Happiness was within her grasp.

But she could not take that step. Not yet. No matter how badly her body wanted to be joined with his. But her blood steamed and her ears hummed. Her fingers curled through his thicket of hair as she pulled his head down lower. Her body was pressed so tightly against his she could felt his erection straining against the zipper of his Levi's.

A low growl seeped from his lips, and he pulled back, his eyes branding hers. "We should stop."

"Yes."

Neither one of them moved.

Shannon tilted her head, sank her top teeth into her bottom lip, held tight to his gaze. His mouth came down again, his tongue seeking and finding that erogenous spot he'd triggered the last time they'd kissed. His hand slipped beneath her open coat, gliding over her breast. Even through the barrier of clothing, Shannon's nipples responded, hardening into achy peaks.

"We have to . . ." She swallowed hard and closed her eyes again at the tidal wave of pleasure crashing over her.

"Uh?" His mouth had moved up, nibbling at her earlobe.

Rockets of sensation shot through her lower abdomen. Her knees were so weak that if he hadn't had one arm tightly wrapped around her waist she would have crumpled to the ground.

She could hear the water splashing in the fountain and the quiet conversations of people around them. She could smell the night breeze ripe with Christmas scents. She tasted so many things—hope, longing, lust. She wanted to lick him all over. Taste him until every cell in her body tingled with anticipation. If they had been somewhere secluded and private, she would have done just that.

"What are you doing to me?" she gasped.

"Same thing you are doing to me. Torturing you."

"I'm breaking out the rules of the Geneva Convention. This has to stop."

"I know," he murmured, his breath vibrating against her skin as he spoke.

"I'm not . . . I don't . . ." She wasn't sure what else she'd intended to say, because all thoughts fluttered from her head when he rimmed the outside of her ear with his devastating tongue. She shivered. Clung to him.

"Imagine me doing that somewhere much lower on your sexy body," he whispered in her ear.

"You're evil. Pure evil."

"Uh-huh." He didn't even bother to deny it.

"I've got to know more about you, Nate Deavers. If we're really going to do this."

"Do what?" he asked, his tone sleepy and suggestive, his lowered lids half shuttering his dark eyes.

"This. Me. You. Dating."

"I'm on board." He stepped back, letting her go.

"What do you want to know?" He spread his arms. "I'm an open book."

Why was she asking? She shouldn't even be thinking about sleeping with him. This was all temporary. There was nothing long-term for her here.

She crossed her arms over her chest. "What are some of your favorite things?"

He put an arm around her shoulder, drew her to him, strolled her over a wooden footbridge aglow with twinkling candy canes. "Christmas morning and Belgium waffles with maple syrup and crispy fried bacon. Fishing off the dock during a summer sunset. Jazz music. Honesty. Openness. Intelligence. Chocolate chip cookies. Old dogs. Flannel shirts. Indian motorcycles. Pumpkin pie. Jack Daniels in moderation. Blue jeans. The smell of fresh-cut grass. Corn on the cob with real butter. Kids. Second chances. Short good-byes and long hellos. Morning sex. But most of all, tawny-eyed women with stupendous legs who taste like candy, smell like heaven, and are pretty darn handy when it comes to putting up Christmas decorations."

"You're just saying that last part because you're here with me." She laughed. No, not laughed. She giggled. Actually giggled, because Nate made her feel like she was sixteen again and having that rush of first crush that she'd never experienced.

He held up two fingers. "SEAL's honor, I'm telling the truth. Can we go back to the kissing now?"

She took another step back. This man appreciated honesty and openness. Something she couldn't provide. At least not yet. "You're sort of obsessed with kissing. You should add that to your list."

"Point taken, but you are standing underneath a mass of mistletoe. It would be remiss of me not to at least try to kiss you, considering the circumstances." He leaned in.

Shannon held up a hand. "Slow down. Talk first. Kissing later."

He sighed. "You're serious about this."

"I am. What bothers you?"

"About what?"

"Life, stuff."

"Cheaters. Secrets. Lies. Hidden agendas."

That pretty well summed her up, except for the cheating part.

"Getting gum on your shoe on a hot summer day. People who think that yellow on traffic lights means go faster. Meanness. Zealots. Fancy gourmet burgers with weird ingredients. Who wants cranberries, quinoa, and feta cheese in their hamburgers?"

"What if I loved hamburgers with cranberries, quinoa, and feta cheese?"

"Then that's one area where we'd just have to agree to disagree. Your turn," he said. "What does Shannon Nagud like?"

Nagud. That stupid name she'd concocted on the spur of the moment. Not only did it lack imagination, it had been plain stupid to use her last name spelled backward.

She leaned over the footbridge, looked down at the water below. The wind ruffled her hair, blowing it back over her shoulder, chilling her cheeks. That was exactly what she needed. A slap of cold air to wake her up.

This little daydream relationship was nothing more than a fantasy. Eventually, she'd be going back to the life she'd left behind. She could go now. There was nothing to hold her here. She didn't even have to confront Raylene if she didn't want to. She could just disappear. Except if she left now she would never get closure.

"Well?" Nate prodded.

"I like closure," she said. "And knowing where I stand. I favor calico kittens. Books. Babies. Deep-dish pizza. Real Christmas trees. The sound of the ocean. PayDay candy bars. The color purple. Summer rain showers. Gladiolas. Peanut-butter-and-strawberry-jelly sandwiches with the crusts cut off. Football. Central Park in the fall. And Betty Boop nightgowns."

"Hmm," he said. "I forgot about the Betty Boop nightgowns. Those are on my like list too. Especially when you're wearing one."

Nate leaned in again, and this time Shannon didn't back away.

"So, did I past the test?" he asked.

"I approve of your favorite things," she murmured.

His hands were in her hair, his palms cradling the back of her head. His cocoa-bean eyes percolated hot and dark. She pursed her lips. Damn her. She shouldn't, but she couldn't seem to stop.

Nate's mouth was on hers again, kissing with a fiery urgency that stole all her reasoning. She kissed him in return, arching her back against him, completely unaware of the people around them.

He touched her, and she burned for him, lust hazing her brain. She couldn't think. All she could do was want and want and want.

"Sweetheart," he whispered, finally breaking their embrace. "I want you more than I want to breathe. But I don't want to rush you. You're right. We need to slow down. Take our time. Savor what's happening between us. So before things get out of hand, I think it's time I took you home."

Chapter Seven

For the rest of the week, Nate courted Shannon in slow, easy measures.

He was determined to not scare her off. He knew she was skittish, and he didn't blame her, considering what had happened with her ex. On the whole, he was pretty distrustful, too, but the way Shannon made him feel overrode his doubts. His gut told him that she was special, and he always followed his gut. It had never led him astray.

The day after their date, Nate came into the Horny Toad for *Monday Night Football*. He brought Shannon a PayDay, and her face lit up as if he'd given her a new car. On Tuesday, he arrived with a deep-dish pizza, and they ate in the back room of the bar, stealing kisses between each bite, their lips smeared with tomato sauce and melted provolone.

On Wednesday morning, he went to J.C. Penney's and bought a purple shirt, because she said she loved the color. She laughed when she saw him in it. He asked her to go fishing. They took hamburgers with them from The Lunch Box—no cranberries, quinoa, or feta cheese allowed. When Shannon caught a small sun perch, she laughed with such joy that the sound had Nate thinking all kinds of seditious things about a long, slow courtship. He wanted her, and he wanted her *now.*

But the Navy had taught him patience, and so he kept waiting.

On Thursday, he asked her to go with him to the annual community tradition of decorating the town Christmas tree that Saturday evening. Shannon's smile of agreement followed him home to his bed where Nate coped with sexual frustration the best way he could. Hand therapy.

On Friday, he couldn't wait to get to the Horny Toad to see her again. He'd made peanut-butter-and-strawberry-jelly sandwiches, carefully cut the crusts off, and wrapped them in plastic wrap. His plan was to share this simple supper with her during her meal break. But when he got there, a part-time waitress was waiting tables.

"Where's Shannon?" he asked, surprised by the nervous stab in his stomach. His first fear was that he'd come on too strong and she'd left Twilight as unexpectedly as she'd arrived.

"She took the day off."

"Oh," he said, disappointed that she hadn't told him. And the sharp edge of that disappointment told him he was sinking deep. Instead of staying for a beer, he just turned and went home.

Clutching a platter of homemade haystack cookies, Raylene walked in Rinky-Tink's with Shannon following right behind her.

The century-old ice cream parlor had been stripped of its creamy treats. Their footsteps echoed loudly on the weathered hardwood floors. The 1950s era décor of the pink-and-turquoise tables and chairs were still there along with photographs of the ice cream parlor throughout the past one hundred years.

"This place must have really been something, once upon a time," Shannon murmured.

"It was," Raylene said wistfully. "Earl and I shared our first banana split over in that corner right there."

"Earl?"

"My high school sweetheart," Raylene mumbled, not wanting to talk about her husband to Shannon. There was too much to explain. She hadn't even realized she'd spoken out loud.

In her mind's eye, she saw her sixteen-year-old self, long blond hair parted down the middle and hanging straight down her back. Wearing a pair of purple hot pants and white, knee-high go-go boots.

Every boy in the place had stared at Earl with envy. Earl in his black leather jacket and scuffed cowboy boots. A cross between a wrangler and a motorcycle-riding bad boy. Except Earl had always had a heart of gold. The bad-boy thing had been an affectation. Trying to look tough to impress Raylene.

"Ray?" a voice called from the rear of the store. "We're back here in the party room."

Raylene led Shannon into the biggest part of the ice cream parlor, where birthday parties were held. On the long folding table decorated with a Christmas-themed, red-and-green tablecloth stretched a wide assortment of cookies. At the end of the table sat a champagne bucket filled with ice and wine.

Raylene introduced her employee to the ladies of the First Love Cookie Club and edged her over to the far end of the table, where the younger, newer members were hanging out—Flynn MacGregor, Emma Cheek, Caitlyn Garza, Christine Noble, and Raylene's niece by marriage, Sarah Walker.

A very pregnant Flynn, who looked as if she was about to pop that baby out at any minute, welcomed Shannon with a one-armed hug and explained the rules of the cookie club. No men. No kids. No store-bought. Let the cookies, gossip, and Christmas spirit flow.

They welcomed Shannon as if she was an instant member of the community. That's what Raylene loved about these women. They made a stranger feel right at home. Raylene took a seat next to Patsy Cross, who couldn't stop talking about her impending wedding. Raylene didn't mind. Patsy had waited over forty years to finally marry the love of her life. But she did tune her out a bit, her mind woolgathering to last Christmas, when her world had come to a crashing halt.

The party was lively. Much teasing, joking, and laughter. The cookies were tasty. The wine was inexpensive but delicious. The company pleasant as always. But all Raylene could think about was what was missing.

Earl.

Her thoughts strayed to the white poinsettias on her office desk. Had Earl left them on her doorstep for her to find? She'd wanted to believe that with all her heart, but there had been no further indication that it was true.

But if not Earl, then who?

Sometimes, when she went out to her car at night she'd get the strangest feeling she was being watched. Not in a creepy way, but in the way you sometimes felt in church. Like God was watching over you, and no harm could ever come to you as long as you kept the faith.

Yeah? When was the last time you were in church?

Raylene had long ago backslid from her Methodist upbringing, but that feeling made her hungry for forgiveness. She shifted her gaze to the end of the table, studied Shannon. The younger woman's face was aglow, as she listened to Emma telling a story about her five-month-old daughter, Lauren.

Not for the first time, Raylene wondered about Shannon. Who was she, really? What was she doing here in Twilight? What was she running from? How long would she stay?

Raylene wasn't a soft touch by any means, but Shannon had gotten to her, and she really couldn't say why. She liked the woman a lot. Which was odd, because they had nothing in common.

And the thought of her leaving sent a nostalgic sadness seeping into her bones. If you were lucky enough to spend sixty years on the face of the earth, a lot of things fell by the wayside. Youth. Hobbies. Habits. Employees. Friends. Family. The love of your life.

Shannon must have felt Raylene's eyes on her, because she shifted her attention from Emma and met her gaze head on.

In that moment, with that particular expression on her face—part curiosity, part puzzlement, and part disdain—she looked just like Lance.

It occurred to Raylene that Shannon was around the same age as her own daughter. The child she'd never seen a picture of. Had never spoken to. Had never even touched.

The old grief rose up, slicing and piercing. She clamped her teeth together and glanced away, fighting back the tears welling in her eyes. What would happen if she tried to contact her daughter now? She'd already lost Earl. Everyone in Twilight had learned her dirty secret.

Raylene had nothing left to lose.

The only thing that held her back was the thought of hurting her daughter. The last thing she wanted was to intrude.

Is that the real reason? Or is it that you're afraid she won't forgive you?

"You're awfully quiet tonight, Ray." Patsy put a hand on her forearm. "Are you all right?"

Unable to meet her friend's eyes, Raylene shook her head.

Patsy wrapped an arm around her shoulder, leaned in close. "It's going to be okay. Really it is."

Raylene pressed the back of her hand to her nose, determined not to cry. How would that look? She had the reputation of being the outspoken, unsentimental one. She was uncomfortable with pity. It made her feel weak.

"Dotty Mae," she called to the elderly lady sitting beside the champagne bucket. "Stop being a wine hog and pass that bottle."

Shannon went back to her apartment with a box of swapped cookies under her arm and a pinch of sadness in her heart. She had really enjoyed herself tonight, and she'd loved meeting the lively women of the First Love Cookie Club. The more time she spent in Twilight, the more enamored she became of the quaint, small-town community.

But she could not afford to fall in love with the place.

Or with Nate Deavers.

Nate.

Today had been the first day she hadn't seen him this week, and she'd missed him. That was bad. Really bad. She was setting herself up for heartache. She was going to have to start weaning herself off him, and soon. Because eventually, she would have to confront Raylene, and her purpose for being here would come to an end. If she was being honest with herself, she'd have to admit that Nate was the reason she hadn't already faced down her mother.

She thought of how Raylene had looked at the party, so sad and wistful. The woman was clearly suffering. She didn't talk about Earl much, but the pain was evident in her eyes. She hadn't expected to feel sorry for Raylene, but she did. She found herself thinking that maybe she should wait until after the holidays to tell her who she was. It would be pretty thoughtless to confront Raylene so close to Christmas.

Shannon undressed and put on her Betty Boop nightshirt. She smoothed it down over her hips, thought of Nate, and smiled. They had a date tomorrow. To go decorate the town Christmas tree. Was it silly that she was so excited?

This isn't your town. He's not your man. You've got a life back in New York. Stop painting a rosy romantic picture here.

But did she really have a life in New York? Her grandfather was gone, her inheritance diminished. Her devious ex had used and discarded her. What was left for her there?

On the other hand, it was the only life she'd ever known. Growing up in that stiff, formal home with grandparents—who, while they had loved her, had trouble showing their emotions—she'd learned to stay calm, cool, distant, detached.

Yet now, at the mid-point of her life, there was a small voice inside her whispering, "You can start over. Build a new life. Become a different person."

Such a hopeful thought.

She lay in bed, tossing the thoughts back and forth, recalling the events of the night. How at the end of the party, all the ladies of the cookie club had toasted the old-fashioned ice cream parlor and told stories of their memories of the place. Rinky-Tink's would be sorely missed. The passing of an era. Leaving a hole in the fabric of the community.

Unless someone bought it and restored the place to its former glory.

Shannon drifted off to sleep and dreamed of ice cream, Twilight, her new friends, and Nate.

Chapter Eight

Nate showed up at dusk, wearing blue jeans, a brown western shirt, and tan blazer. He'd gotten a haircut, and he looked quite handsome standing on her doorstep with long stalks of gladiolas in his hand.

Shannon grinned at him. "Where did you find gladiolas this time of year?"

"Fort Worth."

"You drove all that way for me?"

"I'd drive to New York City and back for you," he said earnestly.

"You're spoiling me."

"You deserve it."

His gentle seduction was so different from the mad-dash whirlwind Peter had caught her up in, but she was still afraid to trust her feelings.

"Nate," she murmured.

"I'm coming on too strong."

"No." She smiled faintly. "You're fine. It's not you. It's me."

"Uh-oh," he said. "That's always a bad sign when a woman says it's not you. That's code for it *is* you."

"Listen, you're an up-front guy, and I appreciate that about you, but there's things about me that I just can't tell you about. Not now."

"You've got secrets."

"I do, and you hate secrets."

He said nothing. Just stood in the doorway holding the gladiolas, looking forlorn. Finally, he said, "Are the things that you're keeping secret something we can get beyond?"

Her heart crawled into her throat. "Honestly, Nate, I don't know."

"Do you want to put these in water?" he asked gruffly, extending the flowers toward her.

"Yes, sure." She took the flowers and carried them to the small kitchenette, filled a tall glass with water. The colorful flowers instantly brightened the drab little room.

"You might want to get a heavier jacket," he said. "The temperature is supposed to dip down in the low forties tonight."

"We're still going?"

"I want to be with you."

"Even if it's only temporary?"

"Yes."

She almost told him then. Let him off the tenterhooks. Revealed who she was. But she couldn't do it. Not until she talked to Raylene.

He touched her shoulder. "Let's just have a pleasant evening and not worry about anything beyond that."

"Thank you." She breathed her relief, and in her

relief she realized why she was really holding back from telling Nate who she was. She was afraid of getting too close. Of letting herself love again, too quickly and foolishly as she'd done before. She was allowing this thing between her and Raylene put a wall between her and Nate.

She'd learned a lot about herself this past year, after her grandfather died, and Peter took her money, and Earl Pringle appeared on Christmas Day to tell her about her mother.

Shannon had come to realize that she was as important as everyone else. She'd taken care of her grandparents, and, truly, she hadn't minded. But she'd put her own life on hold to do so. She'd let her father slide on his parental responsibilities. She made excuses for him. He was a Peter Pan and she'd been grateful for any attention he showed her.

But she'd accepted crumbs, when she could have had a banquet. Because she'd had so little experience at asking for what she needed, she'd been a sitting duck for a con man like Peter.

Ultimately, she was ashamed that she'd been so easily duped. So desperate for love that she'd been unable to see the wolf lurking beneath the sheep's clothing.

That's why she was putting up barriers in a relationship with Nate. Not because she had doubts about him, but because she had doubts about herself.

It was also why she'd waited a year before coming to Twilight. She'd buckled down and done some hard work, examining who she was and what she wanted. And if she was going to become an independent woman who faced life on her own terms, she had to have an equal partnership. She also needed to take things very slowly. Nate, on the other hand, seemed to be at a place in his life where he was ready for a committed relationship, and that just wasn't something she could offer him right now.

He helped her on with her coat and put his hand to the small of her back, as he guided her down the stairs. He was big, but he was calm and quiet, and she felt an overwhelming sense of peace whenever she was with him.

Just having him at her side made her feel better. By the time they reached the town square, with the spirit of Christmas all around her, Shannon felt her anxiety disappear.

"How does this work?" she asked after Nate parked his truck and they walked hand-in-hand toward the twenty-foot tree erected on the town square. "This community tree-decorating thing."

"Chaos." He chuckled. A man of few words.

The sky was clear, and it looked like a million silver stars had been strewn over navy blue velvet. Santa's workshop was a hot spot. Kids lined up to sit on the jolly man's lap and whisper in his ear their most fervent wishes.

Shannon smiled, remembering when life was that simple. You made a wish, believed really hard, and woke up on Christmas morning to the magic of miracles. And then you grew up and learned the truth. There was no such thing as magic or miracles.

Street vendors were set up around the square selling hot chocolate and hot apple cider and steaming cups of coffee. The smell of roasting chestnuts threaded through the air. Mistletoe had been strung from every tree on the courthouse lawn. Couples were stealing kisses here, there, and everywhere.

"C'mon," he said. "They're about to start."

Nate guided her over to where the crowd encircled the community Christmas tree. The mayor was up on a stage with a bullhorn. A rope cordoned off the crowd from the large tree. Boxes of tinsel, ornaments, popcorn, cranberry garlands, and candy canes lay just beyond the ropes. Waiting for the onslaught.

"Ready?" the mayor asked over the bullhorn.

"Yes!" hollered the crowd.

"Light 'er up, Floyd," the mayor said to the man standing beside him with a gigantic extension cord and plug in his hand.

Floyd married the prongs into the socket, and the Christmas tree lit up glittery-golden from top to bottom. The crowd burst into applause.

"Hang onto my belt loop," Nate said.

"What?"

"Hang onto my belt loop."

"Why?"

"Just trust me and do it."

Feeling a bit weird, she hooked her index fingers around the belt loops at the back of Nate's jeans. She couldn't help taking a peek at his exceptionally fine behind. The man had an ass that would not quit.

"Drop the ropes," the mayor said.

The ropes fluttered to the ground, and there was

a huge surge forward. People jostled them from all sides. Nate plowed forward, towing Shannon behind him like a skier.

Now it all made sense. He was right. It was total, joyous chaos. Both young and old and everyone in between were snatching up ornaments and garlands and candy canes and hanging them pell-mell on the tree in no particular order. No rhyme. No reason. No scheme or theme.

"Go for it," Nate said, handing her a large red plastic Christmas ball.

Grinning, Shannon joined the free-for-all. She went for the first bare limb she saw and looped the ball around it. Nate handed her another decoration, and just like that they fell into an easy rhythm, a smooth team. He fed her ornaments, and she hung them. Before they knew it, the supply of decorations had been decimated.

"All the ornaments are on the bottom," Shannon whispered behind her hand.

"Don't worry. Tomorrow some guy in a cherry picker will rearrange everything so it's all balanced out."

"So why have the crazy frenzy if it's all going to be redone?" she asked, a little breathless from the rapid scramble.

"To make decorating our town tree a community affair," he said, reaching over to twirl a strand of her hair around his finger in a gesture so intimate it took the remainder of her breath.

"So what happens next?"

"Just wait."

Even as he said it, people were already joining hands and ringing the tree. Over the outdoors sound system came, "Have Yourself a Merry Little Christmas." Everyone sang along, swaying in time to the music. Nate took her right hand, and someone nudged her left. She looked over and saw Raylene standing there, a sad little smile on her face, palm extended.

Shannon took her hand, and Raylene squeezed tightly as the town welcomed the new Christmas tree in communal song.

It was hokey. And sappy. Far too Whovillian after the Grinch stole Christmas, but it was also incredibly sweet. For a woman who had never been part of a close-knit community, it felt treacherously like home.

Standing there, holding Shannon's hand on one side, her friend Patsy's hand on the other, and singing "Have Yourself a Merry Little Christmas," Raylene felt something she hadn't felt in over a year. Optimism.

She couldn't put her finger on why, especially since she was the town cynic who didn't fall for schmaltzy crap like a group sing-along, but her spirits suddenly lifted and rose with the combined voices and the touch of hands. She and Shannon could have been mother and daughter celebrating the holidays together.

Was it dumb to pretend that Shannon was the child she'd lost? Yes, probably.

Getting maudlin in your old age, Raylene?

She darted a quick glance over at Shannon who

was gazing at Nate with a wary, but awestruck, expression on her face. Clearly, she was falling for the guy but afraid of her feelings.

The song ended. Raylene's link to Shannon broke as they dropped hands and smiled at each other. She hoped that her own daughter had turned out this well.

"You two have a good night." She winked at Nate and Shannon. "Don't do anything I wouldn't do."

"That leaves you a lot of leeway," Patsy observed.

"Yes," agreed Patsy's fiancé, the ruggedly handsome sheriff, Hondo Crouch, as he joined the conversation. "Let's put it another way. Don't do anything illegal."

Shannon blushed, ducked her head.

"We'll try to be good," Nate said, draping an arm around Shannon's shoulders. "But we're not making any promises."

"We're off to hear Sarah do a reading of her new Christmas book at Ye Olde Book Nook. Would you two like to come along?" Patsy asked.

Nate's eyes glittered as he looked at Shannon. "We've made other plans."

"Have a good time." Patsy waved and turned to Raylene. "How about you? Coming to Sarah's reading?"

The peace and hope that Raylene had felt earlier evaporated. Everyone was pairing off, and she was the only one alone in her group of friends. Even eighty-six-year-old Dotty Mae had a new beau.

"My chest is feeling a little tight," Raylene said. "Indigestion. I shouldn't have eaten that hot dog. Give Sarah my regrets."

Patsy put a hand on Raylene's forearms, met her

eyes. They'd been friends so long Patsy could almost read her mind. "Are you sure you want to be alone tonight?"

"I'm fine. Beat it." Raylene waved a hand in the direction of the bookstore across the street where kids in pajamas with books tucked under their arms waited in line with their parents for the book-launch party.

Patsy folded her three middle fingers then extended her thumb and pinky finger and held it up to her ear in a "call me later" gesture.

"Shoo!" Raylene said.

Hondo took Patsy's hand and led her away, throwing "Goodnight, Ray," over his shoulder.

The rest of the crowd had dispersed, as well, leaving bits of litter in their wake. On the other side of the courthouse lawn, the plywood structure of Santa's Workshop was closing up. Young women dressed as Elves put away the faux presents in a giant toy box, so they wouldn't blow off during the night.

Santa stood from his thronelike chair. Every time Raylene looked at the display, she thought of the scene from *A Christmas Story* in which Ralphie got so nervous he forgot to ask for the thing he wanted the most. A Red Ryder B.B. gun.

It was her favorite holiday movie. She particularly liked the part about the leg lamp.

"Your legs are much hotter than any leg lamp, baby," Earl would say every year when they watched the movie, a big bowl of buttered popcorn parked on the couch between them. "You can wear fishnets until you're ninety."

This year there would be no one to watch *A*

Christmas Story with. Earl Junior wasn't coming home. He blamed her for chasing Earl off, and she deserved his anger. Plus, he had a new girlfriend, and he planned on spending the holiday with her family in Seattle.

Santa started down the courthouse steps. He walked with a familiar gait that caught Raylene's eye. For one stupid second, she thought, *Earl?*

Without even meaning to, Raylene started toward Santa, her pulse bounding in her throat. She drew closer.

He descended the last step and hesitated.

Their eyes met.

Green eyes. The same color as Earl's, but the thick white beard cloaked the rest of his features.

You're seeing things. Letting your imagination run away with you. This can't be Earl.

He was eight feet away from her. She took another step, whispered, "Earlie?"

Something akin to panic flared in Santa's eyes. He ducked his head, pivoted on one heel of his black boots, and stalked quickly around the corner of the courthouse.

Raylene rushed after him, her thoughts a wild jumble. *It's Earl. No, it's not. He's got the same green eyes. You're imagining things, because you want it to be Earl. Why did he run off?*

"Earl!" she cried. "Earl, wait."

By the time she made it around the side of the courthouse, no one was there. Santa had disappeared completely, leaving Raylene feeling like a stupid, sentimental old fool.

Chapter Nine

After they left the Christmas tree decorating event, Nate took Shannon to the Marina beach to watch the float procession of lights. Communal campfires had been set up by the city. Couples, parents, and kids ringed the fire pits, roasting hot dogs and marshmallows, waiting for the Christmas water parade to begin.

"This town goes all-out for Christmas," Shannon observed.

"Twilight depends on the tourism dollar. They make the most of every holiday. If you think this is bad, you should be here for Valentine's Day." Nate slipped an arm around her waist. "Will you be here for Valentine's Day?"

"I don't know."

It was an honest answer, but not the one he'd wanted to hear. What could he do to convince her to stay? He could court her until he was blue in the face, but if she wasn't ready, she wasn't ready.

"You want to find a seat by a fire or hug the railing?" He nodded to where a group stood on a pier that jutted over the lake. Outdoor radiant heaters had been positioned in strategic places on the dock to compensate for the cold.

"The railing," she said. "I want a front-row seat."

They found an empty spot at the railing not far from where one of those heaters was spreading out warm air. In the distance to their left, they could see the float boats approaching from beyond the river bridge, festooned in multicolored lights.

Nate stood slightly behind her and tilted his head for a good stare at her fanny that looked so sexy in blue jeans. His palm itched to cup those sweet cheeks. But he wouldn't. He'd promised he'd take things slow. She needed time for her secrets to seep out. He didn't want to rush her, but man alive her sweet scent and that gorgeous ass were driving him crazy. He curled his hands into fists to keep from touching her.

"This is fun," she said in a way that told him she hadn't had a lot of fun in her life. Over the course of their dates, she'd been careful not to say much about her past. He'd let it go, but now it wasn't enough for him. He wanted to know everything there was to know about her. Down to the very last detail.

"I was thinking," Nate said. "It might make it easier for you to tell me your secrets if I told you some of mine."

She turned toward him, her eyes searching his face. "You have secrets?"

He nodded.

"I thought you hated secrets."

"I do. That's why I'm coming clean."

"You don't have to tell me anything."

"I want to," he murmured. "Full disclosure."

"What if I can't reciprocate?"

"I can accept that."

"Are you sure?"

Was he? "I am."

"So let's hear the secrets."

"I was a sneaky kid. At Christmas, I would carefully untape the ends of the packages to read the labels on the boxes, and then I'd tape them back up. My mom caught on after a couple of years, and started putting the gifts in different boxes. One time I thought she'd gotten me a pair of panty hose and I freaked out. Turns out she put a Hot Wheel car in one of those plastic panty hose eggs to mess with my head."

Shannon chuckled. "Where does your mother live now?"

"She passed away a few years ago."

"Oh, I'm so sorry, Nate."

"She died of renal failure when I was in Iraq. She never even told me she was sick." He gazed out at the water, feeling the old pain and remorse. "She didn't want to bother me while I was on a dangerous mission. That was my mom. Always thinking of others. I regret not being with her in the end. That's two secrets if you're keeping track."

"What about your dad?"

Nate shrugged. "They divorced when I was a kid. He's got a whole other family. Lives in New Mexico. Leads walking tours."

"That's different. Siblings?"

"A half-brother and sister. You?"

She shook her head. "Any other secrets?"

"Lots more," he said.

"I'm all ears."

"I told you a couple of mine, can you give a little and tell me about some of yours?"

Her spine stiffened, and her hands curled around the railing. "I was raised by my grandparents."

"What happened to your mom?"

She shook her head. "I don't want to talk about that."

"Okay," he said agreeably, but his curiosity was killing him. "I was engaged once."

"That's not earth-shattering. You're almost forty. I'd wonder about you if you'd never at least been close to marriage before. What happened?"

"Biggest cliché in the book. I came home from the Middle East for our wedding and learned she was three months pregnant. Only problem was that I'd been on a six month deployment."

"Ah."

"She'd gotten pregnant by my best friend. Get this. She still wanted to marry me, though, and raise his kid. I'd be a better parent than Glenn. Those were her exact words."

Shannon wrinkled her nose. "She sounds like a total peach."

"That's one of the reasons why I hate secrets."

"I could see how that might cause some hard feelings on your part."

"It took some time for me to get over that betrayal. I don't love easily," he said, "but when I do, I give the woman I'm with all of my heart. I don't hold anything back."

Shannon inhaled sharply. Nate paused. Had he said too much? But he had to let her know that if something started between them, he was committed to the relationship. If that scared her off, well then maybe that's exactly what he needed to know.

"I'm looking for someone," he said, "and I think I've found her."

She turned to stare at him then, as the first lighted boat moved in front of the pier. Around them people were oohing and aahing, but neither Nate nor Shannon was looking at the water. He held her gaze instead, never blinking or glancing away. This was it. The moment where she told him he was coming on too strong and just walked away. Nate held his breath.

But she did not walk away. Instead, she reached down and took his hand. "I've just been standing here wondering one thing."

"What's that?" he asked, his words coming out all raspy.

"Are you ever going to ask me back to your place?"

Yes, she'd sent the man mixed messages. Telling him to slow down and then asking him to take her back to his place. It was illogical. Impulsive. The kind of thing that could get her hurt. But her body had been yearning for Nate's since that first day in the bar.

Now here she was in his cabin by the lake. Just the two of them. All alone.

"You want something to drink?" he asked, looking as befuddled as she felt.

Slowly, she shook her head.

He came toward her, sex smoldering in his dark eyes. Shannon's legs trembled. Everything about this man made her insides quiver and quake.

Was she truly prepared to go down this road? Accept the consequences of her actions?

She'd made an impulsive choice once before and it had promptly come back to bite her in the butt. Did she dare take another risk? She'd been so risk-adverse her whole life that the one time she'd taken a chance it had ended in complete disaster.

And yet . . . she knew this was right just as surely as she'd ignored the warning signs with Peter. The universe had been giving Nate the green light. Whenever she was with him, he made her feel wanted and cared for. It was an amazing feeling.

He canted his head, studied her, looking at once both incredibly masculine and boyishly adorable. "Shannon," he whispered. "I want this to be—"

"Shh. No more talking." If he kept talking, she would back out, and Shannon did not want to back out.

The fire in his eyes burned hotter, brighter. Nate was so different from the men she'd grown up around. He possessed a strong, stalwart exterior, but inside he was tender, caring, understanding. He was honorable and brave, with an unexpected humorous side; a complex man who at the same time was uncomplicated and direct. He was an ex Navy SEAL who embraced small-town life. He let people be who they were meant to be without condemnation or judgment.

Nate cupped the back of her head as if she were incredibly fragile glass. His dark irises pulled her in until she couldn't have looked anywhere else, even if she'd wanted to. She did not want to.

Her pulse tapped faster than when she danced zumba. *Take me. Now.* Her blood sang even though a tiny vestige of her straightlaced upbringing pushed at the back of her brain. But she was a grown woman. In charge of her own life and her own mistakes. This was her decision, and she embraced it headlong.

He kissed her. His tongue teased her with soft strokes. His callused palm pushed under the hem of her T-shirt and skimmed over her bare belly, as he made appreciative noises in the back of his throat.

They kissed with their eyes open. Both of them old enough to fully understand and accept responsibility for what they were getting into. They weren't kids. Their tongues dueled as he adeptly reached around to unhook her bra. His fingers found her nipples, teased them with gentle pinches.

A soft moan slid from her lips, and she melded her body against his.

"I want you." He kissed the tip of her nose. "Need you."

He tugged her shirt over her head, and then it was her turn, stripping his shirt from his muscular torso. Their gazes hooked as they simultaneously tossed their clothing over their shoulders.

Sexual tension pulsed between them, building to a heated pitch.

Nate went down on his knees in front of her, kissed her lust-swollen breasts. She let out a hissing sound and threaded her fingers through his thatch of thick hair.

His hands encircled her waist. "Beautiful," he murmured against her belly, setting up a ticklish vibration.

"Bedroom," she managed to gasp.

He got to his feet, took her hand, and led her down the wood-paneled hallway into the master bedroom, surprisingly neat for an outdoorsy bachelor. Or what she could see of it in the darkness. The bed was made, the floor clean, the chest of drawers free of clutter. The cooler air in his room felt good against her heated skin.

Nate leaned in to kiss her again in the moonlight falling through the open blinds and cutting broad silvery stripes across the plush carpet. His head dropped to nuzzle her neck, one hand splayed against her lower back. Everywhere his damp mouth touched, she broke out in mini forest fires. If he kept this up, she'd be a five-alarm blaze in no time.

Shannon kept stroking his shoulders, feeling the hard muscles tighten beneath her fingers. This wasn't one of her late night fantasies. It was really happening. She was in Nate's arms. In his bedroom. They were going to make love.

"I haven't been able to get you out of my mind from the minute I first saw you," Nate murmured, his wicked fingers sliding around the waistband of her jeans. He found the snap, worked on it until it popped open. The zipper followed, sliding down like the door of Ali Baba's cave of treasures to the magic words, "Open Sesame."

Shannon looked up into his eyes and reached for the closure of his jeans, his body heat radiating through her fingers. He pulled her to him, pressed her against him. He was hard as concrete.

"I haven't been able to stop thinking about you, either," she confessed.

He whipped off his belt and dropped it, the buckle jangling on the floor. In one bold motion, he shucked her jeans to her knees. She held onto his shoulder, kicked them off along with her clogs. Then he stripped off his own pants, so that they both wore nothing except their underwear.

"I want to wipe all other men from your mind," he said. "I want you to forget about your ex and anyone else who ever hurt you or treated you badly.

"Nate," she whispered, surprised by the strength of emotion closing off her throat. "There is no one else but you."

She'd never experienced a need like this. Such insatiable wanting. It was as if everything she'd ever felt before was nothing but amateur hour. It scared her because it was so strong, so powerful, so easy to just let go and fall into his arms.

Nate stepped to the bed, pulled back the green comforter with a patterned print of flying fish jumping up from streams, and turned down the sheets. They crawled inside together, him on one side, her on the other. The crisp covers smelled of cedar and sandalwood and man. Had he put on fresh sheets that morning? Had he been that confident of himself that they would wind up here?

You're the one who suggested that he bring you here. Stop worrying. Stop second-guessing. Just enjoy the moment.

She kissed him, hungry for his taste. Night after night she'd lain in her bed above the Horny Toad Tavern, imagining this happening. Dreaming of being in his arms, feeling his hot lips on her cool body. She closed her eyes, memorizing every detail of his taste, the way he was touching her, and the things he was doing to her. She never wanted to forget this. The moment they joined for the first time.

She traced her fingers along his scratchy beard. He ran his knuckles over her belly and stopped to draw a heart over her navel before sliding his hand down to slip below the waistband of her panties, touching her in a place he'd never touched before.

"Me too." She giggled and slipped her fingers through the opening in his boxer briefs, strumming over the hard length of him. He wrestled off his underwear, made short work of hers.

Then he took his time, luxuriating over each dip and curve of her body. Stroking her until she was moaning softly in the back of her throat. He touched his tongue to her, running it over tender places she never knew were so sensitive. The sheets whispered. Pillows tumbled off the bed. Condoms came out of the bedside drawer.

She did her own exploring, eager to discover just

what made him whimper and groan with ecstasy. He made beautiful sounds that raised delicious goose bumps on her arms.

"Sweetheart," he panted. "I gotta have you. You're killing me with that wicked little mouth of yours."

His hand touched her knees, and she dropped them open, fully exposing herself to him. He slipped both hands under her hips, pulling her close to him. She arched her back, looking up into his eyes. What she saw reflected in those dark depths stole all the air from her lungs.

Then he was inside her, and they gasped in the same breath as their bodies joined, her femininity fully embracing his masculine thrust.

"Shannon," Nate said. "Sweet Shannon."

He sunk deeper and deeper into her until all separation was gone. They were one, moving like currents on the river, pulling and swaying, urgent and swift, running faster and faster toward the wide-open sea.

Sometime later, Shannon woke in the darkness, Nate's big body beside her. Instant elation grabbed hold of her, and she slipped a hand between her legs, beautifully sore from their vigorous lovemaking. In that moment, she savored the wonder of being here with him.

What if? she wondered. What if this could be more than just lovely sex? What if this could be forever?

The sweet daydream tapped on her brain. What if she could finally have a happily-ever-after? She wanted it so much that she was truly scared to hope. Scared because she couldn't bear to have it taken away.

I want. I want.

The need was so strong, so insistent. She wanted him. Wanted a happy life. Wanted a place to belong. Was it so hard to believe she could have such happiness?

She knew the answer even as she posed the question. Before she could fully open her heart up to the possibility of Nate, there was one essential thing that she had to do first.

Settle her issues with her mother.

Chapter Ten

Unable to bear the thought of going home to an empty house, Raylene went to the Horny Toad. She felt closest to Earl there. It was scary the way she was starting to imagine things now. Supposing that the white poinsettias had come from him, thinking that he was the town Santa. She was hoping against hope. Grasping at straws.

Sooner or later she was going to have to face the fact that Earl was not coming back. She'd lost him forever.

To keep herself occupied, she worked on the staffing schedule for January. Even as she tapped Shannon Nagud's name into the spreadsheet, she couldn't help wondering if the woman would be here in the new year. Shannon was a good worker. Surprisingly, one of the best she'd ever hired. But there was something about the woman, something enigmatic and untouchable beyond those golden brown eyes that told Raylene she had a hidden agenda, and, once her purpose in Twilight had been satisfied, she would be on her way.

That saddened her, too.

The aching in her chest that had started during the tree-decorating event was back. Raylene took some Maalox and rested her head on the desk. She'd go home in a bit when her stomach settled.

She must have fallen asleep, because she jerked away just before dawn, her neck stiff and achy. She sat up, rubbing her sore muscles. The computer was still on, the cursor blinking on the spreadsheet. The name Shannon Nagud.

It might have been her blurry vision. It might have been her penchant for word-find puzzle books. But in that moment, Raylene saw what she'd missed before.

Now she knew why Shannon had struck her as familiar. Why she often caught the younger woman watching her with an odd expression on her face.

Her name wasn't Nagud. It was Dugan.

Shannon Dugan.

The woman she'd given a job and a place to stay. The woman who was the same age as the daughter Raylene had given away.

The realization hit with the force of a bomb, leaving her with absolutely no doubt about the truth. Raylene plastered both hands over her mouth, as a cry of distressed joy leaked from her lips.

Shannon Dugan was her daughter!

In the creeping light of dawn, Nate stirred, and his first sleepy thought was of Shannon. He reached across the sheets, searching for her and came up with empty covers.

He cocked his head, listening for sounds of her in the bathroom, but heard nothing. He sat up, threw back the covers. "Shannon?"

Silence greeted him.

He got up, padded through the house. She was nowhere to be found. He put on his pants, stepped out onto the porch. His truck was gone.

Maybe she went for breakfast, a hopeful part of him suggested. Maybe. But maybe she'd just gotten scared and taken off.

He'd moved too fast. They'd made love too soon. They'd only known each other two weeks. A guy couldn't fall in love in two weeks.

And yet, he had.

Stupid. Stupid.

But calling himself names didn't change the fact that he'd fallen head-over-heels for her. Unfortunately, he had no idea how she felt about him.

Obviously, she'd regretted having sex with him. She'd booked the hell out of here before he woke up. Face it. The woman had issues to work out, and until she did, he'd be waiting on the sideline.

Question was, how long could a man be expected to wait?

Shannon sat in Nate's truck, staring at the front of the Horny Toad Tavern just as she had on the day she'd arrived. Raylene's Cadillac was in the parking lot. What was Raylene doing here at six-thirty in the morning?

Maybe she'd gotten drunk the night before and called someone to take her home.

Maybe. But maybe she was inside.

Go on. You can't create a new future until you make peace with the past.

She blew out her breath, no closer to knowing what she was going to say than she'd been two weeks before when she'd started this ill-conceived charade.

Just go in there, say whatever comes to mind, get it off your chest, then take Nate's truck back to him and see where you stand.

Yes. Right. Okay. The time for avoidance had past.

Except that now, she liked Raylene. Two weeks ago, she'd come here with a chip weighting down her shoulder and now . . . well, she felt sorry for Raylene. For all the things she'd missed out on. For all the things she'd lost. Any bitterness and anger had completely dissipated. She let it all go. Just as she'd let her hurt and betrayal over Peter go.

And it was all because of Nate.

In two short weeks he had taught her more about herself than she could ever unearth on her own. He'd shown her she was resilient and that she was desirable and that she deserved happiness. But she had to take the first step. She had to ask for what she wanted. She was responsible for herself and no one else.

She should have told Nate about Raylene. He would have given her good advice on how to handle it. Why had she been so secretive with him? Was it because she was afraid that if she let down her guard she could never get it back up again?

Stop sitting here and act.

It was time. She'd come to break the chains of the past, and she couldn't have a future with Nate until she took that final step. Feeling shaky but determined, Shannon opened the door of Nate's truck and got out.

The cold morning air frosted her breath and sent a shiver down her spine. The front door would be locked, so she tracked around the side of the building to the rear entrance. She put a hand to the knob just as the door jerked open.

"Yips!" Raylene screeched at the same time Shannon staggered backward, her momentum unbalanced by the opening door.

Raylene gasped, placed a hand to her heart. "Oh, it's you. You scared me to death. I was just coming to find you."

"We must be on the same wavelength, because here I am."

Shannon met her mother's gaze and turned it into a stare.

Raylene's mouth dropped, snapped shut, and dropped again. "Come inside," she said finally. "You're shivering."

She was shivering, and her pulse was ticking behind her eyes like a time bomb. This was it. The showdown she'd been working toward.

"Would you like some hot tea?" Raylene asked, leading the way inside. "I'm going to make you some hot tea."

Hot tea. It sounded so civilized on the surface.

"It's a little too late to be nurturing don't you think?"

Raylene stopped walking. Her shoulders sagged. Slowly she turned around to face Shannon. Her eyes looked stricken, haunted. This was where the showdown was going to happen—in the cramped kitchen of the Horny Toad Tavern.

"I finally figured it out," her mother said. "Nagud. Dugan. I should have put two and two together sooner. You have your father's eyes."

Shannon had waited a year for this confrontation. Had built it up big in her mind as a dramatic face-off. But now that it was underway, it felt so . . . anticlimactic. Raylene was just an aging woman with a heart-load of regrets. And Shannon was a woman who needed to let go of the past in order to build a new future. Nothing could be changed or rearranged. They had to start from here. No going back. No mulligans.

"My grandparents, Lance, all led me to believe you were dead," Shannon said, surprised by the lack of anger.

"Nope," Raylene said. "Not dead. How'd I die?"

They stared at each other, tension tight as a guy wire stretching between them. "I was told that you got pregnant during a one-night stand with my father. That you abandoned me on their doorstep. A few months later you died of a drug overdose."

"Lance never told me that," she mused.

"You contacted my father?"

"I wasn't supposed to. It was my deal with your grandparents. But every once in a while, I'd call, and he'd tell me how you were doing. He wouldn't even tell me your name, though. I didn't realize they'd killed me off."

Shannon cocked her head. She'd thought about this a lot. "I suppose it was to keep me from trying to find you. Looking back, I supposed they were terrified you'd show back up and try to claim me."

Raylene shook her head, despair plucking down the corners of her mouth. "I imagine your grandparents and your father did what they thought best."

It also surprised her that Raylene did not decry the lie that Shannon's family had told her.

"I hated you," Shannon admitted. "For years. My whole life really. Until last Christmas."

"Wh . . . what happened last Christmas?"

"A man came to see me. He told me you were alive and that you were hurting because of what you did all those years ago. He told me why you'd given me away and my grandparents' role in your decision to do so. He also told me that you needed my forgiveness and that I needed to give it to you in order to free myself. But I was in no shape to process that information. I needed time. Time to stop hating you. Time for it fully to sink in that you weren't dead. That you'd been living a whole, full life here in Twilight without me."

Raylene's back was against the sink. She gripped the stainless steel counters with both hands, moistened her lip with her tongue. "I never stopped thinking about you, Shannon. Every day. Every day I thought of you. Not a single day went by that you weren't on my mind. But I truly believed you were better off without me."

"How could you believe that?"

"At the time, I had nothing. My family was dirt poor. Your grandparents could offer you a life of wealth and luxury. I couldn't compete with that."

"It wasn't fair of them," Shannon's voice caught, hitched. She had to pause a moment. "To cut you out of my life like that. For the longest time I thought something was wrong with me, that my own mother didn't want me."

"Oh no," Raylene said. "You were perfect. It was me. I was the defective one. I was trailer trash—your grandmother's exact words—and I had no business being married to a Dugan."

It didn't matter who was to blame. The past was gone. "We can never have a regular mother-daughter relationship," Shannon said.

A single tear slid down Raylene's cheek. "I know," she whispered. "I know what I did was unforgivable."

"I didn't say I couldn't forgive you," Shannon said, tears running over her own cheeks. "Just that we have to start from here to define what our relationship is going to be."

Raylene's eyes rounded. "Wh . . . what? You want to have a relationship with me?"

Shannon nodded. "More than anything in the world."

Tentatively, Raylene raised her arms, but looked braced for certain rejection.

Shannon didn't hesitate. She stepped across the tiled floor to embrace her mother. "I forgive you," she whispered. "I forgive you."

Raylene squeezed her hard, her thin body quaking. They stood hugging for a long, long time. Emotions rising and falling like ocean waves as the implications of the future welled up inside them. Then they were laughing and crying and dabbing at each other's eyes with a plain, white industrial kitchen towel that smelled faintly of onions.

"You've given me the greatest Christmas gift ever," Raylene said. "A gift I don't deserve, but thank you, Shannon. Thank you."

"You're welcome, Mother."

"Mother," Raylene repeated, starting to cry all over again. "You called me *mother.*"

"That's what you are."

Raylene put both hands to her mouth, and it was several minutes before she could speak. "This man who came to see you last Christmas. What was his name?"

Shannon met Raylene's gaze. "It was your husband, Earl Pringle."

Earl.

Earl had gone to see Shannon after their big fight the year before. He'd told Shannon to come to Twilight and forgive her.

Raylene's heart skipped several beats. She laid a hand over her chest, felt the erratic rhythm.

A sudden tightness knifed through her ribcage, spread straight through her back. Emotions had a hold on her. The lies she'd told. The secrets she'd kept. She was being forgiven for all her sins.

It was more than she ever dared hope for. It

seemed, after all these years, that God had finally decided she'd suffered enough and he would answer her prayers.

Joyous bliss exploded in her at the same time a vicious stab of pain gripped her. Sweat popped out on her forehead, and she was instantly sick to her stomach.

"Raylene?" Shannon sounded very far away.

Her breath shot out in quick, hot pants. The pain intensified, dropping Raylene to her knees.

Shannon grabbed her under her arms. "What is it, Mother? What's wrong?"

Mother.

A smile tugged at Raylene's lips as her eyes slid slowly closed. Her daughter had come home. She could die a happy woman in spite of the unrelenting pain twisting through her chest.

All except for Earl. There would be no closure there.

"Mother!" Shannon cried out. "Mother, can you hear me?"

Raylene tried to speak, but it hurt too badly. The pain radiated into her neck, through her jaw and up into her ear.

Shannon had her under the arms and was dragging her somewhere.

Where were they going?

Vaguely, she was aware of being in the main room of the bar. Shannon was fumbling at the locks on the door. "Hang on, Mother. Hang on. I can get you to the hospital faster than an ambulance can get here."

The cold air was a bracing slap. Somehow Raylene managed to stand, as Shannon half-dragged her toward Nate's pickup truck. What was she doing with Nate's pickup truck?

Shannon wrenched open the passenger door and struggled to boost Raylene inside. Her hands were shaking, and tears were rolling down on her face. "Don't die, you can't die. Please don't die before we really get to know each other."

Raylene clenched her jaw in a vain attempt to stay the pain. She reached up to pat Shannon's face. To reassure the poor girl. But lifting her arm was a Herculean effort.

"I've got her," a man's voice said.

Shannon stepped back, and firm masculine hands took hold of Raylene. Familiar hands. Hands she'd known for over fifty years. She blinked, turned her head. There stood Santa Claus, picking her up, gently laying her in the seat.

"Santa?" Raylene whispered.

"Get in the backseat," Santa told Shannon. "I'll drive."

The next thing Raylene knew, Santa was bulleting down the highway, headed for Twilight General Hospital. He turned to look with kind, gray eyes. Kind, gray eyes she'd loved since first grade.

"Earl?" Raylene whispered. But how could it be Earl? Was she dreaming? Earl in a Santa suit, with her long-lost daughter in the backseat? That's when Raylene realized that if these two things had happened, she must be dead already.

CHAPTER ELEVEN

Shannon paced the hallway outside the Medical Intensive Care Unit. The members of the First Love Cookie Club sat in the waiting room, most of them knitting furiously as they waited for word about their dear friend. Several of the ladies had tried to get Shannon to sit with them, and she had for a while, coming clean about who she was. She'd endured their well-meaning hugs, and she was happy they were here, but she was too antsy to stay sitting for long.

If Raylene died before they could really get to know each other, it would be the worst kind of shame. She couldn't help feeling responsible for her mother's heart attack. The stress had simply been too much for her.

Just to have something to do, she headed for the coffee machine in the adjacent snack room. She jammed a wrinkled dollar into the slot, but the machine kept spitting it out. Frustrated, she mumbled a string of curses.

A calm hand settled on her shoulder. "Let me get that for you," drawled a man's voice.

Nate!

She turned. An expression of concern tightened his eyes. "I ran off with your truck," she said.

He nodded. "I know."

"Raylene's my mother."

"I heard. The whole town is buzzing with the news."

"That's my big secret."

"I figured."

"Earl is wearing a Santa suit. He's been living in an abandoned cabin in the woods just beyond the Horny Toad. No one knows why, but if he hadn't shown up when he did, Raylene might have died in the parking lot."

"Now that I had not heard."

"It's true. Earl told me." She looked into his eyes. He took her hands in his. "You came."

"I did."

"For me."

"Nah, I needed my truck to get to work," he teased.

She gave him a small smile. "Thanks for trying to cheer me up."

"I was really worried about you. I thought . . ."

"What?"

He shuffled his feet. "That you'd used me and were done with me."

"I didn't mean to run out on you like I did. I was overwhelmed."

"It's all right."

"Excuse me," a little old man leaning on a cane said. "Could you lovebirds get out of the way so I can get some coffee?"

"Excuse us, sir." Nate waltzed Shannon over to a loveseat in the corner and pulled her down in his lap.

"So what happens now?" she asked.

"We wait to see how Raylene is." He anchored her to him with an arm around her waist.

"I mean after. Between us."

He still had hold of her hands. The air filled with the smell of too-strong coffee. "Depends."

"On what?"

"Whether you intend on staying in Twilight or not."

"You know," she said. "I sort of have this fantasy."

"Hmm. Sounds promising. Fantasies. I like the way you think."

"Sexual innuendo? Really? At a time like this?"

Nate shrugged. "I thought maybe it would help take your mind off things."

"No you didn't. You were being a guy."

"Guilty as charged." He looked sheepish. "Can you guess what I'm thinking right now?"

"Uh-huh," she said. But he was right, she was already smiling.

"So about this fantasy . . ."

"I'm thinking about buying that old-fashioned ice cream parlor that shut down recently."

"Rinky-Tink's?"

"That'd be the one."

"Interesting thought."

"That's where they held the Christmas-cookie swap I went to with Raylene," Shannon said. "I walked in, and the place just felt special."

"So if you bought this ice cream parlor, would that mean you'd be staying in Twilight?" He raised hopeful eyebrows.

"It's just an idea I've been kicking around."

"I don't want to rush you. No pressure, but last night . . . well . . ." He glanced around to make sure no one was in hearing distance and lowered his voice. "Best sex ever."

Shannon felt her cheeks flush. "It *was* pretty earthmoving."

"Gotta tell you, I freaked a bit when I woke up and you were gone. I'm not a one-night-stand kind of guy."

"You're one in a million, Nate Deavers."

"Just as long as you appreciate that fact."

"The reason I left when I did was because I had to go see Raylene and tell her who I was before I could tell you, and I couldn't go another day without letting you in on my secret."

"I get it. I know. Just saying for future reference, don't leave a guy hanging like that."

"I've still got a few issues to work through."

"I'm here."

"I have trouble trusting my own judgment."

"Do you now?" he asked. "Do you trust yourself to trust me?"

She nodded. She did trust Nate.

"We've got a special thing going here. It could just keep getting better and better. I don't want to rush you, but I'm head over heels for you, Shannon, and I don't fall easily."

Nate was falling in love with her. It didn't scare Shannon. Not the least little bit. "I'm falling pretty hard for you too, Nate Deavers."

"Shannon," Patsy Cross called from the doorway. "The doctor came out to speak to us. Raylene is going to be okay. They said we could see her in a few minutes."

"Thank you." Relief sagged through her body. When she leaned her head back, Nate's shoulder was there.

"I've got your back, sweetheart," he whispered. "Never doubt it."

The sound of his voice rumbling through his chest made her feel safe and secure.

Looking into his eyes, she saw all her hopes and dreams. "I belong here," she whispered. "I belong here with you."

"Yes, you do." Nate folded his arms around her, and kissed her for a long, long time. "Yes, you do."

The Watcher sat in the chair beside Raylene, holding her hand and listening to the heart monitor beep. She lay in the bed, looking so small. His tough Raylene helpless. It tore at his soul.

He was still wearing the Santa suit because he couldn't bear to take it off. Even though the doctor had said her heart attack had been mild, that she would pull through, and that with a few lifestyle changes she could live to be a ripe old age, he was still terrified.

Raylene stirred open her eyes. "Earl? Is it really you?"

He nodded.

"What the hell are you doing in a Santa suit?"

Same old Raylene. The woman he'd loved since he was six years old and pushed her down on the playground to prove it. But now came the hard part. Once she knew what had happened, would she still want him?

"Got a job as the town Santa," he said.

"Whatever for?"

"To be near you."

A puzzled frown pinched her brow. "Why didn't you just come home?"

"I couldn't."

"Why not?"

He couldn't meet her eyes. A terrible fear of rejection, the same fear that had kept him in hiding, bunched up inside him.

"Earl." She squeezed his hand. "What is it? Why did you punish me so cruelly? Why did you leave me wondering and fretting about what happened to you?"

It had taken him months to work up the courage to come home, and still he couldn't come right out and tell her.

"Let me tell you what I know," she said. "And you can fill in the gaps. Last year, after you found out about Shannon, you went to find her."

"Yes." His eyes cradled her face. To him, she was just as beautiful as she'd been on their wedding day. He'd always considered himself the luckiest man on

Earth to have such a spectacular woman. When he learned she'd had a baby with Lance Dugan during the time they broke up when she was a Dallas Cowboys cheerleader, it just about killed his soul. He'd been mad. The maddest he'd ever been. But even so, he'd never once stopped loving her.

"You told Shannon about me."

He nodded again.

"What happened after that? Where did you go?"

"I was still too upset to come home," he said slowly, carefully paving the way for the terrible thing he had to tell her. "I went down to Houston and took a job drilling gas rigs."

"Earl Pringle." She struggled to sit up. "At your age? What were you thinking?"

"Lay back down, woman," he growled. "You just had a heart attack. You're in no position to chastise me."

"Shannon came here because you told her to," Raylene said, softening. "We squared things between us. She forgave me."

"I'm glad," he whispered, squeezing her hand. "She'll soon find out what a big-hearted woman you truly are beneath that crusty exterior."

"What about us, Earl? What's going to happen to us?"

He was quiet for a long time. "It all depends on you, Ray, whether you want me back or not."

"Of course I want you back, you old goat. Why wouldn't I want you back? You're the other damned half of me."

He hauled in a deep breath, dropped her hand,

and got up. He felt ridiculous in the Santa suit, but it was his only protection.

"Earl?"

In that moment, propped up on those white pillows, covered by a white sheet, wearing that godawful hospital gown, his tough wife looked so utterly vulnerable that it just about broke his heart. Maybe this wasn't the time or place to break the news.

"You're really scaring me," she said.

He was scared himself. So scared he felt as if he'd been doused in ice water. "I didn't mean to stay away so long. I figured I'd be gone a month, and it would get my point across that I was well and truly pissed off at you." Earl paced the end of her bed, his Santa boots making a snicking noise against the linoleum. "I wanted to work in oil and gas again like when I was a kid. I thought it would make me feel young."

"So how did one month turn into twelve?" Her thin hands, roped with blue veins, worried the sheet.

This was the hard part. He couldn't look at her. He moved to the window, stared out at the parking lot. Nate Deavers and Shannon Dugan were leaning against Nate's truck kissing like there was no tomorrow. They made a cute couple.

"There was an explosion on the rig," he murmured. "Small one. Didn't even make the statewide news."

He heard Raylene's sharp intake of breath. "Earl?" she asked, her voice full of suspicion.

"I was hurt. Knocked unconscious. When I came to in the burn unit, I couldn't remember who I was."

Raylene let out a strangled cry. "You were burned!"

Earl spun around to see she had both hands to her mouth, tears misting her eyes. Oh, damn. He shouldn't have told her now. Not when she'd just had a heart attack. It was so hard. So very hard.

"Oh, oh." The monitor beeped faster.

"Shh, shh. It's okay. Calm down."

"Wh . . . when did this happen?"

"The end of January. I went through months of rehab and numerous surgeries."

"I can't believe you went through all that trauma alone, far from home. Why didn't anyone call me? I could have been there with you. Helped you every step of the way. I feel so horrible that you had to go through that by yourself."

"I told everyone on the job that I had no family."

Raylene winced, and he knew he'd hurt her. "I'm sorry, baby," he said.

"You're not the one who has anything to be sorry about. Every bit of this was consequences of my mistakes."

"No. I made my choices, just as you made yours. After my memory came back, I was too afraid to come home."

She was throwing back the covers, trying to get out of bed. Earl rushed over. "You can't get up, Ray."

Her eyes beseeched him. "Why were you afraid?"

"I was afraid you wouldn't want me anymore." Tears burned his nose. He knelt at her bedside.

"Why in the hell would you think that? Earl Pringle, don't you know I've never loved any other man?"

"You had Lance Dugan's baby."

"I know. Even though we were broke up, you were the one I loved. It was wrong of me. I have no excuse. None." Raylene's lip trembled. "I'm so sorry for the way I hurt you. So, so very sorry."

"I know," he said. "I know. I'm sorry too."

"I still love you, Earl."

"Wait," he said. "There's something you have to see." Earl pulled in a deep breath, braced himself for the horror he knew he would see on her face, and slowly took off the Santa beard.

Raylene's eyes widened, and her hand trembled. She did not look horrified or disgusted, but he could see the devastation in her eyes. She hurt because he had hurt. "Oh, Earlie, how you must have suffered!"

"The worst part was being without you."

Her fingers gently skated across the burn scar that ran from just under his left cheek, past his jaw, and down his neck to his chest and shoulder. "I could have been with you. I could have shared your pain."

"Do you still want me?"

"I'll always want you. No matter what. I love you, Earl Pringle, and have from the time you pushed me down on the playground. We're fated. Meant to be. Yes, we were both damned stupid. Guess that's one of the reasons we're a perfect match."

"Oh, Ray." He hiccuped. "I can't believe I made it back to you."

"I just got one thing to say to you."

"What's that?"

"You hang on to that Santa suit, mister, because as soon as the doctor gives me the thumbs up on having sex, I want you coming down my chimney."

"You bawdy old woman."

"Damn straight. It's one of the things you love most about me." Raylene scooted over, patted a spot on the bed beside her.

Earl kicked off his Santa suit and climbed in beside her. He pulled her into his arms, and she rested her head against his chest. There in Twilight General Hospital, two former high school sweethearts, who'd lost their way, were finally, at long last, reunited for good.

Christine

CHAPTER ONE

Even though she wished she could fast-forward her life and skip right over Christmas this year, Christine Noble smiled at her departing customers.

"Happy holidays," she called over the merry jangle of jingle bells fixed to the door, wriggling her fingers in a wave she hoped didn't look as half-hearted as she felt.

The smell of yeast, cinnamon, nutmeg, and pumpkin permeated the cheerful yellow walls of the Twilight Bakery on that sunny Monday morning. Christine hummed along with "The Most Wonderful Time of the Year" playing on the satellite radio. She took a bite of cookie from the sample pieces she kept on the counter beside the register. A spicy burst of chipotle-spiked chocolate melted sweetly on her tongue. The texture of the cookie had just the right combination of chewy crispness. It was a new recipe. Her own creation. And pretty darn tasty, if she did say so herself.

A casual observer would assume Christine was filled with Christmas spirit. He would be wrong.

Despite the smile on her face, the delightful aroma in her shop, the upbeat song on her lips, and the flavor of the perfect cookie in her mouth, Christine's heart was breaking. Her parents were spending the holidays in Europe with her younger G.I. brother and his wife and kids. She hadn't been able to go, because she was baking the wedding cake for a Christmas Eve wedding. Her darling cat, Cocoa, which she'd had for fifteen years, had passed away three days before. And then there was the letter that had arrived that morning from the last-chance specialist confirming what many other physicians had told her over the years. In spite of all the marvels of modern fertility medicine, Christine would never, ever be able to have children of her own.

She was thirty-one, single, and childless, when what she wanted more than anything in the world was a baby in her arms. What seemed so easy for most people was for her the equivalent of scaling Mount Everest in December without a Sherpa. Futile. Hopeless. Impossible.

What man would ever want a woman who couldn't bear him children?

But life after her accident had taught her one important lesson. Attitude mattered. So she refused to have a pity party. She smiled, and she hummed, and she took pride in her bakery. She tried hard not to think too much about everything she was losing.

The buzzer in the back of the bakery went off. She limped toward the door separating the bakery storefront from the kitchen. The smells were richer in there, robust and warm. She grabbed industrial potholders, took banana-nut cupcakes from the oven, and put them on a cooling rack. They were the last batch of the day, so she turned off the oven and tracked over to the sink to wash her hands. She pulled a tube of lotion from her apron pocket and slathered it over her chapped skin.

The doorbell jingle-jangled.

Her smile had slipped while she was behind closed doors. She quickly pasted it back on and went out to greet her customers.

Four of her friends stood inside the store. Caitlyn Marsh, who owned the flower shop down the street, had her eight-year-old son, Danny, in tow. Emma Cheek, a Hollywood actress who'd moved to Twilight to marry her childhood sweetheart, veterinarian Sam Cheek. Emma had her five-month-old daughter, Lauren, balanced on one hip and her seven-year-old stepson, Charlie, by her side. Children's book author, Sarah Walker, held hands with her nine-year-old stepdaughter, Jazzy.

And there was Jenny Cantrell. She and her husband, Dean, ran The Merry Cherub Bed and Breakfast. Jenny was thirty-seven, six months pregnant with her first baby, and glowing. She had been through a myriad of fertility treatments before conceiving, and she'd been the one to urge Christine to see her specialist. Jenny had been lucky. Christine was not. She dreaded talking to Jenny, because she knew she would ask about the outcome of her doctor's visit.

"Hi, guys!" Christine chirped. *Dial it down a notch. Too perky and they'll get suspicious.*

"We came to cheer you up." Emma ran a hand over Lauren's fuzzy little head. She had bright, auburn hair just like her mother. For a moment, Christine feared they'd somehow learned about the contents of the letter. It was difficult holding onto a secret in Twilight. Then Emma said, "We heard about Cocoa. We're so sorry for your loss."

She struggled to hang onto her smile. "Cocoa was a great cat."

"When you're ready," Emma said gently, "Sam's got a couple of stray cats at the clinic that need a good home."

"Thanks." Christine knew that her friends meant well, but she just didn't want to talk about either Cocoa or her doctor's visit. "So." She rubbed her palms together. "What can I get for you?"

Jenny, Emma, Sarah, and Caitlyn glanced at each other. "You don't have to put on a happy face for us," Sarah ventured. "It's okay."

"What about you guys?" Christine asked the three oldest children, bending to their eye level, palms resting on her upper thighs. "Sugar cookies or gingerbread people?"

"Gingerbread!" Jazzy sang out, her blond curls bouncing. Last Christmas the little girl had been close to death. Thanks to Sarah's parents, who were both heart surgeons, this year Jazzy was the picture of health—rosy cheeks, bright eyes, a hearty appetite.

"Sugar cookie," Charlie said.

"Mom," Danny said, "can I get a cupcake instead of a cookie?"

Caitlyn nodded.

Avoiding her friends' eyes, Christine busied herself with filling their order. Along with the baked goods, she served milk to the children and coffee to the moms, decaf for Jenny.

"Come sit with us." Emma patted the empty spot across from her at the long table.

There weren't any other customers in the bakery at the moment, so Christine didn't have a handy excuse for not sitting down. Reluctantly, she poured a cup of chai tea for herself and joined her friends, Sarah on one side of her, Jenny on the other.

Sarah reached over and gently touched Christine's shoulder. She said nothing, just gave her a sympathetic smile. Out of all her friends, she and Sarah were the most alike, both of them shy and quiet by nature. But where Sarah was bookish, Christine was athletic. Or at least she used to be. The accident had changed the whole trajectory of her life.

If a car hadn't hit her the summer she turned sixteen, she would have gone to the Olympics. She'd have been a world-class sprinter. She would probably have gotten married by now. Had three or four kids. But there *had* been an accident. A bad one, and she'd been left with a permanent limp and a damaged womb.

She splayed a hand over her lower belly and clenched her teeth to hold back the tears.

Jazzy was chattering about landing the role of

Mary in the church pageant and pumping Emma for acting tips. Danny and Charlie were playing rock-paper-scissors and periodically punching each other on the arm. Lauren had cookie crumbs all over her mouth and a good bit stuck in her mother's hair. The baby's eyes met Christine, and she grinned like the sun coming out on a cloudy day.

Christine smiled back, feeling a wistful tugging at her core. Bashfully, Lauren hid her face against Emma's neck, her chubby little fingers still clutching the sugar cookie.

"What did Patsy finally decide on for the groom's cake?" Caitlyn asked.

Patsy Cross was a city councilwoman and owner of The Teal Peacock, an eclectic boutique just off the town square. At one time or another, Patsy had played mother hen to all of them. She didn't have any children of her own, and Christine felt a sudden kinship with the woman who was thirty years her senior. After years of misconnections, bad timing, heartaches, and missteps, Patsy was finally about to marry her high school sweetheart and the love of her life, Hondo Crouch, on Christmas Eve at the First Presbyterian Church of Twilight.

"She's still stuck between Italian cream and German chocolate." Christine folded a paper napkin into a restless square.

"Ooh, hard choice," Emma said. "Both of those recipes are freakin' awesome."

"These cookies are freaking awesome!" Jenny echoed, polishing off her third cookie. "What do you call them?"

"Fandangos."

"I want to order six dozen for the Merry Cherub. My guests will gobble them up."

"I don't have that many on hand. I can have them delivered tomorrow," Christine said, relieved that Jenny was talking about cookies and not doctor appointments.

But no sooner had that thought settled in her mind, than Jenny leaned over to whisper, "How'd it go with Dr. Krishnamari?"

Christine wished she had not gone to see Jenny's specialist. She'd had no real reason to see him. She wasn't dating anyone. But the last guy she'd dated had stopped calling when she'd finally worked up the courage to tell him that she could probably never have children. He wasn't the first to walk away when she'd dropped that bombshell. She'd just held out the smallest hope that maybe the right specialist could offer her encouragement, some miracle of modern medicine. Instead, her last little flicker of hope had been completely snuffed out.

Empathy filled Jenny's eyes. She understood what Christine was going through, but that didn't lessen her pain. Jenny's fertility issues had been resolved, but there would be no resolution for Christine. She would never rock her own baby in her arms. Never watch her son or daughter take those first steps or lose a first tooth or graduate from college. Disappointment tasted bitter as burnt coffee beans. She swallowed it back, forced a smile. She couldn't talk, couldn't make herself say the words.

But Jenny knew. She wrapped a hand around

Christine's wrist. "Don't give up hope. Never, ever stop believing. Dreams really can come true. One day you *will* have children of your own."

Really? How many platitudes could one woman use? Christine wanted to scream, to shout, to knock over a plate of cookies. Jenny meant well. She was a good person. Christine was the horrible one. Jealousy burned through her.

It was easy for Jenny to keep hope alive. *She* wasn't hopeless. She would be holding her baby before spring.

You're feeling sorry for yourself.

Yes, yes she was. Hadn't she suffered enough? Left with a permanent limp at sixteen. Forced to give up the one thing she'd loved more than anything else in the world. Running. God had hamstrung her mobility; now he'd taken her fertility as well. Sometimes life just wasn't fair.

Jenny's hand went to Christine's back, and she silently moved her palm over her shoulder blade in a circuitous, comforting motion. Except Christine wasn't comforted. Agitation set in. Clawing the air from her lungs.

"Christine?" Sarah asked. "Are you all right?"

"Fine." She pressed her lips together. *Shut up. Go. Leave me alone all of you.* "Would anyone like seconds?"

"I do! I do!" Jazzy exclaimed.

Christine smiled at the children, guilt smothering her jealousy. She got up and headed for the counter. Here she was wallowing in self-pity, when last year Jazzy had been on the verge of death. Plenty of people had it worse than she did, and normally Christine accepted her fate. But today, well, that damn letter had left her reeling.

Sarah laid a restraining hand on Jazzy's shoulder. "No more cookies. It will spoil your dinner, and I'm making your favorite."

"Chicken and dumplings, oh boy." Jazzy was up and twirling around like a ballerina, while Charlie and Danny broke out in a duel with imaginary light sabers.

"Luke, I'm your father." Charlie laid one palm over his mouth and made a noise like he was desperately sucking air through a respirator. "Come to the dark side."

"Never." Danny raised his arm to block Charlie's pantomimed assault.

Jazzy pirouetted between the boys.

"Da-da-duh-da." Charlie stomped in time to his own imitation of Darth Vader's theme song.

Danny made light saber noises.

Jazzy, who was spinning faster and faster, slammed into the table.

Coffee mugs jumped, and Christine's teacup leaped from the table. It hit the tile floor and shattered into a hundred little pieces.

Baby Lauren instantly burst into tears. Emma soothed her daughter. Sarah and Caitlyn got up to corral their children. Jenny went for the broom that Christine kept tucked in a corner closet, but Christine intercepted her.

"Don't worry, it's all right, I'll take care of it," Christine said.

"Are you sure?" Jenny's brow crinkled.

"I've got it. Really, everyone, it's okay."

Lauren sobbed her heart out. Emma collared Charlie and propelled him toward the door. "No more high jinks, Darth Vader."

"Aww, Mom."

"I'm so sorry for the mess," Caitlyn said. "Please let me help."

Christine held up a stop-sign palm. "No worries. Really."

"I didn't mean to break your pretty cup," Jazzy wailed, wringing her hands in distress.

"I know you didn't, sweetheart." Christine smiled at her, then squatted to sweep up the glass shards. "Just be careful not to get cut."

Sarah rested her hands on Jazzy's shoulders. "C'mon, Hurricane Jazzy, let's get you home."

"You are so lucky," Emma said to Christine from the doorway, trying to hold on to a squirming Charlie and maneuver the stroller out the door, while Lauren screamed at the top of her lungs. "I'd give my right hand for just five minutes of your peaceful life."

Christine knew that Emma was speaking out of frustration and hadn't meant to hurt her feelings by saying something so cruel. Emma's response had been knee-jerk, and she hadn't meant a word of it, but Christine was feeling sensitive.

She stood up, dustpan in hand, and stared Emma squarely in the eyes. "I'd give the last breath in my body for just one second of your busy, hectic life filled with little boy laughter and sweet baby kisses."

Emma looked embarrassed. She dropped her gaze, mumbled an apology, and herded her brood out onto the sidewalk. Caitlyn, Danny, Sarah, Jazzy, and Jenny quickly followed, waving their good-byes. Finally, the door snapped shut behind them all.

And when the last echoes of the tinkling doorbell faded, Christine was left all alone in the quiet of her empty bakery. She held the shards of the rosebud cup in a blue dustpan, realizing that no matter how hard she tried there would always be a gulf between her and her friends.

A gulf called motherhood.

A gulf she would never be able to cross.

Chapter Two

Cutting horse cowboy Eli Borden glanced at the slip of paper in his tanned, work-roughened hand. Yep. This was it. Twilight Bakery. The place his next-door neighbor, Parker County Deputy Sheriff Ila Brackeen, had gushed about. "Best cake you'll ever put in your mouth."

That's what Eli was looking for—the best birthday cake for the best daughter in the whole world, even if he did have to drive all the way over from Jubilee. Sierra was worth every second of the half-hour drive.

He got out of his work truck, a dual-axel, western-hauler Dodge Ram pickup, and stepped onto the sidewalk. The December air was crisp, but not too cold. Just right for the blue jean jacket he wore. The town square was decked to the halls with holiday themes. A nativity scene on the courthouse lawn sat side-by-side with Santa's workshop. The street lamps were wrapped in wreaths and ribbons. The scent of cinnamon, pine, apple cider, and gingerbread hugged the western-style buildings constructed in the late 1800s.

Through bakery windowpanes decorated with artificial snow, Eli could see a woman inside, hanging cookie ornaments from a small Christmas tree. Behind her, a festive fire burned in an old-fashioned potbelly stove. In that moment, all the oxygen left his body in one heavy whoosh. He stood transfixed, peering in at the cozy scene, the smell of Christmas all around him.

She bent over to loop a plastic chocolate chip cookie over a low branch, giving him an excellent view of the soft curve of her rounded rump. The sight was enough to cause a quick hard tightening below his belt. His body's instant reaction startled Eli.

He crumpled the slip of paper in his fist, bit down on the inside of his cheek, struggled to fight back his arousal. She straightened, thank God, but when she did so, she was standing directly underneath a stand of white twinkle lights. Between the fuzziness of the snow sprayed on the windowpane and sparkling lights, it appeared as if a halo shone above her head.

Angel.

She looked like an angel.

Then she turned, and her eyes met his. For a murmur of a moment it was pure magic. The gentle-faced woman with big blue eyes and an amazing backside framed in an angelic glow. Eli heard soft fingers plucking a melodious harp and cherubs' voices lifted in song. For one strange second he thought he'd died and gone to heaven. It took him a minute to realize a concert was starting on the courthouse steps. A harpist accompanied by the high, sweet chorus of schoolchildren singing *Love Came Down at Christmas.*

Damn spooky timing.

A shudder passed through him. Whoa. What was that about?

A smile lit the woman's full lips. All at once, Eli recognized her.

Christine Noble.

The girl he'd once kissed behind the high school gym two days before his family moved to Jubilee. He'd been a senior and she a sophomore. He'd been thinking about asking her out for weeks. They'd been flirting it up every time they saw each other. But he'd been busy finishing up school and bareback bronc riding. Christine spent every spare moment running track. He'd realized that if he didn't kiss her before he left town, he never would. She had tasted just as good as she looked.

Christine Noble.

Now she was a sweet blast from the past. He hadn't thought about her in years. His stomach lurched crazily and the hairs on his arms lifted.

She raised a hand.

Did she remember him? Or was she simply being friendly?

Only one way to find out, Borden. Get your ass inside. Jingle bells jangled against the door. Inside, Bing Crosby was singing, "Have Yourself a Merry Little Christmas." The bracing scent of yeast and chocolate, cinnamon and vanilla filled the quaint little bakery. Everywhere Eli glanced, he saw something delicious—breads, cakes, cookies, pies, and pastries. A smorgasbord of tasty treats. But nothing behind the counter looked as delicious as the woman standing in front of the Christmas tree, lights still glowing a halo over her head.

"Christine," he murmured.

Her eyes widened along with her smile.

Eli was aware of a high, humming sexual current flowing between them. She was not a great beauty by magazine-cover standards. Her mouth was just a bit too large for her friendly face, and she had a slight gap between her two front teeth. Her soft caramel brown hair was pulled back in a French braid. On some women the high style might look old-fashioned, a bit countrified, but Christine was elegant, ethereal. Her complexion was pale, and her cheeks were quite rosy, as if she'd been standing too near a hot fire.

She took a step toward him, and his heart skipped a beat. He felt oddly exhilarated, the way he did on the back of a cutting horse in action. No holds barred. Going for the gusto.

"Eli," she said in a light, uncomplicated voice. "Eli Borden."

"You remembered," he said, feeling stupidly pleased.

"Best kisser ever." Her lively eyes snapped. "How could I forget you?"

He felt suddenly tongue-tied. If it hadn't been for Sierra's birthday, he might have mumbled "good to see you" and rushed out.

His gaze tracked to her left hand. Bare. That didn't mean anything. She baked. Most likely she took her rings off to knead bread. Because look at her. Why wouldn't she be married? Slim. Sexy. Sweet. Yeah, she'd always been a little shy, but what guy didn't enjoy persuading a pretty woman?

"You still live in Jubilee?" she asked.

"Yep, yep." He nodded.

"I'm guessing you're into cutting horses like most everyone in Jubilee."

"I am. I have my own ranch. Well . . ." He doffed his Stetson, ran a hand through his hair. "Calling my place a ranch is a bit of a stretch. More like a small horse farm."

"Honest as ever, I see." She lowered lashes as long and dark as paintbrushes and sent him a coy glance. It wasn't his imagination. She seemed just as interested in him as he was in her. "So what can I do for you, Eli?"

"Um . . . I . . . um . . ." When was the last time he'd stammered? High school. Just before he'd kissed Christine.

"Did you want to order something sweet?" She raised a hand to brush away a fine sprig of hair that had sprung free from her braid. She wore a blue-and-white-checkered apron that matched the window curtains and put him in mind of an ivory-skinned milkmaid.

Eli fingered his Stetson. "Uh-huh. I want to order a cake for my daughter's fourteenth birthday this coming Saturday. My neighbor, Ila Brackeen, recommended the bakery, but I didn't know that you were the owner."

"It's all mine." She spread her arms. "And the bank's."

He couldn't help noticing how the gesture caused her breasts to lift underneath her white blouse. "How 'bout that. I didn't even know you knew how to bake."

"Turns out it was a natural skill I never knew I had."

"You've done well," he said.

"Thanks." She limped around the back of the counter and took an order sheet from the drawer.

The limp looked pretty bad. A permanent injury? Eli kept rotating his Stetson in his hands, fingers skating over the brim.

Christine cleared her throat. "What kind of cake did you have in mind for your daughter?"

"Um . . . she likes strawberry."

Christine smiled. "Strawberry is my favorite as well."

"Really? I never knew that."

"Why would you?" Her gaze was steady. Unflinching. Good point. He'd flirted with her in high school. Kissed her once. Had a few horny dreams about her, but that had been it.

She limped back to a bulletin board listing the day's specials, picked up a pen and returned to the register.

Why did it hurt his gut to watch her walk?

"Car accident," she said.

"What?" He blinked.

"You're staring at my leg. It was a car accident. Crushed my left femur. Took eleven surgeries to get me to the point where I could walk this well." She spoke matter-of-factly.

"But you . . ." Eli swallowed, thinking about her pain. "You never made it to the Olympics?"

She shook her head, her lips pressed tightly together.

"Christine." Her name rolled off his tongue, but in the silence of the quiet bakery it sounded too tender. Too intimate.

Dammit, he cared. He hadn't laid eyes on the woman in sixteen years, but he cared that she'd suffered. That she'd lost the most important thing in the world to her. Maybe it was because Sierra was almost the age Christine had been the last time he'd seen her. Maybe it was because his daughter loved to run just as much as Christine had. Except where Christine had been a sprinter, Sierra was a long-distance runner.

"So, strawberry cake. What kind of icing?" She clicked her pen, her expression unreadable.

Clearly, she didn't want to talk about it. Didn't want his sympathy. Okay. He got that. Been there. Hated it.

"I'll leave that up to you."

"What kind of decorations?"

"I dunno." He shrugged, clueless. "Nothing Christmasy. Her birthday gets lost in the Christmas shuffle."

"Does your wife have any instructions?"

"What?" He startled.

"About the cake. Does your wife want anything specific?"

Eli met her eyes. "I'm a widower."

"Oh." Her chin trembled a little but her gaze stayed unflappable. She wasn't going to offer him sympathy because she hadn't wanted his.

"Rachel died three years ago," he said, feeling the need to explain. "Eclampsia. After the birth of our twins."

"That must have been very difficult for you."

"It was."

A long silence stretched between them.

"Your daughter, what's her name?" Christine asked.

"Sierra."

"Tell me about Sierra. What is she like?"

"She's a tomboy. Helps me with the horses and the kids. She loves horses. She's my right hand. I don't know what I would have done without her after Rachel . . ." He trailed off.

Christine reached across the counter, laid a hand on his arm. Her skin was so soft, her touch so gentle. "No worries, Eli. I'll make this the best birthday cake ever. When do you need it?"

"Her birthday party is at five on Saturday, but I'm going to have a bit of trouble getting over here to pick it up. My oldest son, Deacon, is riding in his first official cutting event that morning in Fort Worth. Do you deliver?"

"Not usually." She winked. That wink hit him like a kick in the pants. "But I make exceptions for old friends. My part-time help comes in at twelve on Saturdays, I can bring the cake over after that. Will that be okay?"

"Perfect." Eli settled his hat on his head and gave her driving directions to his place. "Thank you, Christine. It was really good seeing you again."

"You too, Eli," she said brightly, but something in her voice told him it wasn't just pleasantry. She really meant it.

And so did he.

Eli Borden.

Christine smiled to herself as she closed up the bakery and walked the four blocks home. Every house she passed was decorated for Christmas—lights dangled from eaves, candy cane arches stretched over walkways, nativity dioramas sprawled across lawns, blow-up Santas waved from rooftops. A few gray clouds crawled overhead, and a lazy wind blew off Lake Twilight. Christine flipped up the collar of her light jacket and stuffed her hands into her pockets.

She hadn't thought of Eli in years, but since his appearance in her shop a few hours earlier, she'd been unable to think of anything else. He was single again.

He was taller than she'd remembered. His shoulders broader. Little laugh lines carved at the corners of his mouth when he smiled. But otherwise the same pulse-pounding reaction she'd always had when she was around him transported her back to tenth-grade algebra class, where she could stare out the window and watch him running sprints with the football team. She'd fallen in love with his loose, effortless stride. Now she became that fifteen-year-old all over again, crushing on a senior way out of her league.

So what? Don't start thinking stupid silly things. When he'd kissed her behind the gym on that fateful sunny afternoon in May, she'd been electrified. And, just as quickly, she'd been crushed when he told her he was moving away. He said he'd been aching to kiss her the entire school year—why had he waited and wasted so much time? But he'd offered her nothing beyond the kiss. Made no promises. She'd only been fifteen, after all, and serious about her running. He'd been seventeen and hankering for a rodeo career. Looks like neither of them had gotten what they'd wanted.

She'd tucked away the memory of that perfect kiss in her heart. If she was honest, she'd admit she'd gauged every other kiss she'd ever gotten against it, and no one had ever measured up. Then today he'd walked into her bakery, swaggering back into her life, and she was feeling all those complicated feelings again. Desire at cross-purposes with what she knew was best. Yet, she had to admit part of her had clung to a childish hope driven by *what-if* scenarios and Twilight's hometown myths of reunited high school sweethearts.

Christine arrived at her cottage, pushed open the wooden gate attached to the white picket fence surrounding her small lawn, and ambled up the cobblestone path.

The heaviness of her lame leg made a soft dragging sound against the brick. She adored the house. It had a decidedly English appearance and deep-down coziness. In the summer, the gardens bloomed with the plethora of plants she cultivated. For now the garden lay fallow, covered up by a display simulating Santa's workshop. Every year, she trotted out the decorations and set them up herself, just like everyone else in her neighborhood.

She unlocked her front door. There wasn't any real reason to lock up in Twilight, crime there being negligible, but it was the sensible thing to do, and Christine was a sensible woman.

Once inside, she caught herself listening for the *thump, thump* of Cocoa's footsteps scurrying to greet her, and then she remembered with a sinking heart that Cocoa was gone.

The house loomed empty without her beloved feline companion. Christine dropped her purse on the floor and with a sad shake of her head, shrugged out of her coat.

There was a message on her answering machine. To distract herself from thoughts of Cocoa, she went over and pressed the play button.

"Hi, honey, it's Mom. Just wanted to touch base with you. Today we're visiting the Black Forest, and your father bought me the most adorable cuckoo clock. We miss you and wish you could have come with us. James and Gretchen and the little ones said to tell you "hi" and that they miss you too. We're all so sorry you couldn't be here. I hate to think of you spending Christmas Day alone. Don't sit home and mourn your Cocoa. Go be with your friends. Bye, bye. We love you. And—"

The machine cut her mother off before she could go on. Christine loved hearing from her mom, but now she felt lonelier than ever. Christmas was still ten days away. So far, she'd managed not to think about how she would spend Christmas, other than attending Patsy and Hondo's wedding on Christmas Eve. Every one of her friends had invited her to spend the holiday with them, but she'd been reluctant to accept. She didn't want to feel like a fifth wheel at their intimate family celebrations.

Tea. That's what she needed. A nice cup of chamomile tea and lemon cookies.

She'd come to associate chamomile tea and lemon cookies with comfort after her accident. The high school principal, Marva Bullock, had brought her tea and lemon cookies when she was at the depths of despair.

"Just know that we're pulling for you, Christine," Marva had told her. "And that you're never alone. You have friends, and we love you."

Those lemon cookies had been so delicious, such a symbol of her friends' caring concern, that it had spurred her to start her own bakery. To her, baked goodies represented love—the giving and sharing of food, the breaking of bread, the crumbling of cookies. Ever since then, Christine kept lemon cookie dough in her freezer, and when she felt blue, she'd slice off a few chunks and bake them up. Soon the fresh, hopeful taste of lemon would lift her spirits.

But when she went into the kitchen and saw Cocoa's bed next to the hutch, her favorite toy mouse tucked in the corner, Christine almost burst into tears. She'd had Cocoa since her accident. The kitten had been a welcome-home present from her parents when she'd gotten out of the rehab hospital. Cocoa had been with her as long as her limp.

Christine's hand strayed to her belly as grief hit her hard. She allowed herself to cry for a few minutes, then she fell back on the bootstrap attitude that made her walk again after the doctors told her she might not.

She swiped at the tears, squared her shoulders. She had two choices. Allow sadness and loneliness to overwhelm her, or put one foot in front of the other and move on.

She'd loved Cocoa, but the cat was gone. Nothing she could do would bring her back. There was, however, a way to bring fresh joy into her life. She remembered what Emma Cheek had told her about the homeless strays at Sam's shelter.

Determined, Christine went back to the foyer, donned her coat and picked up her purse.

She had to see a vet about a cat.

As Christine was adopting a new cat, Eli was struggling to cook spaghetti with his three-year-old twins running about the kitchen playing cowboys and Indians. His son, Abel, wore an oversized cowboy hat that belonged to Eli's older son, Deacon, and a toy cap gun strapped to his waist. His daughter, Abbey, had a Native American headdress and a Pocahontas outfit that she'd worn as a Halloween costume.

Abbey was repeatedly patting her fingers against her mouth and making whooping noises as Abel hollered, "Pow! Pow! You're dead."

Eli grabbed two potholders and picked up the pot of boiling hot water loaded with al dente pasta, intent on carrying it to the colander waiting in the sink. Abbey, acting out her death scene, fell against the back of Eli's leg.

Reflex had his knee collapsing at the impact, and it took everything he had to hold onto both his balance and the pot. A few splashes of scalding water hit his hand. He dropped the pot into the sink and quickly stuck his burned hand under cold running water.

"Sierra," he hollered, "could you come in here and corral your brother and sister before they get hurt?"

A moment later, Sierra appeared in the doorway, arms folded, hands tucked under her armpits, looking thoroughly fourteen and disgruntled. "What? I'm not their mother. Why do I have to constantly be responsible for them?"

He met his daughter's eyes and said what he wished he didn't have to say. "I really need you right now. Could you please just take them in the living room and park them in front of the Wii?"

Sierra sighed, rolled her eyes, and held out her hands to her brother and sister. "C'mon Wyatt Earp and Pocahontas. Let's go."

"Thank you," Eli said. "I owe you."

"Yeah, yeah." She waved a dismissive hand over her head.

Guilt was a tiger, crouching on his shoulders, growling in his ear, *You're a bad father.*

He drained the spaghetti and mixed it with the meat sauce simmering on the stove. He turned off the heat and put garlic toast in the preheated oven and wiped his hand on a cup towel. His fingers still stung from the water burn.

Being a single parent was tough—hands down, the toughest thing he'd ever done in his life. There were so many landmines. So many things a guy could do wrong. So many mistakes. Family members helped out as much as they could, but they had their own lives, their own problems. His parents were retirement age and battling health issues. His dad had heart problems. His mom had beaten breast cancer. His older sister, Tilly, helped him the most, especially with Sierra, but she had her hands full with three active kids of her own.

His family had been telling him that it was time to move on, and he knew Sierra had shouldered far more than her share of the burden. But even as his friends and family played matchmaker, he'd never been able to muster much interest in the women they'd fixed him up with. Eli required a lot from a potential partner. Not only did he have to like her, so did his kids. So far, none of the candidates had gotten that far.

But today, all that changed.

For one thing, he'd seen Christine again after sixteen years, and the old feelings came galloping back. Unresolved feelings they'd never been able to fully explore. For another, his normally cheerful, accommodating teenage daughter had turned surly seemingly overnight. He was putting too much pressure on her, and it was unfair.

He thought again of Christine. Of that long ago kiss behind the high school gymnasium. His mind started spinning *what ifs.*

The next thing he knew, he was picking up the cell phone, dialing information for her number, and asking her out on a date.

Chapter Three

A date.

It was Tuesday night, and Christine had a date. Her first in a very long time. But more importantly, she had a date with Eli Borden.

The skip-hop energy of her schoolgirl crush kangarooed around inside her. Just when she'd been at her lowest point, things had started looking up. She had an adorable new cat to ease the pain of losing Cocoa, and she was already halfway in love with her. A scrawny orange tabby she named Butterscotch.

Butterscotch had assumed Cocoa's bed and toys with an air of haughty feline entitlement. Christine's spirits had already started to lift, when her phone had rung. She'd been watching *It's a Wonderful Life* for the four jillionth time, Butterscotch purring and pawing her thigh with bread-kneading motions.

She'd swiveled her head to peer at the caller ID and just about peed her pants when she saw *Eli*

Borden scroll across the readout screen. A shivery hotness poured over her. *Don't get excited. He's probably just calling about his daughter's birthday cake.*

But when she answered and he asked her out on a date, she was so surprised that he mistook her silence for a *no.*

"Don't feel obligated to say *yes,*" he said. "No pressure."

"Oh, no, no. I want to go. I'd love to go," she said, sounding too eager. Ack! Stop talking.

Now, she stood in front of the bedroom mirror, addressing herself with a critical eye.

"Blue jeans or slacks?" she asked Butterscotch, who watched from her perch atop Christine's bed, tail swishing. She held first the dress slacks to her waist, and then the blue jeans. "It's a country-and-western concert, but the venue is nice, and we're going out to dinner first."

Butterscotch meowed.

"You're right. I agree. Blue jeans for a Christmas concert is too casual. Slacks it is. Good taste. Your listening skills are on par with Cocoa's."

Christine donned the black slacks and a soft pink cashmere sweater that she took from the cedar chest at the end of her bed. She brushed her hair until it shone and dabbed on a little more makeup than usual. She chose a bright shade of red lipstick that she rarely wore, because she feared it looked too flashy. But tonight she felt emboldened. Eli had asked her out.

Knuckles rapped against her front door.

She rushed to slide her feet into flats. Because of

her injury, she could not comfortably walk in high-heeled shoes. She answered the door on his second knock, feeling breathless and eager, her heart pounding crazily against her chest.

Calm down. It's just one date.

But it wasn't just a date. It was her first date with Eli and she wanted it to go well.

His bracing male scent greeted her at the door along with his devastating smile. He smelled nice, like leather and forest pine and amber sandalwood. His rich fragrance wooed her senses, spun her head. In his hand, he held a clutch of orange and pink gerber daisies.

"You remembered." She pressed a palm against her chest, feeling the air in her lungs rise, fall, rise again. "That daisies are my favorite flowers."

His work-roughened fingers touched her wrist as he handed her the flowers. It was slight contact, but oh! Her nerve-endings responded as if it had been full-on, naked-body-to-naked-body contact. Tingling and burning. Aching and sizzling. More. More.

She was hyperaware of him, this tall, lanky man standing on her front porch. Had his jaw line always looked so strong? Had his eyes always been so brown?

He wore slacks and a sports coat, and she was glad she'd decided against the blue jeans. But he also had on a western-style shirt and cowboy boots.

"You look sensational," he said, his dark brown gaze turning murky as he took her in.

"So do you," she said, annoyed to discover she was both embarrassed and beguiled by his compliment.

An awkward moment passed between them. He cleared his throat, shifted his weight.

"Come in, come in."

Eli Borden was now inside her small house, filling her foyer with his manly musk and masculine body. She tracked into the kitchen, taking care to limp as little as possible. He followed her, his boot heels making a shuffling noise against her hardwood floor.

She found a vase to put the flowers in. She thought of other daisies she'd plucked from her mother's flower garden, when she'd played "he loves me, he loves me not" with the petals. Eli had always been the topic of the game. One day he'd come walking past her parents' house while she was out in the garden picking daisies, and he'd stopped to ask her what she was doing.

"Nothing," she'd lied, not about to confess that she was using daisies to forecast the power of his affection for her. She still remembered what he'd looked like standing there on her lawn, a straw cowboy hat cocked back on his head, a bead of sweat straying down his brow, his torso tanned and shirtless.

"Would you like a cup of tea?" she asked. "Or I could make coffee."

He glanced at his watch. "We have seven o'clock reservations at Twilight Cove."

"You don't have to take me somewhere that expensive," she protested. He was a single parent with four kids. He had to be on a budget.

"You let me worry about the expense," Eli said. "This is my treat."

"Really, an expensive dinner isn't necessary."

"I'm trying to court you, woman," he growled. "Work with me here."

His tone was gruff but his eyes were playful. He didn't want any arguments, but at heart he was an easygoing man.

"I can't tell you the last time I had a nice sit-down dinner alone with an intelligent adult for grown-up conversation. You wouldn't deny me that pleasure, would you?" he asked.

"Okay. You win."

"Good call." He took her elbow and guided her outside to the maroon Honda Odyssey parked at the curb.

Christine laughed. "You drive a minivan?"

"Don't make fun. I've got four kids."

But of course it was a mom car, and must have belonged to his late wife. There it was. This ghost between them. Inside the vehicle were kiddy car seats, Happy Meal toys and cracker crumbs on the floorboard. It smelled like family.

"I meant to clean the van," he said. "I'd planned on vacuuming it, but I promised Abbey and Abel I'd read *Curious George* to them before I left."

"Those are your twins?"

"Yes. They're three."

"Don't apologize. Kids ride in this van. Be proud. Think of all the poor people with no kids and spotless cars." *People like me.*

"Never thought of it that way," Eli said. "You make a good point."

At the restaurant, the hostess seated them near

a floor-to-ceiling plate glass window overlooking Lake Twilight. The town was beautiful in December. Buildings, docks, piers, and walkways trimmed with festive lights. Inside, the dining room was candlelit and elegant. White linen tablecloths. Fresh flowers. Poinsettias, amaryllis, chrysanthemums. Red and white and glorious.

"This *is* very nice," Christine said, smoothing out a linen napkin in her lap.

"Told you." He held her gaze, and she felt a smile creep across her face.

Her wrist still tingled from where his fingers had grazed her skin earlier. How was it that one look into his mesmerizing eyes melted her insides like butter, making her simultaneously both weak and strong?

"So," she said, "tell me about your kids."

"You're ready to jump into that with both feet?"

"If we're going to be dating, your children are part of the package. So yeah, let's jump right in."

"Don't you want to edge into this slowly? Dip in a toe at a time rather than just jumping off the diving board into the deep end?"

"I've never been afraid of deep water," she said, "but if you want to start slow, I can do that. What else would you like to discuss?"

"You. I want to know all about Christine Noble."

She waved a hand. "I'm dull. Think of something else."

"You're not dull."

"I am. All work and no play makes Christine a dull girl."

"Why don't you ever play?"

"I love what I do. Baking is my play."

"Okay, you don't want to talk about yourself. I get it. How about our favorite movies or books. Except it's been a long time since I saw a movie that wasn't made by Disney or read a book that didn't start with *once upon a time*." He snapped his fingers. "I know. Fantasy vacations."

"Hmm, fantasies. I like the sound of that."

He arched a sly eyebrow. "Me too."

She flicked out a tongue to moisten her lips. He never took his gaze from her face and he leaned forward as if he found her the most fascinating creature on the face of the earth. Heady stuff, his undivided attention.

"I have a better idea," she said. "How about I tell you what your favorite fantasy vacation is and then you can do me."

"I like the sound of that." He grinned, innuendo in his voice.

"That sounded bad, didn't it?"

"On the contrary, it sounds really good."

She lowered her lashes, unable to handle the heat in his eyes. "Okay, here goes. You spend your fantasy vacation in the forest. Verdant. Vegetation. Twigs snap beneath your hiking boots. The smell of loam pulls primal."

"Poetic. Am I with my kids or without?"

"This is a fantasy vacation."

"Definitely without. Let's park them with my sister, Tilly."

"Kids are parked with Aunt Tilly. They're safe and secure so you don't have to worry. You take off for your camping trip."

"I'm camping now?"

Christine nodded. "Rough camping. No R.V. or cabins for you. Somewhere ruggedly beautiful. Colorado. The Pacific Northwest. Maybe even Utah. You take long hikes in the wilderness and fish in clear mountain streams."

"Am I completely alone?" He lowered his voice. The candle on the center of the table flicked shadows over his face, making him look both dangerous and enigmatic. "Sounds lonesome."

"Not completely . . ." she dared.

"Who's with me?"

"A woman of your choosing."

"So." He reached across the table, rested his hand on top of hers. "You're with me."

"Me?" she squeaked, emotion tightening her throat.

"Yes, because this is your fantasy vacation too."

"We're on it together?"

"We are," he said, his eyes never straying from hers. "So maybe after a few days camping and fishing, we find a nice hotel with spa services. Where you can get a hot stone massage and they put rose petals and chocolates on your pillow at night."

"I'm liking this vacation a lot."

"I'm ready to book it."

"Unfortunately," Christine said. "It's all a fantasy."

"Does it have to be?" He looked so serious that

she inhaled audibly. What was going on between them? It was as if sixteen years had collapsed into sixteen minutes. A deep, wistful longing filled her. Could they have the fantasy?

You could get hurt so badly, Christine. Tread carefully. Watch each step.

When it came to men, she hadn't had a lot of heartbreak in her life because she'd never really allowed herself to get emotionally invested. Except for the man in front of her, and even then, their relationship had been based more on unfulfilled possibilities than any real foundation. One kiss did not a love affair make. But she wanted him. Oh yeah! A lot.

The waiter arrived to recite the daily special, take their drink orders, and leave a small complimentary appetizer. Mushroom caps stuffed with lump crab.

To deal with the out-of-control emotions simmering between them, Christine popped a mushroom cap in her mouth. The earthy taste of mushroom lingered on her tongue, the spongy soft texture tickled her palate, the rich bouquet of butter exploded in her mouth. Salty. Of the sea. Warm.

"Mmm, ooh, these are so delicious."

"You should see the look on your face." He chuckled.

"What?" she asked, bringing a hand to her mouth.

His sly grin was back. "Orgasmic."

She swallowed the crab-infused mushroom, forced herself to smile as if every inch of her body was not flushed with heat and sensation. Delicately, she dabbed at her mouth with her napkin, tried her best not to look overwhelmed, overpowered, over-stimulated. "Can we talk about your kids now? And I expect to see pictures."

Eli's sly grin turned proud and he pulled out his wallet. "This is Abbey. She's all girl. Loves Tinkerbell, tap shoes, grape soda, and wearing costumes. She hates bugs, bullfrogs, thunder, and for her foods to touch. Don't ever fix that child a sandwich, or she'll have a meltdown."

"Eli, she's adorable."

"This is her twin, Abel." He passed Christine a photograph of a round-faced little boy with a silly smile. "He's the clown. Always making us laugh. He loves knock-knock jokes, mud puddles, hot dogs, and he thinks the whoopie cushion is the funniest thing ever invented. He hates going to the doctor, getting his picture taken, and sitting still. It takes hours to get him to go to sleep, but once he's out, he'll sleep through a cyclone."

"What an interesting kid."

"This is Deacon. He's my quiet one. He plays guitar, wants to be a cutting-horse cowboy like his old man, and like most ten-year-old boys, he's a video-game fiend. He struggles in math but kicks butt at science and history. He's in that awkward phase where his face is growing faster than his body."

Christine looked at Deacon's picture. "He's going to be a very handsome man some day."

"And then there's Sierra. She's an amazing kid. She runs cross country, competes in cutting-horse events, and plays slow-pitch softball. My little tomboy. She can cook and clean better than some grown women. She's fiercely protective of her siblings. She's crazy for Mexican food, and I have to force her to eat breakfast." His voice changed tone. "She was the one who suffered the most when Rachel died. The twins never knew her, of course, and Deacon was only seven. He doesn't remember her much. But Sierra . . ." Eli shook his head. "Poor kid's been through so much."

Christine's heartstrings tugged for Sierra. "Anyone can see how much you love your kids. I can tell you're a great father. She'll be okay."

"I hope you're right." Eli slipped the photographs back into his wallet just as the waiter returned with their food order. "I worry about her most of all."

"You are very lucky, Eli," she said fiercely over a steaming plate of shrimp scampi.

"I know." His eyes met hers. "There's only one thing missing from my life."

"What's that," she asked, feeling her neck burn from the heat of his stare.

"A wife," he murmured so softly she wasn't sure she'd heard him.

CHAPTER FOUR

The Cowboy Christmas concert at the Brazos River Music Review located halfway between Twilight and Jubilee made for a pleasant end to an incredible meal. The venue was well known for bringing in topflight musical performances of the country-and-western ilk. Willie Nelson had performed there, as had Faith Hill, The Band Perry, the Tejas Brothers, and Brent Amaker.

The Brazos River Music Review was quickly gaining a reputation as the best country music scene in North Central Texas, giving Billy Bob's in Fort Worth a run for its money. Christine had never been there, but she'd heard that the facility had both an outdoor amphitheater for the summer months and an indoor auditorium for winter concerts.

The night air was brisk, but not frigid. The parking lot was packed, the fresh asphalt black and shiny in the moonlight. There were cowboys in Wranglers and Stetsons, cowgirls in fashionable pointy-toed boots and short denim skirts, older men in bolo ties and western shirts snapped tight against paunchy bellies, and older women in prairie skirts and crisp blouses accessorized with snakeskin and animal prints. Smells of cedar, beer, and nachos rolled through the night along with the scent of peppermint candy canes, spicy cologne, and floral perfume.

On the drive home, they compared notes on the musical acts. They reviewed which songs were their favorites and how fun it had been when The Texas New Notes came into the audience to pull folks up to dance and sing along with "Jingle Bell Rock."

Then, in unison, Eli and Christine sang "Jingle Bell Rock" all the way back to Twilight. By the time they reached her house, they were both laughing.

"That was fun," Christine said breathlessly as Eli pulled to a stop in her driveway.

"It was."

A sudden silence filled the minivan.

"Do you want to come in?" she ventured timidly, wanting him to say *yes,* while simultaneously afraid that indeed he would. "For a cup of coffee," she rushed to add.

"Sure," he said. "That sounds good."

They went inside, and Christine put coffee in the coffeemaker and turned it on. Pivoting, she glanced at Eli who stood with one shoulder propped against the wall, his hands in his pockets, his hungry eyes feasting on her.

As the scent of coffee filled the room, their gazes met.

"Chrissy," he murmured.

Chrissy.

No one had called her that since high school. Her

smile widened. She felt as if she'd been sucked into a time warp and she was fifteen again.

The sound his deep, masculine voice made in the confines of her little kitchen sent ribbons of pleasure uncoiling inside her.

She was overtaken by a supreme sense of ease. Being with Eli was at once both familiar and novel.

"C'mere." He drew her to him and she did not resist.

He lowered his head.

She raised her chin.

His mouth closed over hers. Startled by the intensity of the feelings running through her, Christine sucked in air and along with it, the tangy taste of Eli. She could feel her passion rising, escalating with each sultry flick of his tongue.

He cradled the back of her head in the palm of his hand and pulled her closer against him. His hands were so big. Had they always been this large? Or had hard work and adulthood lengthened and broadened them?

Her fingers fisted against his chest, the crispness of his starched shirt rustled. She tilted her head back, parted her lips, and opened herself up to him. He'd changed in one important way over the last sixteen years. He was even a better kisser now than he'd been at seventeen.

Her hands crept up, arms moving to encircle his neck. Heaven. His lips. She hung on, closed her eyes, savoring the connection, the sweet sensation of kissing him again. Yes! This was the way a woman longed to be kissed.

His taste spun her head, stirred her blood, and

aroused her long-buried sexual appetite. It was the most splendid kiss she'd ever received, and that included the one behind the gym. His kisses fired her system. Turned her inside out.

Turned her *on.*

"Oh, Eli." She sighed into his mouth.

He kissed like an astronaut exploring a new planet, with complete and total dedication. Letting no territory go uncharted, plumbing and searching, eager for every little discovery. The touch that made her knees buckle, the nibbled spot that made her lean into him and shudder, the tender strokes that made her moan for more.

Things were moving way too fast. She knew that, and yet she could not stop. She wanted him with fierceness she had not known she possessed.

"Eli," she said, eyes closed. "I want you."

He captured her face between his palms. "Chrissy, look at me."

Chrissy.

The nickname only he had ever used for her. Reluctantly, she forced her eyes open. As long as she kept her eyes closed it felt more like a sweet dream. If it was a dream, she had nothing more to fear than waking up. But if he was real, if this was real, she could get hurt in oh-so-many ways.

"Do you mean it?" he asked hoarsely.

Yes!

"I could be there with you. I want to go there with you." He peered into her eyes.

"It's too soon," she admitted.

"But we're working on something here. Right?"

She nodded silently; hope a torturous thing. Tenderness engulfed his face. "You are so beautiful."

"I'm not." She shook her head.

"You are to me."

"I limp."

"I don't care."

"There are other things about me that you should know."

"Not now," he said. "There's time. All the time in the world."

"Why does it feel so urgent?"

"Because it's right," he said huskily.

"How can this be happening? We haven't seen each other in sixteen years, but bam! It's as if not a day has passed since the first time you kissed me."

"We have a connection, you and I."

"Is it enough?" she whispered. "This isn't just about you and me."

He gave her another small kiss. "I know. Children complicate things."

"But in a good way."

He studied her. "You truly believe that?"

"More than anything."

"We do have to move slowly, because of my kids, but I definitely want to keep headed forward. What about you?"

"Yes," she said, her heart thumping madly. "Definitely."

He cupped her cheek with his palm and ran his thumb along her jaw. "You're something special, Christine Noble, you know that?"

"No more special than you."

They parted regretfully.

"I'll call you tomorrow," he said.

"We're taking it slow, remember? Day after tomorrow will do."

He smiled slightly. "I can't believe you've been here all along, just waiting for me to show up."

"So close and yet so far." She walked him to the door, then stood in the foyer watching him head to the car, knowing they were on the precipice of something big.

One thing was clear. Either they were going to have the love of a lifetime, or they were going to crash and burn as a couple and break each other's heart.

On Tuesday night after he left Christine's house, Eli tossed and turned and thought of nothing but her. The scent of her perfume—fresh as lemons, homey as vanilla, earthy as pecans—dominated his senses.

What was happening between them was spellbinding, but it was also a bit nuts. Chemistry. Sizzle. Whatever you wanted to call the attraction, it *was* happening too fast, and they'd been smart to back off. But even when Eli fell into a restless sleep, he dreamed of her. Hot, sexy dreams that had him calling out her name.

He woke with a start, his mind in two places. One part of him was resolved to keeping his distance, letting the fire die down so he could adequately assess his feelings. But another part of him wanted to jump in his truck, drive straight to her place, rip her clothes off and pepper her with kisses until they were blind with need.

"Daddy?" A sad little voice pulled his eyes open. Abbey stood in front of him looking forlorn.

Instantly, he sat up. "What is it, honey?"

"I tee-teed in my bed again."

He threw back the covers, got out of bed. "It's okay, honey. Don't worry. We'll get you cleaned up."

Eli picked her up, wet panties and all, and carried her into the bathroom. As much as he wanted to tear off Christine's clothes and ravish her, he would not. His children came first. He had to be sure of his footing with her, confident in their relationship, before he got his kids involved. That was going to take both time and patience.

He would wait. It was the only way this would work. Take their time. New Year's. He'd wait until after Christmas, and then he'd call to see if she had plans for New Year's Eve.

On Thursday evening, as Christine was closing up the bakery, she heard her name being called. A man's voice, familiar but ragged, as if he'd sprinted all the way to Jubilee from Twilight.

"Chrissy."

She turned to see Eli standing there. Her heart reeled. He looked like he hadn't slept since the last time she'd seen him. His hair was mussed, his shirt rumpled, his hands clutched in front of him, fingers interlaced, as if to keep himself from touching her. Shoppers bustled by, laden with packages. There was a chill in the air, and the sky was clouded gray.

"Eli? Are you all right? Is something wrong?"

"I miss you," he said.

"It's only been two days since we saw each other."

"I know. It's crazy. Illogical."

"It's not crazy," she murmured. "I feel it too."

"My kids." He motioned in the direction of Jubilee.

"I know. We discussed it. I'm content to take this relationship on your timetable. We won't rush into anything."

He looked relieved. Took a step closer. "I feel—"

"Out of control?" she finished for him, moving in his direction.

"I feel like I've been given something precious, and all I have to do is close my fingers around it, and it's mine, but I can't move my hand. I'm paralyzed with wanting. I'm not accustomed to this feeling."

Cars motored by on the street, but they could have been standing on an island, so focused were they on each other.

"I'm afraid to trust it," she admitted. She had to curl her hands into fists to keep from reaching out and touching him.

"Me too." He jammed his hands in his pockets, hunched his shoulders against the wind, but he did not drop her gaze. A horse-drawn carriage pulled up and deposited a family of laughing tourists.

"Would you like to take a ride?" He inclined his head toward the carriage.

She should have said *no,* but instead she nodded. "Okay."

All over town, the Christmas lights were starting to wink on. Eli climbed into the carriage and held out his hand to Christine. She put her foot on the step, and he hauled her inside. They sat on the same side of the carriage, and Eli drew the warm blanket up over them as the carriage driver clicked his tongue and the Clydesdale moved forward, his hooves clip-clopping over the cobblestones.

"I've been doing a lot of thinking," Eli said. "About Twilight's sweetheart legend."

"You mean the legend that says if you throw a penny into the fountain and wish for it, you'll be reunited with your high school sweetheart?"

"That would be the one." He slipped an arm around her shoulder and she snuggled against him. "Most people in town seem to believe it, and you've got to admit, it's pretty compelling."

"But we weren't high school sweethearts."

"We could have been. We should have been."

"We weren't."

"If I could go back in time," he said. "We would be."

"Got a DeLorean parked out back, do you?"

"*Back to the Future.* I get it. Funny. We don't need a DeLorean, Christine."

"Don't we? It's the only way I know of to rewind the past."

"We could start from right here, right now. We could get a penny, throw it into that fountain, make that wish."

"How can you be so sure?"

"Nothing's certain. If I've learned anything from Rachel's death, it's that nothing in life is certain." He leaned in closer, his breath warm on her cheek.

"You're going to kiss me again, aren't you?" Christine ducked her head.

"If you'll hold still long enough."

"You shouldn't kiss me. I don't want you to kiss me."

"Liar," he whispered. "You want it more than anything."

"You weren't this cocky in high school."

"Yes I was. You just forgot."

"I didn't forget one damn thing about you, Eli Borden."

"Ah," he said. "You had a crush on me."

She held up a thumb and forefinger half an inch apart. "Not that much."

"I had a crush on you, too."

A shiver ran up her spine. Why hadn't he told her?

"Technically, that makes us high school sweethearts, since you had a crush on me, and I had a crush on you."

"We never dated."

"Wasn't from lack of desire."

"So why didn't you ask me out?"

"You were just a sophomore."

"Oh, right. Couldn't tarnish your senior reputation by hanging out with a sophomore."

"What can I say? I was shallow back then. Peer pressure meant everything."

"And you expect me to believe you've changed?" she teased.

"I have." He dipped his head closer. "I just want to be with you."

There were a thousand reasons why she should

say *no*, but for the life of her, she couldn't think of a single one of them. "Eli," she whispered.

His mouth claimed hers, and Christine was a goner. They kissed under the blanket for the remainder of the carriage ride. When the driver pulled to a stop back in front of the bakery, they didn't stop.

The driver cleared his throat. Loudly. Twice.

"Okay," she said lazily. "You can come home with me."

"I knew my kisses would convince you." Eli grinned.

"Cocky man."

"Don't you know it," he said shamelessly.

"I'm so easy." She moaned. "Hurry before I reconsider and change my mind."

"Not easy," he murmured, his fingers toying with the top button of her blouse. "Sexy."

"Isn't that the same thing?" She did the button up again.

"Not at all." He unbuttoned the button again and pressed his lips to her heated skin at the pulsating spot in the center of her chest, just above her cleavage.

"Ride's over," the driver said pointedly. "That'll be thirty-five dollars."

Eli paid him. They climbed from the carriage. Holding hands and laughing all the way, they rushed to Christine's cottage as fast as their legs would carry them.

CHAPTER FIVE

Once Christine's front door closed behind them, they looked at each other. They did not say another word. Just melted into each other's arms.

It was as if they were caught up in something beyond them. Something magical. Fate. Destiny. Whatever word fit, they felt it.

In a fever-pitch daze, they stroked and touched, caressed and kissed.

Then abruptly, Eli broke away. His hot eyes bore into hers, and suddenly Christine felt impossibly shy. She ducked her head. Felt naked while fully clothed. "What is it? What's wrong?"

"Nothing, sweetheart. Nothing at all. I didn't mean to stare. It's just . . . you're so beautiful."

She cast him a sideways glance, her skin heating up. He sounded so sincere. Like he really did think she was beautiful.

"I have scars."

"Everyone does. Some on the inside, some on the

outside. But sooner or later, life knocks a chunk out of us all." He reached out to cup her chin in his palm and lift her face up to his. "You're even more beautiful because of the scars. You've suffered and survived. You're a true heroine."

It was hard for her to take compliments seriously. Compliments made her wary, but Eli appeared deadly earnest. He kissed her again. He tasted like cool peppermint and hot chocolate.

Tentatively, she traced her tongue along his bottom lip. She slipped her fingers through his thatch of thick hair. She wanted this. Oh yes! But she was scared. What if it all went awry?

Her thoughts were like a thousand-piece jigsaw puzzle thrown into the air. Making love with Eli would be like piecing that puzzle together in front of a warm fire on a cozy December night, making everything whole for a little while. But the fate of a puzzle was to be disassembled, swept into a box, broken back into pieces, and stored on the shelf.

He nibbled her bottom lip, gently rolling it between his teeth. She stepped back. Instantly, he released her.

They stood staring at each other.

"This is probably a bad idea," she said.

"Probably." He nodded.

"You live in Jubilee. My business is in Twilight."

"It's only thirty miles. Not exactly a long-distance relationship."

"That's the question, Eli. Is this a relationship? Or are we just having a good time?"

"Is it necessary to label it?"

She supposed not. "I don't know what I want."

"I do know what I want," he said and started unbuttoning her blouse. "You."

She did not stop him.

"But if you don't want me to go further, just say the word."

She did not say the word.

He made a noise of approval low in his throat, and then they were kissing again, Christine doing her best to ignore the turbulence sloshing around inside her.

His hand centered at the nape of her neck, holding her in place.

She opened her eyes, took a peek, saw that his eyes were wide open, too. His irises were the color of aged whiskey, rich and potent.

Her heart thumped in her throat. They were moving so quickly. Too quickly. This wasn't smart. Not a good idea. Yet here she was, doing it anyway and loving every minute of it.

She'd waited so long to have Eli in her bed. Now that the opportunity was here, how stupid would she be to turn her back on him? She didn't know where her boldness came from, but suddenly it was there. She took his hand and led him into her bedroom. It was warmer in there, friendly as a hearth fire on a cold winter morning. She kept the vents open wider in the bedroom, because she didn't like to be cold as she slept.

They kissed again in the shadows of the scented nightlight, which sent the aroma of coconuts through the room.

"It tastes like Hawaii in here."

"You've been to Hawaii?"

"With Rachel," he said. She wished she hadn't asked. "On our honeymoon. My parents paid for it. We couldn't afford the trip ourselves. We were only nineteen."

"How come you got married so young?" she asked, knowing she was breaking the mood, but powerless to stop herself from asking questions. How much did he mourn his wife? Was he too damaged to move forward? Was she hoping for too much?

"Rachel was pregnant with Sierra."

"She was the love of your life."

Eli's gaze was unflinching. He did not blink. Did not glance away. "She was the mother of my children."

"So." Christine gulped. "Not a passionate love match."

"We grew to love each other."

"You married her because it was the right thing to do."

"Yes, and I don't regret it, but with Rachel, I never felt—" he broke off and finally looked away.

Never felt what? She wanted so desperately to ask, but she did not. If he wanted to tell her, he would. Pushing would either make him resentful or make him lie.

Something rubbed up against the back of her leg, and Christine was so startled by the soft flick of fur that she had to bite back a squeal.

"What is it?" Eli asked, concern darkening his eyes.

"My new cat," she explained, feeling shaky. She

bent down and scooped up Butterscotch, deposited the cat outside the bedroom door, and shut it tight. When she turned back around, Eli looked poised for flight.

But instead of leaving, he moved across the room toward her, covering the few yards in one long-legged stride.

"Chrissy," he murmured in the darkness, and the next thing she knew, he was undressing her. When her dress was unbuttoned, he dipped his head and pressed kisses all over her chest.

She wriggled. Giggled.

"Ticklish?"

"A little." She squirmed.

"Ah, you need a firmer touch." The feather-light strokes of his tongue vanished, morphing into firm, demanding licks.

"Eli, Eli," she chanted.

She heard the crinkle of a foil wrapper, as his erection pressed hard against her. He was prepared. He'd come with protection. Not that he needed it with her.

His scent filled her head, claimed her world. His mouth was soft and warm. His tongue wicked. He laid her down on the bed. They were both sweetly naked. He pinned her with his gaze as his body entered hers.

Their joining was exquisite. He moved slowly, deliberately, taking his time, easing sweet moans of pleasure from her lips with leisurely strokes.

"More," she pleaded. "More."

But Eli was calling all the shots. Each time she tried to urge him to go faster, tried to spur him onward or push him more deeply inside her, he resisted. "Slow," he whispered. "Slow down. Enjoy every second of this."

"You like torturing me," she accused.

"Only in the best way possible, sweetheart."

"I can't take anymore."

"I want you as crazy, out-of-control for me as I am for you."

If that's the way he wanted it, then fine. She would let him have his way. Christine sank her head into the pillow and opened herself up to him fully, allowing her legs to drop open.

"Sweet Chrissy," he murmured. The entire time, he moved deliberately, excruciatingly slow.

She gave him full control. Trusting him. It felt demented, letting herself go. Releasing her fears. Trusting Eli. Trusting the sweethearts' legend. Trusting her own heart to not lead her astray.

Opening her eyes, she watched his face as she surrendered to him absolutely. As her climax swelled and rippled through her in surge after infinite surge, pure satisfaction and extreme gratitude flashed in his eyes.

"We're going together," he said. "You and me. Hang on, sweetheart."

She clung to him, rose and dove with him, strapped her legs around his waist and drove him into her. She wrapped her arms around him. Eli.

Christine gave herself to him in a way she'd never

given herself to another. She set aside her fears. Let him see into the depths of her soul. He'd imprinted himself in her heart sixteen years ago. This was a new chapter. A fresh start. She belonged to him now, and there was no turning back.

Eli slipped his arms around her waist. Ah! She felt so good pressed against him, firm breasts, sexy hips, taut belly, her head nestled against his shoulder. He held her close for a long time, neither of them moving.

He peered deeply into Christine's eyes, and something shifted inside him. The past melded with the present. He spied little flecks of green dancing in those enchanting blue eyes that sparkled and danced with the glow of twinkle lights. Her smile broadened, encompassing her entire face. Rounded cheeks, crinkles at the corners of her eyes. He loved how soft her skin was beneath his palms.

A train. He was on a runaway train. He needed to stomp the brakes, but dammit she felt so familiar and at the same time so novel. She was an intoxicating combination of everything he'd ever wanted and everything he'd left behind.

He traced a knuckle over her chin. She wasn't a dream. Not a figment of his imagination. He could touch her, smell her vanilla fragrance, hear her sweet breathing, and he wanted to taste her too. Here she was. In his life again.

And he wanted more.

Once upon a time, he'd kissed her. It had been a

great kiss, imprinted on his memory. But he'd left town, and they'd been too young. He hadn't tried to take things beyond that kiss. But now? Now, if he took that next step, it would be a leap of faith, to hope she was as involved in this as he was.

Finally, he dropped his arms, and she raised her head to meet his gaze. A rip of sadness tore through him. He saw identical sorrow, befuddlement, and concern in her eyes.

Then, in a mutual merging as natural and inevitable as sunlight sliding into dusk, they drew to each other once more. A certain embrace this time, all tentative second-guessing gone. Their bodies touched, pressed harder together, and surged, all chemistry and heat. Every inch of him ached for more contact. More Christine. More everything. He tightened his arms around her, buried his face in her sweet smelling hair. From now on, whenever he smelled vanilla, he would think, *Christine.*

Her cheek was pressed against his jaw, her breath a shivery warm caress. Her lips kissed the throb of pulse at his throat. Eli groaned, gathering her closer until not a millimeter of space existed between them. A barrage of dormant impulses slammed into him. Desperate need. It bothered him. This desperation. He was afraid to feel again, afraid to open up his heart, afraid of getting hurt. Or worse, somehow hurting his kids in the process. But the unrelenting fierceness burning through his bloodstream refused to let go.

Christine trembled in his arms, pushing closer

still, as if starved for his warmth. He made love to her all over again.

Eli," she whispered a few minutes later, as they lay breathing heavily, bathed in perspiration, the smell of sex and coconut.

"Yes?" He reached out and traced two fingers over the curve and dip of her waist and hip.

"We're in this deep, aren't we?"

"I am," he said staunchly.

"There's something I have to tell you. Something I should have told you before this happened."

Beside her, his body tensed, but he continued his gentle stroking. "What is it?"

She rolled on her side to face him, stacked her hands under her cheek. The nightlight cast just enough glow for her to make out his features in the darkness.

"You look so serious." He leaned over to kiss her nose.

"This is serious."

"I'm listening. You have my full attention."

Quietly, Christine told him her story, the full details of her accident, her recovery, the permanent limp. As she spoke, she relived it all—the squealing tires of the truck, the bone crunching impact, the blurred faces of strangers gathered around her as she lay bleeding on the ground, the intense pain shooting through her leg. And then later there were the surgeries, the excruciating rehab, and hour upon hour of learning how to walk again. She ended her tale with the kicker. The words that had never yet failed to send men scurrying away from her.

"My uterus was lacerated in the accident," she said. "Scar tissue built up over the years. I've seen a dozen specialists but they all say the same thing. I will never be able to have children. I will never be a mother. I am a lost cause."

She paused, watching his face and waiting for the inevitable rejection. Why, oh why had she made love to him before telling him her secret?

Instead, he shifted on the mattress, cupped her face between his palms, and stared deeply into her eyes. "I'm so sorry for what you had to go through."

"I only bring it up just so you know. I didn't want to spring any ugly surprises."

Eli kissed her again, but before they could settle into the warm embrace of their joined lips, his cell phone rang. "I gotta get that. Might be the kids."

She nodded, fully understanding. She felt strangely relieved and at the same time bereft of their kiss. He got up, fished around for his pants, finally found the phone.

"Hello?" He listened for a minute, head cocked. "Settle down. I'm headed home right now, Sierra."

Eli hung up and looked at Christine.

"Your daughter."

"Yes. I told her I'd be home by eight o'clock." He held up his wrist so she could see the face of his watch. It was ten p.m. "She called to tell me I'd broken my curfew. Fourteen going on forty, that one."

"She sounds like a wonderful girl."

He smiled. "She has her moments, but I really do have to go."

"I know. I'll see you on Saturday when I deliver Sierra's birthday cake."

He leaned down, kissed her forehead. "Until Saturday. I'll be thinking of you, and I can't wait for you to meet my kids."

"Me either," Christine said, pulling her knees to her chest and the covers along with them.

"I'll see myself out. You sleep well."

"You too."

It was only when she heard the front door click closed behind him that she realized he'd never commented on her secret.

CHAPTER SIX

At one-thirty on Saturday afternoon, five days before Christmas, Christine drove over the Brazos River Bridge that separated Hood County from Parker County, where Jubilee lay.

The strawberry birthday cake sat in the passenger seat beside her. Since Eli had said that Sierra was a tomboy who liked horses, she had made the cake in the shape of one. A prancing strawberry roan, to be precise, and she was quite proud of how well it had turned out. It was one of the most lifelike cakes she'd ever created.

Her GPS told her to drive another mile and take the next right. Christine slowed when she reached the exit. It was a one-lane country road.

One-lane country roads made her nervous. That's where her accident had occurred. She'd been out running at dusk, and just as she topped the hill—*wham*—the truck had come out of nowhere, slamming into her at full speed.

She gripped the steering wheel more tightly, and her left leg gave a twinge in memory. It had been fifteen years since the accident, but she would never forget being struck, tossed into the air, and flung over a barbed wire fence. Crushed pelvis, shattered leg, lacerated uterus. Her mother crying. Her father's tight face. Her little brother bringing his bedraggled teddy bear to the hospital and tucking it under her arm.

Christine's hand strayed to her lower belly. Because of that accident she would never carry a baby. That was lost to her forever. She needed to fully grieve that loss.

She glanced down for a split second, and when she lifted her gaze to the windshield once more, she saw the girl.

For one bizarre moment, she thought she'd gotten caught in some strange metaphysical time warp, and it was her long-ago self, running along the side of the road in a yellow-and-gray tracksuit, light brown ponytail swishing over her shoulders, Nikes pounding the asphalt. In this strange universe, she was both victim and perpetrator, as the girl suddenly darted across the road in front of her.

She reacted instantly.

Slammed on the breaks. Tires squealed, locked up. Her Ford Taurus shuddered to a halt. The beautiful prancing strawberry roan cake flew from the seat. The box flapped open, and the cake hit the dash with a mighty force, flinging red mush all over the car, and all over Christine.

Her body shot forward at the same time, but

the seatbelt yanked her back. The odor of burning rubber rolled through the car. Christine's stomach lurched, and bile rose in her throat. She slapped a trembling hand to her mouth and sat staring out across the hood of her car, smelling smoking tires and oozing butter cream.

The road in front of her lay empty. No runner. No girl. Nothing except for a terrible memory and a ruined birthday cake.

But the girl had been there. She'd seen her.

Christine blinked. Did you? Did you really see someone? Or did you see yourself as you were fifteen years ago?

It shook her. She couldn't deny it. Why was she having this vision now? Sure, she'd suffered her share of posttraumatic stress. Depression. Anxiety. Nightmares. But she'd been fine for years and years. The old scars had healed. The bad dreams had disappeared.

Why? Why was this happening?

Perhaps the culprit was the latest confirmation from Jenny's specialist that she could never have children. That had to be it. The genesis of her hallucination.

Okay. She'd pinpointed the source, but that didn't make it any less scary. It had been so real. She could have sworn there was a girl running along the side of the road. But if that were true, where had she gone?

The radio was still playing. Bruce Springsteen. "Merry Christmas, Baby."

A hunk of decimated strawberry roan slid off the glove compartment and joined the rest of the mess on the floorboard. What was she going to do? Call Eli and tell him she'd be late? But there was no time to drive back to Twilight and bake another cake. She'd let him down.

Bungled everything.

A car horn honked behind her, and she realized she was still blocking the middle of the road. She glanced in the rearview mirror. Eli's Honda Odyssey was behind her. How was she going to tell him that she'd ruined his daughter's birthday cake over a ghost girl who did not even exist?

Wondering if something had happened to Christine's car, Eli told Deacon to watch the twins, as he pushed his Stetson back on his forehead and got out of the van. He'd sent Sierra to the movies with a friend to get her out of the house while he decorated for her surprise party.

He sauntered up to her car, trying to think of a teasing quip, but he came up empty-handed. Pathetic. It had been so long since he'd flirted that he'd damn near forgotten how.

When he saw how pale Christine looked, the tight lines drawing her mouth, the shadows under her blue eyes, he was grateful that he had not made some silly joke. She appeared seriously upset.

He tapped on her window.

She rolled it down.

"What's wrong?"

"I . . ." Her bottom lip trembled. She swept her hand at her lap, covered in smashed cake. "I'm so sorry, Eli."

Alarm bells flared in his head. "What is it?" His voice came out rough as cornhusks. "What's happened?"

"Sierra's cake is destroyed."

He leaned down closer, saw the mutilated cake mess splayed over the seat, the dash, and floorboard. Relief washed over him that Christine was okay. "Is that all? Are you all right?"

"Her birthday is ruined, and it's all my fault."

"Accidents happen. It'll be all right."

"I let you down."

Eli shook his head. She was so hard on herself. "C'mon over to the house, and we'll get you cleaned up."

"You have guests arriving later, a party to get ready for. You don't have time to coddle me."

"I can't let you drive all the way back to Twilight covered in sticky cake goo. Besides." He tilted his hat back on his head. "I'd like it if you stayed for the party. We can pop your clothes in the wash."

Christine looked down at her clothes. "You've got a point, and I could make another cake while I'm there. Not one as fancy as what I did before, but I'd hate for Sierra to go without a cake."

"It's a deal," Eli said, pleased that she was staying. Yes, the original cake he'd ordered was ruined, but in the big scheme of things that didn't matter. "Make a list of all the ingredients you need, and what I don't have, I'll go borrow from my neighbor, Ila."

He patted the side of her car. "Follow me," he said, and then, whistling a happy tune, he ambled back to his truck, his mind vividly remembering the last time they'd been together. He couldn't wait to get her alone again.

Fifteen minutes later, Christine stepped out of Eli's shower. A knock sounded on the bathroom door. Christine jumped, tightening the oversized bath towel around her.

"Chrissy," Eli called.

"Uh-huh."

"I rooted around in the closet and found something for you to wear while your clothes are in the washing machine. I also assembled all the ingredients you wrote out for Sierra's cake on the kitchen counter."

"Thanks."

"Um, should I hand it to you?"

"Oh, yes, sure." She scurried over to open the door a crack.

His sexy tanned hand appeared, clutching a pink terry cloth bathrobe. That was it? Well, at least she had her underwear to put back on. Worried he might be able to see her reflection through the crack in the door, she snatched at the robe.

Seriously, Christine? Are you that much of a prude? The man has already seen you naked and then some.

It wasn't that she was a prude. Just modest. In fact, during college she'd gone through a mini wild phase, a backlash against her accident. At the time, she hadn't realized why she'd burned through a string of casual flings. In retrospect, she realized she'd been trying to prove that she was still sexy and desirable in spite of her scars. But somewhere along the way—maybe it was when she woke up in the bed of a man whose name she'd forgotten—her behavior wasn't empowering but making her feel lonely and empty, and she'd stopped seeking self-esteem through sex.

Her fingertips bumped against Eli's and she heard him exhale audibly at the same time she sucked in a big gulp of air. They'd touched, and she was naked underneath the towel. It was so sexy. Erotic in an innocent way. Kids were in the house.

Confused, elated, jealous, jumbled, joyous. Erratic emotions skip-jumped through her. She put on her bra and panties. Slipped into the robe and belted it at her waist. It smelled faintly of mothballs. Not a particularly elegant aroma, but at least it didn't smell of another woman. She put on her flats and stepped out into the hallway, feeling strangely exposed even though she was completely covered.

Shyly, she followed the sound of voices to the kitchen, where Eli and his three youngest children were putting up groceries. From the doorway, she cocked her head, admiring their relay system of shelving groceries.

Grocery sacks were in the middle of the floor. Eli's twins, Abel and Abbey, removed items from the sacks. Abel handed canned goods off to Deacon. Deacon then stacked the items in the pantry, while Abbey handed off refrigerator and freezer items to Eli, who was bending over at the crisper, affording Christine an eyeful of gorgeous cutting-horse cowboy butt.

Her cheeks blistered. She almost turned and scurried back to the safety of the bathroom, but Eli straightened, turned, and lifted his gaze to hers. An automatic grin lit his lips.

"Hey," he said.

"Hey." She stuffed her hands in the pockets of the bathrobe.

He stood transfixed, his eyes taking her in. Unnerved, she pulled up the collar around her neck. She wished she had never braked for the phantom runner and sent birthday cake flying about her Taurus.

"I cleaned out your car as best I could." He did not glance away. Did not even blink.

"Thanks. That was nice of you." Brilliant conversationalist. Got any more dazzling witticisms lurking in your brain?

"All done, Dad," Deacon called, breaking Eli from his trance.

"Good job, kids. Deacon, why don't you take your brother and sister into the game room and play Super Mario," Eli suggested.

"Wow, sure." Deacon grinned.

"I'm usually pretty strict about video-game time," Eli explained. "They have to earn the privilege. But since you're here—"

"The kids don't have to leave," she said in a rush. The thought of being alone in the room with Eli made her breathless and bothered. They hadn't talked since she'd spilled her big secret Thursday night, and she was feeling awkward around him. "I thought they might like to help bake Sierra's birthday cake."

"Yay!" said Abel and Abbey. They jumped up and down.

Deacon looped his fingers through his belt loops, took on a manly stance that was a miniature copy of Eli. "If they want to help make birthday cake, Dad, can I play Mario by myself?"

"Thirty minutes." Eli tapped the face of his watch. "No more."

"Yes, sir." Deacon scooted from the room.

"Cake!" the twins chimed in unison.

"Can you handle this?" Eli nodded at his offspring. "While I put up streamers for the party?"

"Oh, yes," Christine said, the thought of spending time with two lively three-year-olds tweaked her heart. "We'll be just fine."

Eli grinned and headed out of the room. "Holler if you need help. They can be a handful."

That's what Christine longed for most—to have her hands full of kids. She rummaged around in the kitchen and found everything she needed to remake Sierra's birthday cake. Since Eli didn't have ingredients to make a strawberry cake, she'd gone for the old standby, red velvet. Everyone loved red velvet, right?

The children hopped around her like exuberant grasshoppers. She fashioned aprons for them from cup towels and clothespins, then pulled kitchen chairs up to the counter for them to stand on.

Christine preheated the oven and then went to work. Abbey cracked eggs into a big blue Corningware bowl and grinned with pride. "Wow, Abs, that was an awesome job," Christine said, discreetly fishing out the bits of eggshell.

"I Abs," the little girl announced to her brother, wearing the nickname like a badge of honor.

"Ooh, Abel," Christine praised. "Good job." She'd assigned the little boy to buttering the cake pans and he'd managed to butter his cheeks too. He beamed up at her, and she realized these kids were hungry for maternal attention.

"Whatch you name?" Abel asked.

"Christine."

Abel gave his sister a happy smirk. "Christine say I do a good job."

"I do a good job, too!" Abbey protested.

"Yes, yes." Christine hugged first one and then the other. "You both did wonderful jobs. Now let's mix it all up and pour it in the pan and you each get to lick a beater."

They cheered that idea, and a few minutes later the twins were sitting in their chairs busily licking cake batter off the beaters. It was so touching how easily little children were won over. Smiles, praise, cake, a hug or two, and they were putty. Just as she popped the cake into the oven, Eli reappeared.

"How's it going?" he asked.

"Great."

Eli took one look at his children, faces covered in cake batter, and he burst out laughing. "They look happy," he said.

"So do you." It was true. The corners of his eyes crinkled, and he'd come into the room whistling,

"Always," by Bon Jovi. A popular song when they'd been in high school.

"I'm feeling good." Eli held her gaze too long. His eyes were warm, inviting. "You look good."

It was only then that she remembered she was wearing the bathrobe.

Deacon drifted back into the room, his nose twitching. "Something smells good."

"Cake!" declared the twins, as if the evidence wasn't smeared all over their faces.

Christine pulled in a deep breath. What a lovely family. She couldn't have dreamed up one any better. She wished they were her family, but that was a big leap from Eli's bed partner to his wife.

Wife? Aren't you getting ahead of yourself?

"You okay?" Eli asked.

She smiled brightly. "Yes, why?"

"For a second there, you looked sad."

"Just thinking about Sierra's cake," she lied.

"Done, Daddy," Abbey said and held out the mixer beater she'd licked clean of batter.

Her twin did the same.

Eli shook his head. "I can see baths are on the agenda before we get this party started."

"I'll help you," Christine volunteered. "While the cake bakes."

"I've got it," Eli said.

"I don't mind," she said earnestly. Honest, she wanted to bathe his kids. Dumb as that might sound to some. "It is my fault they're in a mess."

"Okay, sure." Eli smiled and reached for the hem of his daughter's shirt. "Hands up, Abigail."

"Abs," she told him.

He looked amused.

"I sort of gave her a nickname," Christine explained.

"Abs!" Abbey said and pointed at her chest.

"It seems to have stuck," Eli chuckled. "If you want to go ahead and run the bathwater, I'll get these monkeys stripped."

Five minutes later, she and Eli were kneeling side-by-side washing his naked children. The twins splashed and giggled. Eli reached over to grab soap for a washrag, and his shoulder brushed against Christine's. She just about came undone.

The soft grunt that sprang from his lips told her that she wasn't the only one affected by the contact.

"Rub-a-dub, three men in the tub," Christine sang, anything to keep her mind off the sizzling tingle shooting through her shoulder.

Abel caught onto the song immediately and joined in.

Christine's eyes met his, and in that moment they both stopped soaping up messy kids. "You have a wonderful family, Eli. You are so lucky."

"I know," he said, his voice husky.

A dinging noise sounded.

"What's that?" Abbey asked.

"The timer on the oven," Christine said.

Abbey's big brown eyes, the same color as her father's widened. "Why?"

"It tells me the cake is ready."

"Why?" Abbey raised a handful of bubbles,

squinted one eye closed and peered at Christine through the bubbles.

"So the cake doesn't burn."

"Why?"

"This could go on all day," Eli chuckled. "Go check the cake. I'll finish up with these two."

"Why!" Abbey hollered as Christine left the bathroom.

Still grinning, she opened the oven door. The red velvet cake was perfect. She extracted it from the pan, sat it on a cooling rack, and busied herself with making frosting. Chaotic thoughts played pinball in her head as she measured and mixed powdered sugar and cream cheese.

Eli.

Whenever she was around him, she felt all weak and noodly. Like pasta boiled too long in salty water. And she started thinking dangerous things—like the possibility of happily-ever-after. Like the sweetheart legend coming true for her.

She glanced at the clock. It was almost four. Eli's guests were expected at five. Her clothes. She had to change back into her clothes.

Where was the laundry room?

"I put your clothes in the dryer," Eli said, coming into the room carrying a clean toddler in each arm.

"Mind reader."

"Sorry, I forgot about them. I should have put them in sooner." His gaze strayed to the bathrobe that cut a low V at her cleavage. "Then again, there are some advantages to a forgetful mind."

Christine's cheeks flushed, and she quickly turned back to the frosting. Was this what a hot flash felt like? A storm of feelings, rushing and pushing against your skin?

Deacon came into the room. "Grill is ready to go, Dad."

"Thanks, Son."

Christine shook her head, amazed.

"What?" Eli asked.

"Your kids are perfect."

"You haven't met them all yet."

"Yeah," Deacon said. "Sierra's a real pill."

"Don't talk bad about your sister," Eli chided.

The back door flew open, and every head in the place swiveled to see who'd arrived. It was a teenage girl, wearing a gray-and-yellow tracksuit, with a long brown ponytail swishing behind her.

The same girl who'd darted in front of Christine's car. She hadn't been a figment of Christine's imagination. A vicious scowl marred her pretty features. She sank her hands on her hips, stalked across the floor, and planted herself right in front of Christine. "Just who the hell are *you*?"

Chapter Seven

"Sierra Colleen," Eli scolded his eldest, ashamed of the way she was treating Christine. "Apologize to our guest."

"She's not *my* guest."

He clamped a firm hand around Sierra's wrist. He hated to scold her. She'd been through so much. Losing her mother had affected Sierra far more than it had the younger children. Still, he wasn't going to tolerate rude behavior.

"This is Christine Noble," he said. "She's a friend of mine from high school."

"She's wearing Mama's robe. Why is she wearing my mama's robe?" Sierra's voice bordered on hysteria, and Eli saw the situation from his daughter's point of view.

Christine looked stricken. Her hands flew to cover her mouth.

Eli shook his head. Sent her a silent message with his eyes. *This is not your fault.*

"Is that your car out front?" Sierra demanded. Without waiting for a reply, she jerked from his grip and launched into another barrage of agitated speech. "She almost ran over me, Daddy. Did she tell you that she almost ran over me?"

Daddy.

Whenever she called him Daddy, he unraveled. It was like she was Abbey's age again and looking at him as if he was the sun and the moon and the stars all rolled into one. Usually, she called him Dad. Lately, once in awhile, she even called him Eli. Testing. Seeing what she could get away with. Mostly, he picked his battles. Let it go. Raising four kids alone wasn't easy, and he relied on her.

"She darted in front—" Christine pressed her lips together. "No. It wasn't her fault. I didn't have my eye on the road."

"Damn straight it wasn't my fault," Sierra glowered.

Eli understood what had happened. Sierra loved running along the roadside, but she could be impulsive like any fourteen-year-old. She'd darted in front of Christine's car, and Christine had slammed on the brakes. That was how the birthday cake had ended up in Christine's lap. His daughter's recklessness scared him.

"Tell her to take off my mother's robe!" Sierra stood foolish and proud. Trembling with anger and indignation. Christine stayed quiet. He could tell by the studied expression on her face that she was weighing the situation, trying to find the right words.

"We were just about to frost your birthday cake," she said calmly. "Would you like to join us?"

Sierra's gaze flickered to the red velvet cake, to her brothers and sister, then back to Eli. He saw his daughter's body tense, knew she was revved up. There was no soothing her when she got caught in the onslaught of teenage emotion. He thought about how this must look to her, Dad's girlfriend in her mother's bathrobe, making a birthday cake with her younger brothers and sister. Taking her place. Usurping her role.

Dad's girlfriend?

Even as the thought settled into his brain, Eli knew it was true. He wanted Christine to be his girlfriend. He'd wanted it sixteen years ago, but circumstance and their young age had intervened. Now, the main obstacle was standing right in front of them. How could a good father place his own wants and needs above his child?

"Hell no, I do not want to ice a cake with you," Sierra snorted, nostrils flaring and arms folded over her chest. "This is the shittiest birthday ever."

"Sierra!" Eli said sternly. "You apologize to Christine right now for your language and disrespect."

"Eli," Christine's voice cut through him. "It's all right. I'm sure my clothes are dry now. I'll go change, frost the cake, and head home."

"No," Eli said. "I want you to stay."

Sierra's chin jerked up, and unshed tears shimmered in her eyes. "It's my birthday, and I don't want her here, and I don't want her stupid cake." She turned and stormed from the room.

He realized then that this was more than just teenage drama. Something else was bothering Sierra. For one thing, she was supposed to have been at the movies with her friend when she'd been running alongside the road. Why had she not been at the movies? He'd get to the bottom of this, but he didn't want to leave Christine hanging.

Christine's gentle smile told him that she understood completely. "It's all right, Eli. Go to her."

"But—"

"She needs you."

He hesitated.

"Go on."

"Thanks," he said. "For understanding. Can I call you later?"

"I don't know if that's such a good idea." She nodded in the direction Sierra had disappeared.

"Please, don't write us off. Not yet."

"We moved too fast," she said. "We knew it was a mistake, but we did it anyway. We allowed ourselves to get caught up in our emotions, but this isn't a fantasy, Eli. It's the real world. You have children and they matter. The decisions you make affect them. We had a good time. We got closure on that long-ago kiss. It's enough. It has to be. For the sake of your daughter."

Even though it ripped his heart right out of his chest, Eli knew she was right. This thing between them was too powerful. It burned too hot. If they weren't careful, too many people could get hurt. Better to stop their affair now, when a minimal amount of damage had been done.

Why, then, did watching her walk away hurt so damned much?

"I screwed up," Christine mumbled to Butterscotch as she got down a can of Fancy Feast. "I listened to my heart and not my head. But I can't be in love with him. How could I be in love with him? We barely know each other. Yes, we knew each other in high school, but that was a long time ago. We're both different people now."

Butterscotch meowed and butted the calf of Christine's bad leg with her furry head. She dumped the cat food in a bowl, and Butterscotch pounced on it as if she hadn't eaten in a week.

Christine washed her hands, and then she preheated the oven. "Yes, it hurts, but it will go away. Sure, his kids are adorable, and Sierra's just upset because she perceived I was taking over her mother's role. I understand completely."

She took a roll of lemon cookie dough from the refrigerator, sliced off half a dozen cookies. "You know, it's really a good thing that we broke up. I've been distracted all week because of Eli Borden, and I only have five days to get Patsy and Hondo's cake made. That should be my focus. Baking is the one thing that saved me when everything else was falling apart."

The timer dinged, letting her know the oven had preheated to the correct temperature, and she slid the cookies in. She put water on for chamomile tea. "And yes, it was dumb of me to start fantasizing about spending Christmas with Eli and his kids. Totally stupid. It'll be me and you this year, Kitty, but that's fine. We don't need anyone else, do we?"

Butterscotch purred happily.

"That infertility thing probably scared him off, too. I mean, I know I'm officially the one who broke up with him, but he never called me after I told him. Although, to be fair, it was only two days. Still, I'm sure it gave him pause."

Christine pulled a palm down her face. "So here's the deal. We're not going to mope. We're going to smile and go back to work, and eventually we'll forget all about Eli. We're going to drink chamomile tea and eat lemon cookies and remember what Marva taught me. That we're never really alone. We have friends, and they love us."

She sat down on the floor, and Butterscotch crawled in her lap. She sat there scratching her soft fur, salty tears streaming down her face. She cried until she could not cry anymore. When the smoke detector went off because she'd burned the lemon cookies, Christine got up, turned off the oven, threw out the cookies, and started over.

Eli talked to Sierra, but he couldn't get to the bottom of what was making her so moody lately, nor would she tell him why she hadn't gone to the movies with her friends as she was supposed to do. So he persuaded his sister, Tilly, to come talk to her.

Tilly came out of Sierra's bedroom as the party guests were starting to arrive and crooked her finger at Eli to come over for a private conversation.

"What's wrong with her?" he asked.

"Here's the deal, baby brother, your daughter started her period while she was at the movies, and she's too embarrassed to tell you. That's why she left. That's why she was running. That's why she hid out. That's why she's been extra moody."

Eli slapped a palm to the nape of his neck. "She needs a mother."

"I'll do everything I can for her. I've already given her some of my feminine products, and I'll take her to the store later."

"Man, isn't she too young for this stuff?"

"Nope. In fact, she's a little later than average."

"I thought they taught girls this stuff at school."

"Not like you'd think. But Sierra's smart. She googled it. But she just needs a woman to talk to."

"Thanks," he said. "I appreciate your help."

"She'll be out in a little while for the party. She just needs some time to adjust to the changes in her life."

"Don't we all?" Eli mumbled.

Tilly helped him with the party, and he made idle chitchat with the guests, but his thoughts were firmly centered on Christine. How many women would have baked a second cake for his daughter? How many would have helped him bathe his kids? How many would put up with sassy lip from his teenage daughter with the same level of kindness and understanding that Christine had shown?

He thought about how she couldn't have children of her own, and a knot of sadness gripped him. He'd handled everything wrong. He'd blown his chances with her by moving too fast, and it was a grand loss because she made his blood pump harder than it had pumped in years. She reminded him of the seventeen-year-old he'd left behind. She possessed a deep, centered calmness that quieted his anxiety. When he was around her, he worried less. With Christine, he had an abiding feeling that no matter what happened, everything would be okay.

It was a powerful combo. Pretty woman who made his pulse race. A woman who met his emotional needs, as he met hers in return. A woman who liked his kids and they liked her back. Except for Sierra. That was the sticking point.

It was scary. Opening his heart up again. Risking rejection.

But he'd moved too fast before. He hadn't stopped to consider the ramifications of his actions. He had a lot to think about. Mostly, how he was going to convince Sierra to give Christine a fighting chance.

Christmas Eve. It took every ounce of courage that Christine possessed to go to Patsy's wedding. While all her friends were living their dreams of being reunited with their high school sweethearts, she was miserable because her happily-ever-after had slipped through her fingers. But once she was there, she had to admit it was one of the most beautiful weddings she'd ever attended, and the wedding cake she'd made was the star of the reception.

Patsy looked luminous in the white gown, studded with lace and pearls. Shaking her hand in the receiving line, a lump rose in Christine's throat. "You look like a fairy princess."

"A damn old fairy princess," Patsy chuckled.

"You've waited a long time for your happy wedding."

"Forty-three years. I can still hardly believe it." Patsy clasped Christine's hands in hers. "Don't give up hope. Never, ever stop believing. Dreams really can come true."

Funny. It was the exact same thing Jenny had said to her on the same day she got that awful letter, ending all her hopes and dreams.

Not *all* her hopes and dreams. She was the one who'd broken things off with Eli.

But she'd done it for a reason. The well-being of his children was more important than her desires. Those kids deserved to be happy, and if she couldn't be the one to mother them, she didn't want Eli holding on to her. He needed to rebuild his family. Too bad she couldn't be the one to help him do it.

Once the music started and couples edged out onto the dance floor, Christine decided to go home. She couldn't dance, and everyone was paired off. She felt lonelier here than she would at home, alone with Butterscotch watching *It's a Wonderful Life*.

Telling her friends she was going to the bathroom, she instead headed for the exit. Just as she started down the church steps, Eli was coming up them.

She stopped. Was he here to see her?

"Chrissy," he said. "Were you just leaving?"

His brown-eyed gaze ate her up, and she was having trouble breathing. "Yes," she whispered.

"Can we talk?"

She shivered in the cold and glanced over her shoulder. "We could talk in the vestibule."

He reached out to take her hand, and she didn't resist. That was the problem. She'd never been able to resist him. That's how she'd gotten in this mess in the first place.

Once they were secreted away from prying eyes, Eli took her other hand. He held them both. Squeezed tightly. "I need you, Christine," Eli murmured. "I made a mistake when I let you walk away. I told myself it was best for Sierra. That I didn't want to risk hurting her. But the truth was that I used her as an excuse to protect myself, because *I* was terrified of getting hurt. Losing Rachel was tough enough, but you made me feel things again. Things I'd never felt before. Strong, scary things. You resurrected my heart and hopes, and, along with it, my fears."

Christine stopped breathing. It startled her to hear him admit it. His dark brown eyes searched her face, beseeching her to give him another chance. She could not turn away.

"I've loved you since I was seventeen," he continued. "I didn't have the courage to admit it then, but I'm admitting it now. I know it's too soon. I don't care. It's the way that I feel, and I know that it's right. We'll work it out with Sierra. She's just at a tough age. Eventually, she'll come around."

"Eli." She finally took a breath.

"I know it's asking a lot for you to love me back. We're just barely getting reacquainted after sixteen years, but I feel something powerful, and I know you feel it too."

Joy washed over her, but it was so intense, she had to close her eyes to absorb the meaning. Her fingers curled around his hands, and she clung to him like a shipwreck survivor on a raft.

"You don't have to love me back." His deep voice rumbled through her ears. "But I had to tell you how I felt. If you give me a chance, I'd like to spend the rest of my life making you happy."

Eyes still closed, she listened to what he was saying. Listened with all her might. Heard his words echo through her ears again and again. *I love you. I want you.*

"I know I've got a lot of baggage. Four of them to be precise."

Christine's eyes flew open. "Those kids are certainly not baggage. They are precious each and every one."

"Including Sierra?"

"Especially Sierra. She needs me most."

He shook his head. "That's one of the things I love most about you, Chrissy. You have such an understanding heart." He tightened his arms around her. "And the way you love so easily and completely."

Emotions tangled up inside of her like unwound yarn. Concern, hope, trepidation, amusement, happiness, but the sweet, delicious warmth shimmering through her was much more than that. Her entire body vibrated with a hot strumming light burning bright as the star atop her Christmas tree.

"I love you, too, Eli Borden," she whispered. "I've

loved you since I was fifteen years old. And there's nothing more I'd want on the face of this earth than to be mother to your darling children."

"Are you asking me to marry you?" he chuckled.

"Not at all," she said. "We really do need to take things slow this time. I just want you to know I'm in for the long haul."

"So am I, Chrissy. So am I."

Then he took her in his arms and kissed her for a long, long time.

Epilogue

Christine spent Christmas Day with Eli and his children. As she watched them open their gifts, she couldn't help wishing she could slow-motion her life so she could extend this moment of utter joy. The twins were bouncing from Christine to Eli, showing them what Santa had brought. Deacon was chattering a mile a minute about all the cool video games he'd gotten.

Even Sierra had apologized for her behavior and was actually sitting next to Christine on the couch. When she opened the running shoes Christine had gotten her on a late Christmas Eve dash to the stores, Sierra sent her a sideways glance. "I heard you used to be a sprinter. You almost went to the Olympics."

"I did," Christine said.

"Do you think you could help me with my cross-country training?"

"I'd be honored." Christine smiled.

They cooked Christmas dinner as a family. Everyone helping out. Abbey and Abel set the table. Deacon made the bread. Sierra tossed the salad. Eli fried and carved the turkey, and Christine made everything else.

As they sat at the table, holding hands and giving thanks for their meal, it occurred to Christine that she had indeed gotten everything she ever wanted. A job that not only enriched her but helped her spread joy to others, children to love, and the man of her dreams.

She smiled, thanked God, and was darn glad that once upon a time, she'd had the foresight to fling a penny into Sweetheart Fountain and make a heartfelt wish for true and lasting happiness.

GRACE

Chapter One

The perfect Christmas starts with the perfect tree . . .

Flynn MacGregor Calloway put a palm to her aching back, wrapped her other arm around her pregnant belly, canted her head, and studied the spindly-branched, lopsided Scotch pine. After much wrestling and a few choice words, she'd managed to get it set up in a corner of the living room in the cottage she shared with her husband, Jesse.

She'd wanted to surprise him, so she'd waited until after the morning wedding of Jesse's father, Sheriff Hondo Crouch, and his bride, Patsy Cross, before she'd slipped down to the Christmas tree lot and using Jesse's pickup truck drove the tree home. Jesse had volunteered to drive the newlyweds to DFW airport to catch a plane bound for a Hawaii honeymoon and had taken their sedan because four people and luggage fit in it better. That gave Flynn plenty of time to get the job done.

The glow from the icicle lights dangling on the eaves outside slanted through the window and shone through some of the more meager limbs.

Okay, so it wasn't quite a Charlie Brown tree, but it was close and clearly not what Maven Styles, the author of *How to Host the Perfect Christmas,* had in mind when she declared that an impeccable holiday began with the perfect tree.

Then again, Maven Styles probably wasn't on a newlywed student's tight budget that required her to wait for Christmas Eve when they marked down the trees. Flynn had picked this one up for five dollars and she was proud of her bargain. Maybe not proud, but it was a real tree, not artificial, and seven feet tall. She should get points for that, right? All it needed was a few decorations to spiff it up.

She couldn't regret cutting corners. The baby had been a surprise, a very welcome surprise to be sure, but their finances had taken an added hit because of it. Between scraping together money for her college tuition, the cost of rebuilding Jesse's motorcycle shop after the fire, exorbitant health insurance for the self-employed, and getting ready for the baby's arrival, they hadn't much money left to spend on holiday celebrations. Their situation was a temporary setback, she knew that, but part of her couldn't help feeling wistful that their last Christmas with just the two of them was going to be as sparse as that scraggly Scotch pine.

Stop feeling sorry for yourself, she scolded. *Plenty of people have it much worse.*

By tightly pinching pennies all year and keeping an eagle eye out for sales, she'd managed to save just enough to buy Jesse a new leather jacket to replace the one he'd worn since high school. She couldn't wait to give it to him on Christmas morning. For now, it was wrapped and stowed in the trunk of their car. He'd had so little growing up that she ached to give him everything his heart desired. Which was why she'd checked *How to Host the Perfect Christmas* out of the library, hoping she could pick up a few pointers.

A cardboard box filled with decorations from her childhood sat on the floor. Flynn peeled back the tape and opened the flaps. Her mother had had the habit of either buying or making one special ornament to commemorate each Christmas.

As she removed them from the box, each decoration stirred a memory—the candy canes made out of bread dough and shellacked (crumbling a bit now with age) that she and her younger sister, Carrie, had helped their mother bake in 1992. The twin wooden toy soldiers her mother's best friend, Marva Bullock, had given her after the twins, Noah and Joel, were born; and the last ornament her mother had ever purchased, a delicate red glass ball inset with a tiny nativity scene.

Air stilled in her lungs. Although her family hadn't known it at the time, the red glass ball represented the last perfect Christmas before her mother had been diagnosed with amyotrophic lateral sclerosis.

Tears misted her eyes. *Oh, Mama. You'll never know your grandchildren.* With a knuckle, she wiped away the tears. Should she put the ornament on the tree? It would stir painful memories every time she looked at it. And yet the ornament was a shining reminder of that one perfect Christmas when her family was last together and whole.

Flynn nibbled her bottom lip. What would Maven Styles recommend? Hmm.

The light caught the red glass, glittered prettily, highlighting the sweet scene of Mary gazing upon the baby Jesus with rapt eyes. Beautiful. It was so beautiful and, honestly, too precious to risk. Gently, she nestled the ornament back in its packaging.

For the next half hour, she strung lights, hung ornaments, and draped garlands, filling in the branches, transforming the tree from leftover to magnificent. Jesse was going to be so surprised.

After she finished, she stepped back to look over her handiwork. Ah, much better. Except for a glaring bare spot near the top of the tree. One more ornament should take care of that. She peered into the box.

Only the red glass ball remained.

She pursed her lips, glanced from the box to the empty branch and back again. The bare spot bothered her sense of symmetry and, honestly, since she was trying to make her own perfect Christmas, shouldn't her mother's last ornament have a place on her tree? Life was bittersweet, after all. The good and the bad mixed in a complicated mosaic of joy and pain.

Carefully, she climbed up onto the stepladder and stretched long in order to reach the unadorned limb.

Just then, the front door swung open and Jesse walked in.

One look at her handsome husband and Flynn's heart reeled. Whenever they'd been separated, even for a few hours, it was like this. He took her breath away, time and again.

How she loved this man!

He'd lost a few pounds over the last few months, working two jobs to make ends meet, and his hair was a bit too long since, to save money, he'd gone from getting it cut every six weeks to every two months. The cold and wind had reddened his cheeks and the tops of his ears. For the life of her, she couldn't coax him into wearing a ski hat or gloves, but he had the collar of his old leather jacket pulled up tight against his neck.

Jesse halted in his tracks, his festive smile dying on his lips and two furrows digging between his eyebrows. "What *are* you doing?"

"Surprise!" She gestured from the stepladder like Vanna White revealing letters on *The Wheel of Fortune*. "The tree only cost five dollars and—"

His frown deepened. "You're nine months pregnant putting up a tree and climbing up on a stepladder while you're here all alone. What on earth were you thinking?"

Her smile bobbled and her stomach sank. "That I'd surprise you."

"I don't need these kind of surprises."

"I'm fine," she whispered. "It's fine."

"You could have fallen." He stalked across the room toward her.

Her pulse revved. "But I didn't."

"What if you had? What if something had happened to the baby?"

"You're overreacting."

"No I am not," he said gruffly and put his hand to her lower back, while he held out his other arm to her.

She placed her palm in his and he helped her down. His touch was tender, but his eyes were troubled.

"Imagine if I came home to find you on the floor. I—" He broke off, shook his head.

Heat pushed up her face. Her stomach vaulted into her throat. He'd never scolded her like this before and it hurt her feelings, but he was right, one hundred percent. She'd been so excited about setting up and decorating the tree that she hadn't even considered it might be unsafe. "Jesse . . . I . . . I'm so sorry. I didn't think."

"We're going to be parents soon. We can't be selfish. The baby must always come first."

Stricken, she mumbled, "Of course. I know that."

His distant gaze fixed on the Christmas tree, but he was looking past it, through it. He'd been raised in a string of foster homes, hadn't known who his real father was until he was an adult. Was he thinking about the care that no one had taken over him?

Flynn cupped his cheek with her palm. "Jesse?"

He shifted his attention back to her. "We both have a lot of adjusting to do."

"We can handle it," she said. "Together, we can do anything."

He rubbed his hand against her upper back in a circular motion, gave her a soft smile, and drew her into his arms. She rested her head against his chest as best she could with the bump of their baby between them, and breathed in his scent mingling with the smell of Scotch pine.

After a moment, he pulled back, slid his arm around her shoulder, and eyed the tree. "It is pretty," he said, "and a good bargain. I'm sorry I bit your head off, it's just that there's so many things that can go wrong."

"Shh, it's okay. I understand."

He kissed her forehead. "We need to get a move on delivering those Angel Tree gifts. The Weather Channel is predicting the ice storm might hit sooner than they first thought. Tonight instead of tomorrow morning."

"On the plus side, we'll have a white Christmas. I mean how many times do we get a white Christmas in North Central Texas?" she asked. "It's going to be perfect."

"Not if we get caught out in it. I already stopped by the community center and the Angel Tree volunteers loaded up our car with food and gifts. Where's your coat? I'll get it for you."

"Front closet."

As he moved down the hall, her gaze flicked back to the Scotch pine. The red glass ball had slipped down the branch and it hung there, fragile and tremulous. In the face of Jesse's displeasure with her she'd neglected to securely anchor the ornament to the branch.

It was about to fall.

Gasping, she waddled as fast as she could toward the tree.

But she was too late.

The treasured glass fell from the branch, smacked against the hardwood floor, and shattered into a million tiny slivers.

CHAPTER TWO

The perfect Christmas and a charitable heart go hand in hand . . .

The car smelled of turkey dinner with all the trimmings that they were delivering to a needy family. Jesse reached across the seat for Flynn's hand, and squeezed it tightly.

She gave him a forgiving smile and squeezed back.

He was still shook up over finding her up on that stepladder. He knew she was just trying to give him a festive Christmas, like the kind he'd never had growing up, but if anything had happened to her, he would never have forgiven himself. Why hadn't he already bought a tree and put it up so she wouldn't have felt obligated to do so? He'd screwed up. Let her down.

"I'm sorry about your mother's ornament."

She blinked, forced a smile. "Thanks."

"You still miss her a lot."

Flynn nodded. "Don't you miss your mother?"

"I barely remember her."

"Still, you must feel something. Especially at the holidays."

He shrugged. What was it with women that they always wanted to talk about feelings? "Do I wish she hadn't died? Hell, yeah. But it happened and I can't change that, so no point digging up the past."

"Sometimes, I worry that something might happen to me and our little one will have to grow up without a mother."

"I won't let anything happen to you," Jesse said fiercely. "Not as long as I have an ounce of air left in my body."

"You can't protect me from everything. My dad couldn't protect my mother from ALS."

"Nothing is going to happen to you, Flynn. We're going to have a wonderful life."

"You always know what to say to make me feel better. I love you, Jesse."

"Love you too," he rasped, and cast a sideways glance at his wife.

Her hazel eyes glowed with a special light since she'd become pregnant, and her curly brown hair had thickened. She'd been pretty, but now? She was stunning.

He slipped his hand from hers and placed it on her belly. The baby kicked against his palm, and a loopy grin took hold of him. This was a miracle.

Once upon a time, he figured he'd spend his life alone, and now he had all this. How had he landed a woman like Flynn? It boggled him. Scared the hell out of him too.

His heart jumped into his throat, choked him. He didn't deserve her. He was a scarred, damaged man who'd spent ten years in prison, even if it was for a crime he hadn't committed. He knew his faults and flaws, and he was terrified that one day, she'd see them too and leave. He loved her so much. Maybe too much, if that was possible. If he lost her, it would be the end of him.

And now, there was someone else to love. Someone else he could lose. Dad. A father. Him? What a huge concept to wrap his head around. Nine months wasn't nearly enough time to prepare. They'd taken childbirth classes and learned about all the things that could go wrong. It was a miracle, really, that anyone was born safe and healthy.

But it wasn't just the difficulty of childbirth that worried at him. He didn't know the first thing about being a good father. He'd had no role model. No road map to follow. What if he screwed it all up? Raising a kid was serious stuff.

The baby kicked again. They'd decided to wait and find out the sex when it was born, so he had no idea if he was about to have a daughter or a son.

"She's active today," Jesse said.

Flynn nodded. "He's eager to meet his daddy."

"Can you believe it? Only a week to go."

"Babies arrive on their own timetables. Could be longer."

"We need to settle on a name. I'm still up for Hondo if it's a boy."

"If we're going to use family names, I want to name him after you." She reached out to comb her fingers through his hair. "Jesse could work for a girl too."

"We could do what your parents did when they merged Floyd and Lynn into Flynn."

"So Jesselyn?"

"Or Flesse," he teased.

"Horrors!" She laughed. "I've always felt it's best to give a baby a name that's all their own. That way they don't have to live up to anyone else's expectations."

"So we're back to square one on the names?"

"I'm not too worried about it. I think as soon as we see our wee one, we'll know exactly the right name."

"I love your confidence," he said. "You give me courage."

"Ha! If you only knew how insecure I feel sometimes."

He touched the tip of her nose with his index finger. "You've got nothing to feel insecure about. You're going to be a great mother."

"You didn't think that thirty minutes ago when you caught me on that stepladder."

"I overreacted. You got the directions?"

Flynn dug around in her purse for a piece of notepaper and unfolded it. "After we pass the Brazos River, take a right into the Post Oak Shores development."

They crossed the bridge, traveling from Hood

County into Parker. Normally, the recipients of the Angel Tree charity had to live in Hood County to qualify for the program, but this family had just moved after being evicted from their home three days earlier. It wouldn't have been fair to cut them off because their situation had gotten even worse.

Heavy-bottomed clouds bunched, turning the sky dark an hour before nightfall. He switched on the radio, searched for a station that was giving the local weather.

The weatherman announced, "This doozy of an ice storm is expected to hit Dallas/Fort Worth and the surrounding areas around nine o'clock tonight, so get home and stay warm, folks. But don't worry, kids, it's not going to stop Santa from making his rounds. He's got Rudolph to light the way."

Flynn rested a hand on Jesse's arm. "Relax. We'll be home long before the storm hits."

"Who says I'm tense?"

"You're clenching your jaw."

He rubbed a hand over his chin. "You know me so well. I can't help wishing I'd left you at home."

"C'mon. You couldn't do that to me. The highlight of my Christmas Eve is seeing the faces on those Angel Tree families when we arrive with their gifts and food. Giving is the best part of Christmas."

"Which is why I didn't bother trying to get you to stay home," he said. "In the meantime, I'm allowed to worry until we're back safe and sound."

"Okay, Daddy," she said. "I'll grant you a little fretting."

Daddy.

Jesse grinned. He sure liked the sound of that. Imagine. He was about to have a family of his very own. He turned into Post Oak Shores. It was a poverty-stricken community, composed mostly of thin-walled shacks and rundown trailer houses. Many of the yards were littered with junk cars and overgrown weeds, but a few were lit with Christmas decorations.

"Take a right at the fork in the road. It's the third trailer house on the left. Lot number sixteen," Flynn read from the directions.

Jesse took a right and slowed down. Outside number sixteen sat a twenty-year-old Chevy with balding tires and a dented front fender. In the bare patch of ground that passed for a yard was a plastic Big Wheel faded from orange to faint yellow and a wading pool filled with stagnant water. The porch steps leading to the trailer house look rickety. Probably eaten up with termites. He hated the thought of Flynn climbing them.

"I'll be okay," she said, reading his thoughts. "We're doing a good thing."

He knew that. It was the reason he was here in the first place, sad memories of the time when he and his mother lived in such dumps. He swung into the driveway, and his headlights swept across the side yard where a thin woman was trying to heft an axe to split a chunk of wood. She swung and missed. Momentum spun her around so fast he feared she was going to chop off her leg.

"Oh my," Flynn said. "That looks like an accident waiting to happen."

The gaunt woman set the axe down, straightened, and ambled toward the car as they got out. Her hair was pulled back into a haphazard ponytail and she wore oversized rubber boots and several thread-bare sweaters layered over each other. She hunched her shoulders against the blowing cold. Her cheeks were windburned, her hands chapped. "You folks with the Christmas Angels?"

"We are," Flynn confirmed.

The woman plastered her palms over her heart and looked as if she was about to burst into tears. "Thank the Lord! I thought since we moved outta Hood County we might not be gettin' a visit."

"Don't worry," Flynn said softly. "Your kids are going to have a good Christmas this year."

"I'm Myra. Myra Scott." She shook their hands as they introduced themselves. "Y'all come on in. Sorry the place ain't much."

"No need to apologize," Flynn said.

Jesse reached into the backseat for the Styrofoam cooler, and Flynn held out her hands to take it from him.

"I can carry that," Myra said. "You don't need to be totin' my groceries in your condition."

Jesse passed the cooler to the woman and went back for the oversized cotton bag packed with presents.

"I can carry something," Flynn said. "I'm not helpless."

"Sweetheart, relax. You don't have to do every-thing."

"Please."

"If you insist, there's still a bag of nuts and oranges in the floorboard."

She beamed. "Thank you."

He nodded for her to go up the porch ahead of him. He wanted to stay behind her so he could catch her in case the stairs gave way. Dammit, why did she have to be so stubborn? He would have been much happier if she'd agreed to stay home. Then again, she wouldn't be his Flynn if she weren't a bit bullheaded. Her ability to dig in and do what needed to be done was one of the things he admired most about her.

The trailer was just as cold inside as it was out. Three kids—a boy about six or seven, a girl slightly younger, and a baby around nine months old—shivered around a potbellied stove, the fire inside burned down to embers. Explained why their mother had been out chopping wood.

The kids eyed them as their mother moved clutter from the counter, but they didn't come over to investigate. He wondered about their timidity. He could tell from their eyes they'd seen too much of the rough side of life.

"Set it here," Myra said.

"No heat?" Jesse grunted.

She pushed back a lock of hair that had fallen across her face and looked sheepish. "Furnace don't work. Potbellied stove gets the job done. Excepting I have to chop the wood and I'm none too good at it."

Jesse's gut twisted. He couldn't go off and leave the frail woman without any heat source for the holiday, especially with an ice storm on the way. He pulled all the money he had from his wallet, money that he'd earmarked for a tank of gas on the way home, but no matter, they still had a quarter of a tank, plenty enough fuel to make it the twelve miles back to Twilight from here.

He laid the two twenties on the counter. "This is to help get you through. I'll call a furnace repairman out here the day after Christmas and pay for the repairs. In the meantime, I'll stock you up on firewood."

Gratitude and relief mixed with the shame on Myra's face. "Thank you, mister. Thank you."

Flynn sent him a tender look. *I love you,* she mouthed silently, and then said brightly to the mother, "Let's get your kids fed."

An hour and a half later, the trailer house was stocked with enough wood to get them through the next couple of days, the family had eaten the meal Flynn had put out for them, the healthy helping of leftovers had been put away, the dishes washed, and the presents stashed under an artificial tree that looked as if it had come from the dollar store a decade ago. The room had warmed in the heat from the roaring fire Jesse stoked. The kids were sucking on candy canes and watching a Christmas program on an old tube TV. This was as good as life got in a place like this.

Time to go. The ice storm was bearing down and he had his own family to think of.

Flynn slipped into her coat and gathered their belongings. Myra kept thanking them profusely, and both of the older children came over to hug them as if they were beloved relatives, and damn if his eyes didn't mist a bit. Too bad he couldn't wave a magic wand or say abracadabra and make their lives easier.

The second they stepped out into the night, icy wind cut through them, colder than ever. Flynn shivered and clasped her mittened hands together, her breath coming out in frosty puffs. Jesse took her elbow and guided her down the rickety steps to the car.

"That was really kind of you," Flynn said as he started the engine. "Stocking that woman up with firewood."

"You think I could just walk away and leave them without any heat?"

"No," she said, reaching over to stroke his arm. "That's one of the things I love most about you, Jesse. You always try to do the right thing."

Her words lit him up inside. Hell, she made him feel so warm and cozy and like the luckiest son of a bitch on the face of the earth. "We gotta get home before this ice storm hits."

"Those people are going to have a happy Christmas because of you."

"Hey, you were just as much of part of this as I was."

He had just pulled out of the Post Oak Shores development and turned onto Highway 51, when out of the dark a pair of red and blue flashing lights lit up his rearview mirror. The Jubilee Police Department.

He groaned. "C'mon, man. Not tonight."

"What is?" Flynn craned her neck. "We weren't speeding. Did you run a stop sign or something?"

"No. Maybe I've got a taillight out." He moved over onto the shoulder of the empty road and the police cruiser pulled in behind him.

A prickly sensation, as if a tarantula was crawling over his skin, spread up the back of his neck. He waited with his hands on the steering wheel while the patrol officer stalked to the window. It had been three years since he'd been released from prison, but he still couldn't shake the adversarial feelings he had for law enforcement.

The trooper rapped on the glass.

He put the window down. "Good evening, Officer."

"You Jesse Calloway?" The trooper widened his stance, his hand resting on the duty weapon at his hip. His name tag read Penninger.

Jesse winced. Uh-oh. No automatic let's-have-your-license-and-registration. This was not a routine traffic stop. "I am."

A second trooper came up on Flynn's side of the car. Jesse chuffed a breath.

"May I see some ID?" Officer Penninger asked.

"What's this about, Officer?" Flynn stretched across the seat to peer up at the trooper.

"Ma'am, I'm not speaking to you."

The muscles in Jesse's throat seized and it took everything inside him not to double up his fists. *Don't disrespect my pregnant wife, you tool.* He bit his tongue and motioned for Flynn to sit back.

She looked frightened, shivered.

"It's okay," he murmured, and patted her arm.

"ID," Penninger demanded.

Jesse fished his wallet from his back pocket, took out his driver's license, and passed it to the officer. *Stay cool.* This was not worth spending Christmas Eve in jail over.

"You were just at the residence of lot sixteen on Morning Glory Trail, correct?"

The knobby bones of Jesse's spine turned to ice cubes. "That's right."

"Were you aware that it's the residence of a known drug dealer?" Penninger scowled.

Jesse gripped the steering wheel tightly, and from the corner of his eye kept watch on the second officer.

"Myra Scott is a drug dealer?" Flynn exclaimed.

"Not her. The guy whose house trailer she moved into. We got a tip there's a drug deal going down there tonight and we've had the residence under surveillance, and lo and behold, an ex-con who went to prison for cocaine distribution shows up." Penninger tapped the brim of his hat. "Makes you go hmm."

"Excuse me?" Flynn scolded. "If you've been watching that trailer, then you must have seen how that woman is struggling to provide for those children. Why didn't you do something to help her? Call CPS if you believe these kids are going to end up in the middle of a drug deal."

Jesse loved his wife dearly, but he wished she would stop talking. He ran a palm down his face. "Honey, this is not our battle."

"Well," Flynn said. "They've pulled us over about it, so seems to me they've made it our battle."

"You're married to a convicted felon. Getting pulled over goes with the territory," Penninger said snidely.

Jesse's biceps turned to stone. *Don't rise to the bait. Just don't do it. He wants you to give him a reason to slap the cuffs on you.*

"He was innocent of those charges," Flynn said, leaning back across the seat.

Officer Penninger lowered his head, fixed a marble stare on Flynn. "Not to sound like a jaded cop or anything, but all convicts say that, ma'am."

"In this case it's true. My husband was framed and we know by whom." Flynn looked mad enough to spit bullets. "You're profiling my husband."

"But your husband was never pardoned, that makes him an ex-con no matter how you slice it."

"Please, cut her some slack, Officer," Jesse said. "As you can see, my wife is nine months pregnant."

"Don't make excuses for me," Flynn bristled. "I have a right to get testy over police harassment."

Penninger shifted his gaze from Flynn to Jesse. "We simply want to ask you a few questions, Mr. Calloway."

"There's no reason to ask him questions. We were delivering Christmas gifts and food with the Angel Tree foundation of Hood County."

"This is Parker County."

"Clearly. No one in Hood County would make the mistake of pulling us over for nothing."

Penninger decided to let that go. "Mr. Calloway,

this is nothing complicated. If you've got nothing to hide, you shouldn't have a problem with following us to the Jubilee Police Department to answer a few questions."

"I'd rather take my wife home first," Jesse said. "It's late and an ice storm is on the way."

"Or we could take you in with us, and let your wife go on home," Penninger said. "We'd happily give you a ride home if everything checks out so she does not have to come out in the weather to pick you up."

He did not like that option, but it didn't look like Penninger was going to give him a choice.

"I can't believe you're doing this on Christmas Eve," Flynn interjected.

"Mrs. Calloway, your husband was in the residence of a known drug dealer. That's a clear violation of his parole. It's not my intention to put him under arrest, but if he chooses not to cooperate . . ." Penninger shrugged, his implication clear.

Flynn shrank back against her seat, her face pale. "Are you threatening us?"

Gently, Jesse put a hand on her shoulder. He understood why she was hot under the collar. Hell, he loved her fierce loyalty, but the only way to deal with this was to play their game. "It's okay, sweetheart. They're just doing their job. I'll go with them, answer their questions, and be home before you know it."

"Your husband has made a wise decision."

Flynn snorted. Glared.

Reluctantly, Jesse undid his seat belt, kissed

Flynn, got out of the car, and followed Penninger back to the cruiser. He hated sending her off in the dark alone, but sour feelings went much deeper than that. This incident drove home the fact that no matter how hard he tried, he could never really escape his past.

CHAPTER THREE

The perfect Christmas demands the perfect music . . .

Bing Crosby was wishing everyone a white Christmas as Flynn started the car with trembling fingers. Frustrated, she sat there letting the engine idle while she collected herself. She knew Jesse was right to cooperate, but knowing that didn't make her feel any less awful.

In the rearview mirror, the taillights of the cruiser winked out in the darkness, taking Jesse from her. She closed her eyes, remembering when she was sixteen and a similar patrol car had whisked him away from her for ten long years.

It's gonna be okay. You'll get home. They'll let him go. You can stay up late, have eggnog and cookies, and play some Christmas music. The whole evening isn't ruined. Not yet. Not yet.

A soft sound pelted the windshield, an onrush of

icy vibration. No, no. She opened her eyes. Oh no.

Sleet.

Buckets of it.

Home. She had to get home. Now. But home was eleven miles away.

Tightly gripping the wheel, she bit down on her bottom lip and pulled onto the empty highway. Was it a good thing or a bad thing that there were no other cars on the road?

That's when she noticed the gas gauge read a quarter of a tank. It should be plenty to get her home, but it was just something else to make her antsy.

As she neared the Brazos, a thick mist rolled off the river, engulfing the car in a headlight-dousing fog. She inched along at twenty miles an hour, every muscle in her body tuned tight.

The baby, as if sensing her distress, kicked.

She spared a second to put a hand on her belly, even as she kept her gaze trained on the road. "Don't worry, baby. Mommy isn't going to let anything happen to you."

The car skidded.

"Whoa!" She sucked in a startled breath, immediately clamped her hand back onto the wheel, and eased up on the accelerator. *Concentrate, concentrate, you have a promise to keep.* She had no idea if she was even on the bridge yet. She'd never seen a fog so dark and thick.

Bing was gone and Bruce Springsteen was telling her that Santa Claus was coming to town. Maybe so, but St. Nick better not be on this road. Not if he valued his sleigh.

The baby kicked again.

"I'm sorry, wee one. I know you want out, but you've got another week to go before it's time to pop from this toaster."

Even though she couldn't see it, she knew the bridge lay just ahead. This was the hardest part of the drive home. Once she made it over the bridge, the fog would lessen and she'd be able to see again.

The tempo of sleet fall quickened until it sounded as if a hundred long-nailed typists were simultaneously keyboarding *War and Peace*. The wheels hung on a patch of black ice; the protesting engine revved a whining complaint.

Flynn's heart galloped. Was it turn into a skid or turn away from it?

The car kept sliding in a perverse ballet, skating toward the right. If she was on the bridge, she'd soon whack into the guardrail, and if she wasn't, she'd go off into a bar ditch. *Please let me be on the bridge.* Better to dent up the car and still be able to drive home than get stuck in a gully.

What to do? What to do?

Turning into a skid was counterintuitive, but she had to do something. She was going to do it, but what did turning into a skid mean? Did you turn the wheels in the direction you were sliding or the opposite direction?

No time to think. Act! She wrenched the steering wheel to the right.

The car stopped sliding, gained a little traction.

She blew out her breath. Whew. Now what?

The baby threw a punch.

"I know, I know, I'm trying my best to get you home, sweetheart."

The daunting fog was a blanket, blocking any visibility. Nightmare. She was going to have nightmares about this for weeks to come. *Oh, Jesse, where are you when I need you most?* That wasn't fair. None of this was his fault. He'd wanted her to stay home but she'd insisted on coming along. She'd put him in a no-win situation.

Tentatively, she pressed down on the accelerator. The car jumped and instantly fishtailed. Adrenaline raced through her body, hot and jittery. *Stop! Stop!*

Tires whisked against the ice, a spine-curdling, glassy *whoosh.* Panicked, she jammed on the brakes.

Mistake. Big mistake.

The wheels completely locked up and the car spun a one-eighty, shot sideways, and glided downward. To the river? Was she going into the water? Dear God, please help!

The car crashed into something with a brain-rattling jolt, pinballed off that something, and spun again.

Powerless, she clung to the steering wheel, a whimper of despair seeping past her clenched teeth.

The front fender bit into hard ground. Thankfully, not water. But in the process, the passenger door flew open and her purse, which contained her cell phone, bounced out into the pea-soup fog. She heard a splash. Gulped.

As she sat there contemplating what to do next,

Josh Groban crooned softly, "I'll Be Home for Christmas."

Well good for him, at least somebody would.

The Jubilee police dropped Jesse off at his house around eleven. It had taken a call to Warden Neusbaum at Huntsville prison to fully convince them that Jesse was not involved in any drug deal, and Neusbaum had been a hard man to locate on a holiday weekend. If Hondo hadn't been on a plane to Hawaii, the misunderstanding could have been cleared up in a matter of minutes. As it was, Jesse struggled not to be resentful. Penninger had apologized to him, after all.

The Christmas lights on the house twinkled gaily, but the inside of the house was dark. He'd expected Flynn to be waiting up for him. The uneasiness that had started when he'd tried to call her and kept getting her voice mail crept over him again. To cut costs, they'd gotten rid of their landline. He hoped she'd simply forgotten to plug in her cell phone. The pregnancy had made her a little forgetful lately. Maybe she was exhausted and had gone on to bed. It had been a long day, what with Patsy and Hondo's wedding, but if that was the case, why hadn't she at least texted him when she'd gotten home okay?

He trudged up the icy steps trying not to let worry do him in. *Don't borrow trouble.* She was most likely sound asleep. He couldn't wait to slide under the covers and snuggle up beside her.

That's when he saw the dog.

A blue merle Australian shepherd lay curled up

on the welcome mat. He stopped, and an uncontrollable smile crossed his face. He'd always wanted a dog. Had Flynn surprised him for Christmas? No. She wouldn't have left a dog outside in the cold.

The Aussie jumped to his feet, tail wagging madly as if he'd been waiting for Jesse his entire life, and rushed over to him.

"Any other time, dog, and I'd be over the moon." Jesse bent to scratch the pooch's head. No collar. Fur matted. Skinny. He looked homeless. "You remind me a bit of myself before I came to Twilight."

He opened the door and flicked on the light. The dog waited at the threshold, looked at Jesse expectantly. "It's Christmas Eve, you really think I wouldn't say c'mon in?"

The dog trotted inside.

"Flynnie," Jesse called, opening up the pantry for a can of tuna. "You awake? We've got company. Come see."

He peeled off the pull top on the tuna can and set it on the floor. Immediately, the Aussie devoured it. He moved to throw away the pull top, spied a library book on the hutch beside the trash can. *How to Host the Perfect Christmas.* Aw, Flynnie. Always trying to be perfect. Didn't she realize that in his eyes she could do no wrong? Not ever. No matter what.

Shaking his head, he stepped on the lever that opened the trash can, and red glass shards from Flynn's mother's Christmas ornament glittered up at him from the garbage. Dammit. He'd forgotten about that. Flynn really had had a rough day.

"Flynn," he called her again.

No answer.

The uneasiness that had abated when he'd seen the dog turned to dread. Jesse rushed down the hall, his pulse spurting hot blood through his veins.

He flung open the door. The bed was neatly made up. Flynn had never arrived home, that meant she was stranded out there somewhere in the ice. He spun on his heel, ran for the door. The dog kept step with him.

"I don't have time for you," Jesse muttered, but Aussie stayed glued to his side. He couldn't leave the poor thing in the house alone, but neither could he leave it shut out in the cold. "All right, you can go with me."

Walking as quickly as he dared on the icy ground, he headed toward the detached garage. Nope, her car was not there, confirming his fear that she had not made it home. After what seemed like an eternity, he was on the road with the dog riding shotgun. As he drove, he used his hands-free device to try and call Flynn again. When that failed, he called relatives and friends. No one had seen or heard from her that evening.

He cursed himself up one side and down the other. Cursed the Jubilee police and the drug dealer. For good measure he cursed Beau Trainer, the man who'd framed him in the first place and had stolen ten years of his life.

When the police had brought him home, they'd taken the straighter route down 171 from Jubilee to Twilight, instead of Highway 51 which he and Flynn had been on, so he wouldn't have seen her if she'd been stuck on the side of the road.

Jesse fisted his hand on his thigh. If any harm came to Flynn there was going to be hell to pay.

Picking up on his mood, the dog whined and pawed the dashboard. The radio came on, playing "Merry Christmas Darling" by the Carpenters. A song about a loving couple forced to spend the holiday apart.

Ah hell, ah damn. No way. He was going to find Flynn and she was going to be okay. Determined, Jesse snapped off the radio before he lost it completely.

Chapter Four

Ultimately, the perfect Christmas
is about those we love . . .

Flynn tried for what seemed like a solid month to find her purse. Inching to the icy water's edge in the deep, dark fog, forever aware that one slip could potentially end the life of both her and her baby. But the phone was her only salvation. Essential.

She'd felt blindly along the icy ground, touching tree branches, sharp rocks, and brittle patches of grass until the relentless damp, treacherous ice and bone-deep cold had forced her back inside the car. Now, she huddled in the passenger seat, wrapped in Jesse's new leather jacket, teeth chattering, boots wet, toes Popsicles, engine idling, heat cranked up to the max, and praying the car didn't run out of gas.

The first labor pain hit her with the force of a

lightning bolt—hot, hard, and burning bright. She cried out, grasped her abdomen. No, no, no. This could not be happening now. The baby wasn't due for another week.

"Babies come on their own timetable," Dr. Butler had said.

She closed her eyes. Maybe it was just those Braxton-Hicks contractions the nurse educator talked about in childbirth classes. False labor. Yes, that was it. Had to be it. The baby was definitely *not* coming. Not while she was stranded by herself in the ice, on Christmas Eve. N.O.T. Not happening.

The second pain ripped through her. She gritted her teeth to keep from screaming. It had been less than two minutes since the first contraction. This was not good. Not good at all. Damn the Jubilee police all to hell for taking Jesse away from her. He was a good man. He didn't deserve the stigma.

Be calm. Calm down. Think of the baby.

The baby hadn't moved in awhile. She stroked her belly, cooed sweet nothings. Okay, she *had* to make another attempt to find her purse, get to her cell phone, and call for help, but the thought of going back out into that freezing, foggy night weighed on her as heavily as lead boots.

Tears pushed at the backs of her eyelids, but she couldn't give in to self-pity. Despair was not an option. Jesse would come looking for her; that was a certainty. That was unless the police decided to detain him overnight.

No. Can't think like that. He will come looking for you. He is probably already looking for you.

At night. In the fog. During an ice storm. Not to mention that she'd clearly crashed into some kind of ravine near the river bridge. What were the odds that he would find her before she had the baby?

Whenever she imagined her first child's birth, this scenario had never come to mind; so much for expectations.

The third pain clamped down on her and wouldn't let go. It wrenched the air from her lungs, left her gasping and grasping. *Oh Jesse, hurry, hurry.*

When the fourth pain hit shortly on the heels on the third one, she realized she'd better get in the back while she still could, use that cloth bag they'd had the Angel Tree presents in to protect the seats. Unless something changed soon, it was looking more and more like she was going to have to deliver this baby herself.

Driving in the ice was slow going, but Jesse had no other option. Going fast could end him up in a ditch and he simply could not take that risk, even though plodding along went against everything he had inside him. He wanted Flynn and he wanted her now.

Patience. His patience was what won her in the first place. Ten years he'd waited for her, and she'd been worth every tick of the clock.

As he neared the Brazos River, a thick fog rolled toward him. Flynn was out in this? His bones ached and his stomach roiled. *Hang on, sweetheart, I'm coming.*

By the time he got to the bridge, his hands were

shaking. How was he going to find her when he couldn't see beyond the hood of his truck? He'd scanned the bar ditches since he'd started down 51, but no sign of her. She had to be somewhere between the Hood County side of the bridge and Post Oak Shores. Where to start?

Retrace your steps. Go back to where you left her and start from there.

The bridge was icier than the highway. No sand trucks had been out here. The pickup fishtailed and it took every bit of concentration he could muster to focus on driving across the frozen bridge. By the time he reached the other side, he was as wrung out as if he'd sprinted five miles. If he was this worn down, what had Flynn been through?

The Aussie whined, sounding a lot like Lassie did when little Timmy got into some scrape or another.

"You sure you want to hang out with me, boy?"

The dog licked the back of his hand.

"We're going to have to search on foot. In this pea soup, it's the only way." Jesse didn't know whether to pull over to the side of the road and risk getting stuck or leave the truck in the middle of the road and take a chance that no one would come along. Better to get stuck than to cause an accident.

He pulled over onto the shoulder as far as he dared with zero visibility and got out of the pickup. Before he could shut the door, the dog bolted out of the truck and ran off, the mist gobbling him up. So much for loyal companion.

Which way was north? He stood in the fog, trying to get his bearings and feeling utterly alone. Finally, he pulled out his phone and in a Hail Mary, called her again.

Voice mail.

"Flynn, where are you?"

Far off in the distance, Flynn thought she heard the faint ring of her cell phone, but maybe it was just her ears ringing. Labor pains could make you see sounds, taste textures, and smell colors. Son of a biscuit, it hurt. She'd chewed her bottom lip raw and sweat drenched her clothes.

"Looks like it's just me and you, kid," she mumbled, and massaged her belly. Even that small effort was too much and her hand flopped limply to her side.

Conserve your strength. You've got a big job ahead of you.

Contraction after contraction rolled through her. No one had told her it was going to hurt like this. She thought she'd deliver in a nice hospital, with an epidural. Life had a way of mucking up the best-laid plans.

When the urge to push came it was so unrelenting, she felt kidnapped. It was the strongest impulse she'd ever experienced. She tried to remember what she'd learned in prenatal classes, but her brain was numb, every bit of energy given over to childbirth. She closed her eyes, barely able to draw in air.

"Flynn!"

Her eyes flew open. Was she hallucinating or was someone calling her name? The voice sounded muffled, distant.

"Flynn!"

Yes, someone was definitely calling her name. She opened her mouth to answer, but another contraction grabbed her with such force all she could do was grunt.

"Flynn! Can you hear me?"

It was a man's voice, but still too far away to hear clearly. Could it be Jesse?

Her pulse quickened and a rush of adrenaline swept through her. She raised her head and for a second, she was Superwoman. "Here, I'm he—"

Pain cut her in two.

A dog barked, but she was so engulfed in her toil that the sound barely registered. She clenched her fists, gave in to the overwhelming urge to push. She had to get this baby out.

The barking grew louder, more insistent. Whose dog was that? What was it barking at? What—

The baby's head was crowning. She could feel it. No stopping now.

She squeezed her eyes closed and poured every ounce of attention into the biggest job of her life.

The barking stopped.

The car door wrenched open. "Flynn."

Jesse!

She opened her eyes and there stood her husband, his jaw hanging open, his face the color of paste, but he was the most beautiful sight in the world.

"Finally," she gasped. "We got our timing right."

He delivered his own baby.

Jesse couldn't wrap his mind around that reality

even as he held his wriggling daughter in his arms. He'd swaddled her in the leather jacket Flynn had meant as his Christmas gift.

She'd been born ten minutes after midnight on Christmas Day. An ambulance was on the way from Twilight, but for the moment, it was just the three of them. Well, four. The Aussie sat dutifully beside the car.

He was in the backseat with Flynn, everything suddenly quiet after the noise of the last few minutes, sweet silent night. Jesse glanced from his daughter to his wife and his heart grew too large for his chest, pressing against his lungs so full and tight that he could scarcely breathe. This was the most incredible, miraculous thing he'd ever gone through and they'd done it together. It made all the sorrow and turmoil he'd suffered in his life worth it. *They* made everything worth it.

Joy burned his eyes. "Flynn, you did so good. I'm so proud of you. I . . ." His throat tightened.

There weren't enough words in the world to tell her how much he loved her, how important she was to him. Each day he woke up next to her was a gift from God, and now he had another wonderful girl to love.

"Not so bad yourself, bad boy," she teased, somehow managing to look radiantly beautiful in spite of her exhaustion.

"A daughter." He shook his head in awed disbelief. "We have a daughter."

"And no name to give her."

"I have a name," Jesse said. "A name that represents every good thing you and the baby have brought into my life."

"So are you going to tell me what you've named our daughter?"

"Grace," he said. "I want to name her Grace. Because of your love, Flynn, I feel like grace has pardoned me from an empty life."

"Oh, Jesse." Tears filled her eyes.

He tucked their sleeping daughter in the crook of his arm, took Flynn's hand, and squeezed it tight. He was a lucky, lucky man. Her love had awakened him, made him whole.

"Grace," she whispered, and looked at their baby. "I couldn't think of a more perfect name."

"Fatherhood changes a man," he said. "I was so scared that I wasn't going to be a good father. I mean, I wanted to be and I hoped to be, but I didn't have a role model for what a good father was. I was scared that I couldn't live up to the challenge, certain I didn't deserve such an honorable role. But now . . ." His voice cracked.

She smiled. "Why, Jesse Calloway, here you are going all poetic on me?"

"You are the most amazing woman."

"No more amazing than you." She reached over to stroke his cheek with her soft palm.

For the first time ever, he understood what the phrase "my cup runneth over" meant. He had so much joy and love inside him that it simply could not be contained. Love flowed from him, bright and

true and strong, and he truly wished happiness for every single man, woman, and child on the face of the earth.

Flynn frowned.

Alarmed, he tensed. "What is it? What's wrong?"

"Is that a dog I see?" She leaned across him to rub the frost from the window. "It is! You got me a dog for Christmas. You know how much I love Aussie shepherds. Grace is going to have such fun growing up with a dog in the house. Jesse, you are the best husband ever."

"I wish I could take credit," he said. "But the dog just showed up at the house."

"Then Santa brought him. How amazing."

"More than amazing. If it hadn't been for the dog, I wouldn't have found you when I did. His barking led me to you through the fog."

"What shall we name him?"

"You let me name our daughter." Jesse waved his hand. "Be my guest."

"Rudy." She nodded. "Short for Rudolph, since he guided you to me through the stormy night."

"I'm on board with that."

She kissed him then, softly, gently, perfectly, and if the sound of an ambulance siren hadn't cut things short, Jesse could have gone on kissing her all night.

Maven Styles might not have approved, but Flynn couldn't think of a better way to celebrate Christmas. Their daughter's birth might not have been conventional, but now they'd always have an exciting story to tell. The doctor had examined them both and pro-

nounced both mother and child healthy and sound, and recommended spending the day at the hospital only as a precaution.

She sat propped up in her hospital bed, their daughter sleeping in her arms, her family and friends crowded around, gifts piled so high that the nurses glared whenever someone brought in another one. Good thing Jesse insisted she have a private room. Her well-wishers would have crowded out a roommate.

Patsy and Hondo had just Skyped them from Maui and all the members of her mother's old knitting club were there—Marva Bullock, Belinda Murphey, Terri Longoria, Dotty Mae Densmore, and even Raylene, who was also in the hospital, recovering from a mild heart attack. Earl rolled her into the room in a wheelchair with an IV attached. Raylene teased that there was vodka in it. Everyone was glad she was going to be okay. Raylene's long-lost daughter, Shannon, and her boyfriend Nate came too, and Flynn liked them both already.

Carrie and her ex-husband-turned-fiancé, Mark Leland, were squeezed into a corner of the room, surreptitiously sneaking kisses. Christine Noble and her ready-made family stopped by to bring Grace a birthday cake, and the sweet-natured baker had never looked happier with her handsome Eli.

Noah and Joel showed up to meet their niece before they went off to share Christmas dinner at the homes of their respective girlfriends. Amid the boisterous hubbub, her father came in with his lady companion, local librarian Barbara Duffy. Her

father was four years clean and sober and she was so proud of him.

Flynn looked from the tenderness in Jesse's eyes to all her friends and neighbors, to the sweet little baby snuggled in her arm, and she felt utterly peaceful. She felt a quiet, calm strength that she had never experienced before becoming a mother, and the feeling stirred her to the depths of her soul.

Only one thing was missing from this picture and that was her own mother, but nothing was ever one hundred percent perfect, was it? You had to take the special moments when they appeared, wrap them in the tissue paper of memories, and tuck them close to your heart, because these special moments were what made life worth living.

"Flynnie," her father said, "I've got a special Christmas present for you." He passed her a small square box covered with gift paper so old it was faded and brittle. "Your mother bought and wrapped this the year she was diagnosed with ALS. She asked me to give it to you the Christmas you had your first child."

She sucked in a deep breath. "Oh, Dad."

Murmuring their good-byes, her guests slowly gathered their things and drifted from the room, giving Flynn and her family their privacy. Finally, only her father and Jesse remained.

Jesse took Grace from her arms and stepped to the foot of the bed.

"Go ahead," her father urged. "Open it."

She met Jesse's eyes. He nodded.

Butterflies fluttered in her stomach as she untied the ribbon, peeled back the yellowed Scotch tape, and lifted the lid.

Inside the box was a Christmas ornament. An exact match to the ball that had broken, except this one was imprinted with the words "BABY'S FIRST CHRISTMAS."

A single tear slid down her cheek.

Underneath the ornament lay an envelope with her name on it. She picked it up. The smell of her mother's perfume, Wind Song, wafted out and punched her right in the gut.

Gulping, she opened the envelope, took out the card.

To my beautiful daughter Flynn,

If you're reading this, you're a mother now, and for the first time, fully able to understand what a precious gift a child is. I pray you have a wonderful husband who cherishes you as much as your father and I do.

My deepest regret is that I won't be around for this momentous occasion, but do know that I am with you in spirit. When you hang this ornament on your Christmas tree it will unite your past to your present, and when you pass it along to your son or daughter, it will link us both to the future. Be happy, darling, and know that you are well and truly loved.

—Your adoring mother, Lynn

Unstoppable tears streamed down her face.

Holding Grace cradled against his chest, Jesse rushed to her side. "What is it? What's wrong?"

She looked at her concerned husband and the tender bundle of joy he held. "Nothing. Everything is absolutely fine." She smiled through the tears, because they were truly tears of utmost joy. "This is the most perfect Christmas ever."